STILL IN LOVE WITH HER

MAGGIE & VINCE, #1

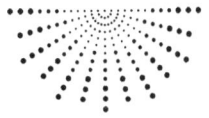

Z.L. ARKADIE

Z.L. ARKADIE BOOKS

ISBN: 978-1-942857-83-9

❀ Created with Vellum

ACKNOWLEDGMENTS

Thanks to the following:

Edited by Red Adept Editing

Cover Design by Z.L. Arkadie Books

PART I
HE LOVES ME

ENTER THE TWILIGHT ZONE

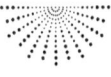

MAGGIE

I haven't seen Vince since my cousin Curtis's wedding, which was nearly a month ago. I've been in New York and London, working like a mad woman to boost the ratings for two new shows that have been added to Prime D TV's *Sizzling Summer* lineup. I've held viewings on Mondays, Thursdays, and Sundays. I've pulled consecutive all-nighters interpreting empirical data and writing reports. I've worked with teams to produce crawls, commercials, and press boxes. I've been pulled in so many directions that my head has been bobbling all over the place. I hardly consumed anything other than protein bars and Colombian coffee. When I had a moment of downtime, I tried to call Vince, but he didn't answer his phone. However yesterday, I received a jaw dropping email from him that said, "other than work, which you care more about than me, I think we should go our separate ways."

That's why I hitched a ride to L.A. on Jack's jet early this morning. Vince is leading the state-of-the-company meeting today, so I know he'll be in Conference Room 11 at ten a.m. As soon as I arrive, I take a cab to Vince's house in Malibu. The Range Rover Vince bought me for my thirtieth birthday is parked in the garage. I can hardly believe I hit the big 3-0. Two years ago, I never thought I'd be standing in my shoes, successful at life and, I hope, at love.

I go inside to get the car keys off the hook. The curtains are open because Vince likes a lot of light in the house. The floors and furniture are so shiny that I could eat breakfast off them. The faint scent of his cologne is in the air.

"Vince!" I call three times. I'm positive he's already left. He's a consummate early bird.

I stop at the Starbucks on Pacific Coast Highway and grab a cup of coffee and a breakfast sandwich. I finish both with time to spare while braving the stop-and-go traffic all the way to the company's mirror-glass building on Avenue of the Stars in Century City.

Darren, the valet, opens my door and says "Maggie's back in town."

"In the flesh," I reply and wink.

"Are you still taking names and kicking ass?"

"I never stop," I say as I gallop toward the glass doors.

The elevators are always crowded in the mornings, and today is no exception. I carve out a space for myself and read my emails on my cell phone.

"Good morning, Mags," a deep voice whispers in my ear.

I jump and turn to face Robert Tango's trademark smirk. "Morning," I say in a lackluster tone.

He's behind me. I'm pretty sure a woman in a blue suit was standing in that spot when I got in. He must've maneuvered his way over to me. His hands are on my hips, and now my ass is against his cock, which is getting firmer by the second. I look at the woman next to me to see if she notices Robert getting off on my ass. She's not paying attention. No one else is either.

"You're a pleasant surprise, Mags," Robert says.

"Do you know what's going on with Vince?" I ask.

"What's going on with Vince?"

I jab him in the ribs with my elbow. "Stop that," I whisper.

He chuckles. "Stop what?"

He's always screwing with my head.

"You know what." I shift my hips forward.

The doors slide open, and four people exit. I step away from Robert and glance at his package.

He puts his mouth close to my ear. "You're the one who pushed your ass against me."

I snort. "In your dreams."

He chuckles. I think he's delighted to get a reaction out of me. I have to stop feeding into his bullshit.

"Don't you ever wonder?"

"Wonder about what?" I ask, although I know exactly what he's talking about.

"Fun doing what?"

"You and me and how much fun we could have," he says.

Robert flexes his eyebrows. He's wearing a royal-blue silk shirt and nice-fitting navy slacks. He always looks scrumptious. Once or twice, or ten times or more, I've admired how attractive he is. However, I have no intentions of hooking up with Robert Tango.

First, I love Vince. Second, Robert's a scoundrel who's banged almost every attractive woman in this company. I'm surprised there haven't been any sexual harassment complaints. I'm sure they'll come rolling in like an avalanche sooner rather than later.

"No," I reply.

He smirks. "You should. Not too many men know their way around a woman's body the way I do."

"That's because you're a scoundrel." I spin on my heels and walk away. I can't do this anymore. Robert has given me my first headache of the day.

He keeps up with me. "I still need to meet with you today."

"About what?"

"Sizzling Summer."

I roll my eyes. "Sizzling Summer? When did you start having anything to do with real work?"

"I want to talk to you specifically about Hanna's show."

I scoff. "I told you the show was going to flop before it premiered, but you were fucking Hannah, so you blew me off. My opinion hasn't changed. I can't improve audience reception because the show stinks. Cancel it."

"Damn it, Maggie, we're meeting today. What time are you available?"

I stop in front of my office. "I don't know. Call Mavis, and she'll pencil you in."

He snorts cynically. "*Pencil* me in?"

I glance across the maze of cubicles at Vince's office. There stands Vince, facing a woman I've never seen. She has a lot of copper-colored hair cascading down her back and is wearing a very tight dress that extends past her knees. She's very thin. I can't see her face, but the fact that she's standing so close to him gives me a sinking feeling in the pit of my stomach.

"Who's that?" I ask Robert.

Vincent's gaze meets mine. I smile, but he looks shocked to see me. I look away from Vince to face Robert's smug smile.

"That's Emily. Vince's old girlfriend from high school."

"What is she doing here?"

"She's our new corporate PR director."

"What happened to Pamela?" I ask.

"Pamela isn't *corporate* PR. She's departmental."

I glare at Vince and this woman named Emily. I think I'm jealous, which is a pretty new emotion to me. "What the hell? Did you guys make up that title?"

Robert snaps his fingers in front of my face to regain my attention. I turn my grimace on him.

"Pamela needed some help with the corporate side of things. Emily handles our images," he says.

"Whose image?"

His mouth stretches into that naughty smirk of his. "She's done a lot of work on Vince's."

"What are you insinuating?" I snarl.

Robert has a dazed look in his eyes. I've seen it before, usually when Vince is near, so Robert has to zip it and stop coming on to me. I turn to see Vince only a few steps away.

"What are you doing here?" Vince asks.

"Why haven't you returned my calls or answered me on Skype?" I reply.

He glares at Robert then checks his watch. "The meeting starts in ten minutes."

"I didn't ask when the meeting starts. I asked—"

"I know what you asked."

I'm taken aback by his harsh tone.

"Follow me, Maggie," he says and steps away, confident I'll obey his order.

I glower at Robert one last time before trailing after Vince. I wonder if this is the end of us. If so, then what did I do wrong? I thought everything was good between us when I left the wedding. I had to leave early to catch a flight to London. We even grabbed a quickie in a utility closet before I hopped into a cab for the airport. He'd banged me against the wall among the dirty mops and brooms. Our passions ran so high that we clawed and bit at each other, frustrated that we couldn't sink into the other's skin. But right now, his mood is so severe that I feel as though his heart is light-years away from loving me.

We go into Vince's office. He closes and locks the door behind me then shuts the blinds. My heart is racing a mile a minute. I'm flushed and dizzy. Is he really going to break up with me right before the meeting?

"What—" I gasp as Vince shoves his hand under my blue sheath dress. Since I don't wear panties, his fingers slide right inside me.

"You're wet," he says.

Robert may have made me melt a little by grinding my ass, but I frown and choose to ignore Vince's comment. "What's going on with you?"

Vince's mouth is caught open. He's staring into my eyes, and I can see his thoughts turning. If only I knew what they were. His behavior is very odd.

I feel the tension in my forehead. "Are you okay?

Did something happen?" Is this the part when he tells me he has an incurable disease?

Our lips enfold. We don't break eye contact as we kiss tenderly.

Then he stops, blinks, and mutters something that sounds like, "I can do this." Vince undoes his pants and takes out his dick. It's erect and slippery at the head. "Get on your knees."

My frown deepens. "What?"

"I said get on your knees."

"I'm not getting on my knees. Are you crazy?"

"You're so fucking obstinate. If only you would…"

He pulls my dress all the way up, lowers me onto the sofa, separates my legs, and slams his dick into my slipperiness. We lock eyes for a long moment. Then he pounds me. I stare into his eyes, trying to figure out what's gotten into him. I feel the first traces of an orgasm, and my eyes close as I release a moan.

"You like that?" Vince slams into me harder, faster.

"Yes…" I suck air.

He rams his thickness deeper inside me and holds my hips against him. "Oh." He grunts and jerks.

I'm breathing heavily, shocked that he didn't get me off before he came, especially when I was so close. He's never done that before. Vince pulls out of me. My legs drop to the floor, and he zips his pants.

I'm still perplexed. "What the hell was that?" I get up to grab a tissue off his desk to clean myself.

He grabs my wrist. "Drop it."

I flinch, taken aback. "The tissue?"

"The tissue."

My frown deepens. "Have you fallen on your head? Is that what's wrong with you?" He hasn't removed his hand, so I drop the tissue.

There's a knock on the door.

Vince looks over his shoulder. "What do you want?"

Langley tries to open the door but it's locked. "The meeting starts in four minutes."

"Is that it?" he says.

She hesitates. "Well, yes."

"Got it."

I shake my head. "Did an alien abduct my boyfriend and replace him with an evil twin?"

"I'm not your boyfriend, Maggie. Do you remember I asked you to marry me?"

Shit. I'd thought his proposal was tucked away safely in my drawer along with the ring. "Yes…"

He sniffs disdainfully. "There are lots of lessons I need to teach you."

"You have lessons to teach me?" I say sarcastically.

"If you want to fuck Rob, then go right ahead, but I'm not going to make you come until you learn how to get on your fucking knees when I tell you to."

Did he just accuse me of wanting to bang Robert? I'm generally a quick thinker, but I'm still trying to process everything that just happened. I watch, stunned, as Vince fixes himself up.

He indulgently runs his thumb across my bottom lip. His lips comes close to mine, but he doesn't kiss me. "Don't be late." He strolls out of the office, leaving the door wide open.

I peek at Langley, who's sitting at her desk and staring at my exposed vagina. I lower the bottom of my dress, rake my fingers through my hair, and grab my satchel. I avoid eye contact with her as I sweep past her desk, heading toward the conference room. The meeting hasn't started, but everyone is here. I make the rounds, and people express how pleasantly surprised they are to see me.

Samantha from the ads department pulls her lips squeamishly. "Especially in light of things."

I want to ask in light of what, but I'm afraid of

the answer. The only empty seat is next to Robert. I've had enough of him for one day, so I tap Angela from finance on the shoulder. "Could you take the seat up front? I have to sneak out in a little while and link into a conference call." I show her my best smile. "I don't want to disturb the meeting after it gets on the way."

"Absolutely," she says, ogling Robert.

Every woman in the room would like to sit next to him. He's probably banged half the women in here.

"I need you up front, Maggie," Vince says as Angela stands.

Angela gives me a consoling look. I hate that smirk Robert wears as I approach and sit beside him. I take my pad out of my bag and scribble, *What did you say to Vince?* on the top page.

Robert flips the page. *I say a lot to Vince. We're buddies.*

I scoff. *You're a buddy who tries to fuck his friend's girlfriend!*

A buddy who has fucked his buddy's girlfriend.

I furrow my eyebrows. Robert and I have never had sex. He leers at Emily as if he's trying to tell me something.

"Okay, let's start," Vince says.

Robert's knee hits my leg and settles against it. I shift, turning my body away from his. Vince always winks at me before he starts a meeting, but today, he doesn't look in my direction. Instead, he winks at Emily, who winks back. My mouth falls open as my heart takes a dive. I want to run out of the room crying. It's no secret that we're a couple, so our colleagues exchange looks. They realize he's snubbing me, so on top of hurt, I'm embarrassed. I keep my eyes on the blank sheet of paper in front of me.

Vince runs down the list of our new video/media projects. I'm listening but pondering my last conversation with Monroe. She'd suggested that I quit my job and go into business with her as an image consultant. She said it's right up my alley. I know how to sell anything to the public, so why not people? I actually liked the idea. However, I assumed Monroe was just trying to get me to make major changes in my life so we could spend more time together. I hardly see her anymore, and she's made it very clear how much she doesn't like that.

"By the way, I want to formally introduce Emily Callahan," Vince says. "She's been around since last week, and everyone in the L.A. office has noticed her, I'm sure." He and Emily share another smile.

A bitter laugh escapes me. Everyone looks at me.

Vince has blatantly disrespected me on so many levels. If he thinks I'm a little debutante he can make jealous by flirting with other women after only half fucking me, then he's wrong. I shoot to my feet and gather my things. I don't care who's watching or what they think.

"Maggie, no leaving before the meeting ends," Vince says.

I flip him the bird. "Fuck you."

"Sit down," he says as if he's the prime minister of Maggieville. "I'm telling you as your boss."

I hang my bag on my shoulder and tuck my notepad under my arm just so I can flip him off with both hands. "You're not my boss. I quit, you jackass. On so many levels, I quit you."

I'm feverishly hot as I walk out of the room, because my anger has spiraled out of control. I don't expect Vince to chase me since he tried so hard to humiliate me, but just in case, I take the stairs, running down twenty-seven flights. My face is damp from tears and sweat when I reach the bottom. I'm surprised to see Vince standing out front speaking to Darren. I turn left and right, searching for another way out. I run down the escalator to the parking garage. People look at me as if I've gone insane, and indeed I have. I make it to the green level and rush past the parked cars, searching for an exit sign. Once I see the way, I run out into the heated morning.

I lean against the wall to collect my breath. I can't believe the morning I'm having. Just like that, Vince has replaced me with a debutante. Maybe he was just with me to get his kicks. He always knew that in the end, he would settle down with someone like Emily. I should've known he hasn't changed. That's why Robert thinks it's his turn to have me, because Vince is over me. What a jackass.

I walk without thinking about where I am going. I turn down a street with very little traffic, take out my cell phone, and call Monroe. I can always count on her to pick up on the first ring.

"What's up, Mags?" she says.

"He… Vince…" I'm blubbering.

"Where are you?" she asks, sounding panicked.

"I'm in L.A."

"Where in L.A?"

I look for the street signs. "I'm on Galaxy Way."

"Don't move," Monroe says and hangs up.

I lean against an iron gate, bury my face in my hands, and bawl. I feel so used and abused. Deep down, I knew before I arrived that my day would probably end with Vince and I breaking up, but I never thought he would treat me as if he hadn't an ounce of love for me. He was a real jerk. So Emily *was* the "girlfriend" Robert was referring to in the note, and not Vince's old girlfriend but his new one. I've been replaced.

I want to cry harder, but instead I wipe my tears and get a grip. I feel like the girl in one of those movies where the popular boy seduces her just to get his kicks. But in the end, the unpopular girl realizes that she didn't need his ass in the first place. I don't need Vincent Adams. My life will keep going. I have the rest of it to find the real thing one day. I set my stone-cold glare on the street. Monroe should be here soon.

2

CAUGHT IN THE RAT TRAP

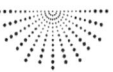

MAGGIE

"Ⓦhat the hell? Has he been reading novels and shit?" Monroe laughs, making light of my situation.

I grimace. "Why do you say that?"

I'm at Monroe's house. She and I are sitting against the headboard in the guest room she keeps for me. I'm wearing one of her sexy nightshirts since all of my clothes are in my suitcase, which is in the back of my Range Rover.

She flings her hands as she talks. "It's popular in books today. Submissive and dominant shit. I'm surprised you don't know this. Isn't it your job to know that shit?"

"Submissive and dominant what? Jerks? Assholes?"

"No, it's sex-slave shit. He tells you what to do, and you do it. And if you disobey him, then he punishes you."

"Punish me?" The more details she feeds me, the more off course she sounds. I don't think Vince would ever try to emulate such nonsense, although I'm not sure if I ever knew him at all. "Who does that kind of shit in real life anyway?"

"You'd be surprised."

I lift my eyebrows. "You've done it?"

"I don't submit to cock. And usually it's the people you least expect who do."

I'm confused. My brain isn't as sharp as usual, so I have no idea what that meant. "Whatever. I just don't know what I did for him to betray me like that."

Monroe rubs my back consolingly. "I'm sorry, Mags. Vince is a stupid ass. You're not an easy one to catch, and he had you."

I smile with the sides of my mouth turned down. "You're so good for my self-esteem. But he accused me of wanting to fuck Robert. I can't believe I let Robert grind my ass on the elevator." I shake my head. "I mean, he was really getting in there. It was... gross."

"Uh-oh," Monroe says.

"Uh-oh what?"

Monroe tilts her head. "You liked it. You like him."

"I don't hate him, but he drives me crazy."

"I know you, Mags. You like him, *like* him."

I sigh hard. "Am I curious?"

"Yes you are!"

"Yes I am but it's never going to happen."

"You're like a guy who wants to fuck his girl-friend's best friend." She looks at me askew. "So are you going to do it now that you've broken up with Vince in front of the entire company?"

Jeez. I pause to think about what I did. "I must've lost it."

Monroe laughs. "Well, when someone pisses you off to that point, watch out! I mean, you don't get there quickly, but when you go, you blow."

I cover my face with a pillow. "I made a fool of myself!" I shout into its fluffiness. "Oh my God, I don't have a job!"

"You don't need one. You're Jack Lord's cousin."

I lower the pillow. "I'm not going to mooch off Jack."

"Or we can go into business together. I already have a client lined up." Her eyes shine with hope.

"I've been counting on you mentioning that."

"And?"

"I just need to put this day behind me, but I'm ready. I think we should do it."

"You do?" she asks.

I shrug. "Why not?"

"For real, Mags. You're not fucking with me?"

"I wouldn't fuck with you."

"Then let's shake on it." She holds up her hand. "And don't shake on it if you don't mean it."

I shake her hand. "I mean it."

"There's no turning back now. It's a done deal."

"Okay," I say.

"Okay."

We grin at each other. I really like the way this decision makes me feel. I've made it under duress, which is never a good thing to do, but so what? Since leaving the tutelage of Cruella La Bitch, I've learned to take life by the horns and try like hell to bend it to my will.

I pat Monroe's thigh to signal a change in conversation. "Oh, congratulations on *The Great Dame*. I heard it got good ratings as a made-for-TV movie."

Monroe smiles proudly. "It did."

I smile. "And there's Emmy talk for best made-for-TV movie and a best actress nomination for Mandy Hill."

"Can you believe it? The way that chick bumps coke, you'd think her brains would be too fried to remember her lines."

"She's an addict?"

Monroe nods. "She has a serious problem. I like her, you know. She's crazier than I am!"

"That's indeed crazy."

She elbows me. I laugh.

"A group of us were thinking about putting together an intervention for her," Monroe says.

I flinch, taken aback. "Wow. You're that close to her?"

"We're friends. Not like you and I—we're sisters."

I grin. "That's what I want to hear."

She rolls her eyes playfully. "But deep down, Mandy's a good person. By the way, I noticed you were wearing the Valentino dress I gave you. Really, Mags, are you still wearing my hand-me-downs?"

"I still don't like to shop."

"I know. It's part of your psychosis."

I grunt. "I still don't understand what the hell you're saying when you say that."

"I'll tell you what, Vince isn't going to let you go. He's going to ride your ride until the wheels fall off."

I shake my head. "No, we're done. He used me. And the way he fucked me this morning… And the way he embarrassed me… He's just an asshole I'd rather forget."

Monroe rolls her eyes as she shakes her head. "Listen, the next time he tries to get you to submit, do it."

"He's not. We're done. He has a new girlfriend."

"Sometimes you can be so smart yet so dense. He's not done with you. He was trying to get your attention, and it worked!"

I frown. "Huh?"

She takes my shoulders. "Apparently he wants you to submit to him. So just do it."

I squirm out of her grasp. "No, and why are you asking me to do that? It's warped."

"Men like that shit. It turns them on."

"Well, it doesn't turn me on. And if that's the case, then why do all the bitches have the best guys? Huh?"

"I'm a bitch, and I've had horrible luck with men," she says. "Let's start with Charlie. I bet Angelina would climb a tree if he asked her to."

"Not even the least bit true. But he is into her tits in a strange way. Charlie and Jack are alike—they fixate on tits and ass and shit like that. They're both

Scorpios. I'm positive that has something to do with it."

Monroe lifts her shirt. "But I have great tits."

I roll my eyes playfully. "Yes, you do. You bought a great pair."

She elbows me. "Screw you."

"It's not even that hers are real and yours aren't. Their fixations are specific. It can be a mole or the way the nipple is shaped. I've seen Angel's tits. They slope like a slide. She's got great ones."

"Don't tell me that. I'm already jealous of her."

"You shouldn't be, especially if Charlie's the reason."

"Humph, but Charlie's a Scorpio?"

"Um-hum." I gaze off thoughtfully. "I can't figure out what sort of mojo Daisy is working on Jack. When they're together, they fuck twenty-four seven."

"Maybe it's her kitty-cat."

We both burst into laughter. I'm laughing because hot damn, I think that's it!

Monroe pats my thigh. "Get some rest, because I'm having a party tonight."

I sigh. "Not tonight, Roe. I'm not in the mood."

She leaps to her feet. "This isn't going to be your run-of-the-mill fun, bump, and fuck party." She smirks. "Well, all of that will happen, but we're going to be on the outside looking in."

I frown. "Huh?"

She flexes her eyebrows. "Rest and then come to my closet," she sings. Monroe dances out of sight.

I pull the blanket over my shoulders and turn on my side to stare at the wall. My head is sleepy, but my heart won't let me rest. Vince hasn't called me. Double fuck Vincent Adams. I probably should've gotten involved with Robert Tango instead. At least with him, there would be no blurred lines. He's always been clear about what he wants from me—legs spread, insert dick.

I flip onto my other side and try to get comfortable. It's not working. My muscles are too tense. I kick off the blanket, sit up, pull off Monroe's come-fuck-me T-shirt, and go for a swim. I lap the pool until my arms and legs grow heavy. I dry myself with a towel and then wrap it around my head.

Back in my room, I check my phone. I have missed calls from everyone except Vince. *Jerk.* I stretch across the bed, lying on my stomach, and close my eyes. Inch by inch, I creep off to sleep.

Robert Tango and I are in the elevator, riding up to the twenty-seventh floor. It's dim, and cheesy red light flashes. I'm in that slinky, back-out dress

Monroe gave me. I've tried it on several times, but the message it sends is far too distracting for my taste. Robert strides across the small space, and his hooded gaze is so sexy. He spins me around, lifts my arms over my head, and slaps my palms against the wall. I gasp when his healthy erection stabs my ass.

"You want this, don't you?" His warm breath blows in my ear.

His tongue traces circles and lines down my back. He's moaning, getting off on dry-humping me. I toss my head back, and the sounds of our whimpers crash around us. I want to milk his dick. *But why?*

"Yes, why? Why do you want me to come, Maggie? All over your pretty little ass?"

"I don't know," I whisper.

"I can tell you why."

"Then do tell."

His sexy chuckle warms my ear. "You like being liked."

I shake my head. "No."

Up and down, his dick rides the crease of my ass. "Yes."

"No."

"Then why won't you spread your legs and let me

have you?" His hand snakes up my thigh. "Why, Maggie?" he barks and stops stimulating me.

The ache I felt when I saw Vince wink at Emily returns. "Because..."

"Because what?"

"I only love Vince. I only crave him."

"But he doesn't want you. And you want me."

A dick impales me and makes me want to erupt at first thrust.

I wake with a stop. The room is dark. The towel is off my head, and I've managed to curl into the fetal position. Thank goodness that was only a dream.

My phone rings, and I spring off the bed to answer it. "Hello?" I ask without checking to see who's calling.

"Mags, did you really quit or are you battling a case of the crazies?"

Ugh. I roll my eyes. It's Robert. "I really quit."

"You do know you signed a contract."

"You do know that I know Jack Lord."

"You do know I can make it impossible for you to find another job."

"Again, you do know that I know Jack Lord?"

"Fucking Maggie! If you ever appreciated the opportunity Vince gave you, then you would do it right."

I sigh hard. Monroe calls my name.

"Be there in a second," I say to her.

"You're coming to see me?" he asks.

I recognize that tone. "You see, this is one problem I have at A&Rt—*you*."

"You're the one who said you were coming over."

Although I can't see it, I know he's smirking. "I was talking to Monroe."

"Oh?" He sounds intrigued.

"Actually, the two of you would be perfect for each other."

"But I want you, Maggie. You can't dock me for being honest."

"If you have a crush on me, keep it to yourself."

He laughs. "A crush?"

Why the hell am I entertaining this conversation? "Call it what you want."

"I have an ache for you."

"Have you told Vince that you have this"—I draw air quotes—"'ache' for me?"

"Vince knows I want you."

"Then why..." I shake my head, confused. Then why hasn't Vince punched Robert's lights out? Why are they still friends?

"Listen, Mags, come back to work."

I shake my head emphatically. "I'm done."

"Give us two weeks. You're an important part of our company. If you jump ship, people will feel the waves. Vince will be in L.A. for the next couple of weeks. Work out of New York."

I squeeze my eyes shut, trying to forget the dream I just had.

"Maggie, what are you doing?" Monroe asks, poking her head in the room.

I point at the phone in my hand.

"Is that Vince?" she whispers.

I shake my head and mouth, "Robert."

Her eyes expand, and she leans against the doorjamb.

"I have to go," I say. There's no way I'm letting Monroe hear this ridiculous conversation.

"So are you giving us two weeks?"

"Okay. As long as I don't have to see those two together."

"Then I'll see you Monday?"

"Wait. I don't want to see you either."

Monroe chuckles.

"You're going to have to see one of us. Pick your poison," he says.

I sigh. "Okay. I pick your poison. See you Monday." I end the call before Robert can say something that will make me change my mind. I shake a finger at Monroe. "Do not."

She draws a line across her lips. "Why are you naked? Have you been playing with yourself?" She's clearly entertained by that idea.

"No. I went swimming."

Her eyes roll up and down my figure. There's something weird about the way she's looking at me. "Well, don't put any clothes on. It's time to get you dressed for the party. The caterers have already set up, and the strippers are arriving."

"Strippers?"

"They're the cheese to trap the rats."

Again, Monroe has thoroughly confused me.

3

EXIT THE TWILIGHT ZONE

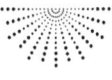

MAGGIE

I shower, washing the chlorine out of my hair and off my skin. I blow-dry my mane bone straight. It's still not as thick as Monroe's, but my hair is shiny and soft as butter.

"You're so damn hot," Monroe says as I study myself in the mirror.

What's strange is that I'm wearing a dress similar to the one I wore in the dream I just had about Robert, except this one is powder blue.

"This is the last straw," I say. "It's time I woman up and buy my own clothes."

"Nah, let me buy your rags, Mags. You have no idea how to dress that sexy body of yours, and I do." Monroe slaps me on the ass.

"I must admit," I say, turning this way and that, "this dress looks really good on me."

"Really good? You look hot!" She slaps my ass again.

Monroe and I talk about Dash, the new guy she's seeing, as I sit on the chaise and watch her get dressed.

"Have you heard me say 'gnarly' yet?" she asks.

"Only dozens of times."

"I like that word." She threads an earring through the hole in her earlobe. "I always knew I was made to be a Californian."

"Well, that is definitely the defining factor. I mean, no one, and I mean no one, says 'gnarly' like Californians."

"And oh, can he fuck. No one fucks like Californians."

"That's because they get a lot of practice."

"And practice makes perfect!" Monroe leaps into her closet. "I think the night should culminate with you getting laid. You can either join me and Dash in here, or I can hook you up with someone else."

I flinch so hard that I nearly strain my neck. "Join you and Dash? You're talking about girl-on-girl with me?"

Monroe reappears. "Although I've eaten pussy,

yours is off-limits to this mouth. But I would eat your tits because, well, you have nice ones."

I laugh so hard that I spill off the arm of the chair. Maybe both of us have lost our marbles today. "When the hell have you eaten pussy?" I manage to get out.

"I don't tell you everything I do." She points at me. "Just for that reason, right there."

"What? I'm not judging you. I'm not going to let you eat my tits either."

"You should try it. A soft woman's tongue and teeth devouring your sweet nipples?"

"What?" I say as if that's the most ridiculous thing I've ever heard.

"Let me try it now."

"Wait." I throw up a hand. "You're not going to tell me you love me or some shit."

"No way! I mean, I love you, but I like dick —mostly."

"OMG, as the kids say."

"Mags…"

My eyes widen in horror as she walks toward me.

"Dash is going to bang you and taste and I'm going to do this." She pulls the material from over my breasts, exposing my firm nipples. "Look at that,

You're not used to letting go. You don't let your body do what it wants to."

"Monroe..." I feebly object. I'm curious as hell about how far she's really going to take this.

"Shush."

I watch the tip of my tit disappear into her mouth. She was right. It's a soft, titillating sensation, although the jury is out on whether or not I like it. Tongue, teeth, and suction stimulate my nipple. A gasp escapes me, and Monroe sticks her fingers into my wetness.

"Um," she moans. "Damn, Mags, you taste like a vanilla Popsicle. I want to eat this so badly." Her finger taps my clit. "But like I said, you're off-limits. I've been thinking about why I've been wanting to do this."

She sucks my other nipple. Should I tell her to stop? What the hell is going on? Did I disembark at LAX and land in the Twilight Zone? She sucks and bites my nipples while her fingers bang me like a jackhammer. For a moment, I forget it's Monroe making me feel this way. I pitch my head back and suck air.

"Shit!" I grab her hand. I'm so close to coming, and if she gets me off, that would definitely put weirdness between us. "Stop."

Monroe's tongue laps my nipple one more time, and she rakes it between her teeth. "There, out of my system."

"You're crazy, you know."

"I know! So are we awkward now?" she asks.

I raise my eyebrows. "Very."

"But you liked it. Don't say you didn't."

"It felt good but wrong—for me. If you want pussy, then have a buffet but mine isn't on the menu, or my tits."

She cracks up. "No. I'm good." She tilts her head thoughtfully. "I think you cured me of my pussy craving."

A laugh escapes me. "I'm heading downstairs."

"No, really, Mags, this is good. Now we can work together without me wanting to do what I just did."

"Is that how you're reasoning it?"

"What I did is going to happen to you more often than you blink. Men. Women. Our clients are going to want to make your beautiful ass moan."

"So you're saying that was a test?"

She shakes her head. "No, that was me wanting to get you off."

I laugh. "First of all, I'm rethinking working with you. I love you, but you can be just as wacky as Robert Tango."

"Could you stop calling me wacky, crazy, and insane?" she asks.

I study her serious expression. "Okay."

"Thanks, and I'm sorry. I won't do it again unless you ask me to."

"I'm not going to ask."

"Then I won't do it."

I study her with one eye narrowed. I sigh. "All right then."

She smiles. "Now how was I compared to Vince?"

"You're an expert."

She nods. "I know. I'm so good with a woman's body. I think it's because I know what I like."

I raise a finger. "Just don't ever touch my vagina again."

She laughs. "Deal. But what about Dash?"

I'm very close to calling her crazy. "I thought you liked this guy?"

"I do, but we have an open relationship." She looks off as if she just had a thought. "Tonight, you'll have him all to yourself. He's my gift to you. And may he fuck Vincent Adams out of your system."

I ruffle my eyebrows and ponder her words. Monroe takes off her white, see-through lace dress and puts on a short, tight black rubber dress instead. Her hair is flowing, and her legs are long, but she doesn't turn me on in the slightest. I'm not surprised she made a move on me. Monroe would fuck a peanut if it could be done. However, the nipple stimulation and masturbation she gave me has made me horny. I want Vince even though he's long gone.

"Okay," I say.

Monroe emerges from the bathroom. "Okay what?"

"If Dash is that good, then I'll fuck him."

She grins. "Oh, he's that good."

"Okay then."

IT SEEMS AS IF EVERYONE ARRIVES AT THE SAME TIME. If they've made it inside, then they've passed through metal detectors and three burly doormen, whose body checks consist of feeling under the nut-sack and in butt cracks. A deejay is spinning music, and buck-naked girls swing on poles. I know a number of the guests. They're actors, agents, music artists, athletes, and their muses. I stand on the stairwell checking it all out. Round tables are set up. There's enough coke to get us all twenty years upstate. I see a man's head bobbing up and down against a guy's lap. The receiver's name is Delta Foster, the action-film heartthrob.

"You're looking at Delta?" Monroe says after stepping up behind me. "There are rumors that he prefers cock. As you can see, they're true."

"I see…" I'm transfixed by Delta Foster.

Delta's sucking air like a fish out of water, and no one seems to care. It could be because it's happening all over the place. One woman is against the wall with a guy giving her pussy a go. I count three more incidences of the same thing. There's actual fucking going on too. No one seems to mind.

"Someone could take a picture of him getting his cock sucked right now, broadcast it all over the world, and as an image consultant, you could still convince people that he's as straight as an arrow. Couldn't you?" Monroe says.

"Huh?"

Delta blows. The other guy has come all over his mouth as they kiss.

"Is he our client?" I ask.

"Bingo."

I shake my head with certainty. "No way."

"Mags, come on. Don't be a wimp. This kind of challenge is right up our alley."

"Is misleading the public a challenge?"

"The public image of a public figure is never the truth. People can't handle the truth. They don't like bitches, arrogant egomaniacs, crybabies, junkies, or dumbasses. They don't want to know the truth."

"And which is Delta?"

"A hundred percent egomaniac, three-quarters junkie, and half dumbass."

I snort and roll my eyes.

"Just hear him out first. Deep down, you know that you love the kind of challenge he presents."

I twist my mouth thoughtfully. "I'll hear him out, but before or after he gets his rocks off again?"

Monroe laughs. "Tomorrow. By the way, have you seen Dash?"

"I have not a clue what he looks like."

"He's right..." Her arm shoots past my face, and my eyes follow her finger. "There."

Monroe points at a guy with shaggy blond hair and a rugged five-o'clock shadow. He's wearing a navy button-front shirt that hugs his frame and nice-fitting gray slacks. He's sexy, but my eyes devour the better-looking guy standing behind him and staring at me.

"Oh shit," Monroe says.

"What's he doing here?" I ask.

"I can get rid of him." She slaps my ass and starts down the stairs.

I grab her shoulder. "That's okay. I want to talk to

him." I walk past her feeling as if my head is floating above my shoulders.

Vince doesn't take his eyes off me.

"Hey," I say when we face each other.

Vince hugs me and looks around the room as though he's trying to figure out what in the hell is going on. "Can we go somewhere and talk?"

I tilt my head. "This way."

Vince rests his hands on my hips. Being handled by him feels so good, but it's also infuriating because of the way he treated me. He follows me up the stairs, down a long hallway, through an alcove, and down a short corridor. From there, we walk down steps, but Vince grabs me before we make it to the bottom.

He pins me against the wall. "What the hell was that today?"

I shake my head as the pain floods back into my heart.

"Maggie, Emily and I are not together."

"It didn't look like that to me."

He stares in my eyes then gazes down my body. "You're wearing this fucking dress? For who?"

"For me."

Vince licks his lips and pulls up my dress. He looks down. "No panties?"

I shake my head. His eyes are hooded as he unzips his pants, finds his dick, curls an arm around one of my legs, and lifts it. He grunts as he sinks his dick into my creamy wetness.

"Damn it," he mutters, pumping in and out of me. "Oh…"

Our kissing is primitive. We tug at each other's tongues and bite each other's lips. I feel as though it's been forever since we've kissed and never since we've kissed like this.

"I'm going to come." He impales me as he shouts, "Fuck!"

Vince and I pant against each other's mouths. He pecks at my lips. I feel his seed dripping down my inner thighs just as it did this morning.

"Are you going to leave me now?" I ask.

"No," he says, out of breath. "I'm not done with you yet."

"Why did you treat me that way this morning?"

"It was a bad idea." He looks down the stairs. "Where are you taking me?"

"Somewhere quiet."

He puts my leg down and fixes my dress. "You look sexy. If I hadn't come, then you would have looked like this for other guys."

"You don't get to be jealous after what you did to me."

"Yes, I do, Maggie." He massages my thigh and sucks air between his teeth. "Hurry up and take us where we're going."

Vince and I wobble down the stairs, intoxicated with desire. We make it to the bottom, and I open the door to the dungeon. It's a small room with a large window that looks over the canyons. A king-sized bed is pushed against the wall, each side of the bed has two cylinder shaped lamps dangling from the ceiling and a black furry rug rests at the foot of the bed.

"Is that a stripper pole?" Vince asks, pointing at what's obviously a stripper pole on top of a platform next to the fireplace.

"Um, yes."

"You ever use it?"

"Um, no."

"That's what I like to hear." Vince's eyes land on my body. "That fucking dress." He runs his fingers down my bare back.

His hard dick presses against my hip. I close my eyes and feel his fingers stroke my skin. They journey to the front and caress my nipples with constrained urgency. A squeal escapes him. He walks me to the bed, lays me down, and inches my dress up my thighs, enjoying the view. This is why I could never screw Robert or Dash.

His tongue laps my clit. I clutch the sheets as he sucks it, swirls it, and flicks it with his tongue. I scream and pull at the sheets. He pins my hips against the bed and does it faster. He moans and jabs his fingers into my wetness. Then he stops cold turkey and crawls up the bed to lie beside me. His pants are still unfastened, and his dick sticks straight up.

"Really?" I say, still breathing heavily.

"Maggie, we have a problem."

"I would say so."

"You want to do whatever the fuck you want, when you want," he says.

"It sounds like, for you, that's an unfortunate consequence of me being a free human being."

He snorts. "You have a sharp tongue."

I try to sit up, but Vince holds me down. I look at him askew. "What's this new act of yours all about?"

"It *is* an act."

"I know!"

"Which means you quit your job over an act."

"Correction, I made an ass out of myself in a room full of our colleagues over your act. But was

Emily in on it? Because she seemed pretty convinced that there was a you and her and not a you and me."

He's silent for a while, facing my chest. "Are you wearing a new perfume?"

"No…" Then I remember. "Oh, Monroe sucked my tits."

He balks. "Get the fuck out of here."

"Apparently she's fluid."

"Humph."

"Humph, what?"

"How did you like it?"

I shrug. "It was like eating chicken."

He chuckles. We grin at each other.

"You want to know the truth?" I ask.

"Yeah," he says with a sigh.

"It felt weird but good. She can really suck nipples."

"Better than me?"

I stretch my lower lip, squeamishly.

"Fuck no!" His tone is disbelieving.

I nod. He pulls the material down from over my breasts, exposing them. The band of my dress pushes my tits up, and they look luscious sitting high on my chest.

"Her mouth is softer, more sensual," I say.

"Like this?" He slips between my legs.

His tongue is like velvet on my nipple. The stimulation is gentle as he makes the same circles Monroe did. His strong hands grip my ribcage as he bites a little and slowly rakes his teeth across the sensitive tip. I groan in pleasure. He repeats what he just did over and over. Just like Monroe, he puts his fingers between my legs.

"How was that?" he asks, stroking my slit.

I smirk. "You're number one."

He plunges his fingers inside me, stroking my G-spot. Flickers of pleasure swirl under my hood.

"Am I?" He increases the stimulation.

I gulp and nod vigorously.

"Are you coming?" he asks.

I'm afraid to answer. He just might stop if I say yes. I concentrate, because there's no way I'm not going to finish this time. He stops.

I groan. "Really?"

"I can't reward you for bad behavior, baby. Get on your knees," he orders.

Damn it, whatever game he's playing is beginning to work. I just want to be fucked by Vince. So I get off the bed and plant myself on all fours on top of the rug. "Okay, I'm on my knees."

"Be quiet, or I'm zipping up and leaving."

I'm so close to challenging him, but he's already

demonstrated that he'll take drastic action if I do something he doesn't like. I sigh and roll my eyes.

"The eye roll and sigh are strikes one and two. I want to fuck you silly. Look at this." Vince steps in front of me and grabs his rock-hard dick, stroking it up and down.

I want it inside me too.

"If I don't see you in person, in real life—skin on skin, then I don't want to see you at all," he says.

"You don't—"

"I said shut the fuck up." He must be able to see how disturbed I am by his tone, because he sighs remorsefully and says, "Strike one for me. I shouldn't speak to you that way. I just want to get one thing clear before we start." He sets my engagement ring in front of me. "Put that on."

I gaze up at him. I've been keeping the ring hidden away in my panty drawer at his house. I sit on my knees, slip on the ring, and show him.

Vince takes my hand. "Wear it. Now get on the bed and spread your legs, wide."

I vacillate between doing what he says and telling him to go to hell. The game he's playing is profoundly conflicting. I stand, and we're face to face. The feathery breath he releases is like satin on my lips.

"Wait," he says.

I gulp. Vince takes my dress by the hem and slides it up my thighs. His hands make my skin shiver, and his rock-hard erection pokes me. My nipples yearn for his mouth. My clit whimpers for his touch. My sex screams to be penetrated by him. What a wicked game Vincent Adams is playing, and at the moment, I have no doubt that I'm all in.

Vincent Adams

No matter how hard Vince's dick got or his mouth watered at the sight of Maggie's beautiful body, he was determined not to fold under the pressure. The point was to make her ache for him, and not just moderately but excessively. He'd driven to Monroe's house defeated, ready to apologize to Maggie for all the shit he'd done to her, even the shit he lied about.

He hadn't seen her since her cousin Curtis's wedding when she'd left him nearly an hour after the bride and groom said, "I do." Later that night,

Vince had gone with Charlie and two of Charlie's friends to a small dive bar. Vince got three scotches closer to the moon, pissed that Maggie had banged him in the closet then left his dick high and dry. He felt as if he was the most sexually frustrated, loneliest motherfucker on the planet. Then Charlie's friend, Thatcher Collins, asked him when was he marrying that "hot goddess."

"I asked her," Vince said.

"And what did she say?" Thatcher said.

"She said yes."

"She doesn't wear a ring. I checked."

"Me too," Peter Reece said.

"Every guy in the building checked. She's fucking hotter than hot," Thatcher said.

"She's not that hot," Charlie mumbled.

Vince snorted and gulped all the liquid in his glass. He raised the empty glass and called to the bartender for another.

"I haven't seen her in a while. Where is she?" Thatcher asked.

"On her way to London," Vince muttered, hating having to say it out loud.

"There was a reason why Maggie was single when you first met her," Charlie said. He took a swig from his glass, not realizing all eyes were on him.

"Is she a crazy psycho bitch?" Thatcher asked, sitting on the edge of his seat.

Vince raised a finger. "Hey, she's not a bitch."

"Sorry, guy. Didn't mean it that way. Look at her. What does she have to be bitchy about anyway?"

"Thatch," Charlie said, "Maggie is a bitch. You cross her, and she'll stab you with her stinger. Don't let the Heidi costume fool you."

Vince frowned into his scotch. He wasn't going to rebut Charlie—needling each other was the nature of the two cousins' relationship. Vince and Angelina had learned to stay out of it. Deep down, Maggie and Charlie loved each other until it hurt, but they'd been taking jabs at each other so long, they don't know how to stop the insults. But Vince was conflicted as hell. Before Maggie had come along, the idea of marriage made him break into hives. Listening to his sisters warn him that his clock was ticking and he didn't want to be bouncing babies on his bad knees when he was a senior citizen gave him a migraine. But every man he knew wanted to fuck Maggie, married or single. She had a universe full of options, and sealing the deal would make him her only choice.

"Deep under Maggie's surface lives the soul of a

cranky cat lady with no cats," Charlie continued since he was on a roll.

Thatcher laughed his head off. "Why doesn't she have any cats?"

"Because she'd have to feed them and buy kitty litter and shit. Sorry, Vince bro, but the question isn't when you're going to get married; it's when are you going to get so fucking fed up that you finally dump her ass."

"I'm never dumping her," Vince said.

"I'll remember that when you eat those words. Look, I love Mags. I really want the best for her, but she's not wearing your fucking ring, is she? Maggie doesn't believe in marriage. I'm surprised she hasn't told you that. The best relationship she's ever had was with herself."

Vince crumpled his eyebrows. He couldn't dismiss what Charlie was saying. Maggie made the worst girlfriend, but when they were together, it was fantastic.

She didn't wear the engagement ring. *He was determined to make her wear the fucking ring.* He wasn't one of those guys who wanted her to stay home barefoot and pregnant, but they had to live some kind of life together, like normal couples. He was tired of being penciled in on her *fucking* calendar.

Half the time it wasn't even her calling to make the plans; it was Mavis, her assistant. He had moved heaven and earth to lick up the crumbs of time that she had given him, but crumbs could never fill the belly. He wanted to feel fulfilled when it came to loving Maggie. He deserved way more than she was giving.

"Does she love you?" Thatcher asked.

"Yes, she does." Vince was sure about the answer to that question but he looked to Charlie for consensus anyway.

Charlie snorted. "She loves him."

"Then make her remember it. I'll give you some tips," he said. "But they can backfire if she doesn't love you." Thatcher had told him about borrowing tricks from BDSM culture, dominant and submissive practices. "It's some sick shit but it works on hot chicks like her who are used to men falling all over them."

"Maggie'll never be some guy's slave," Charlie chimed in. "If she does, I'll kick her ass. Plus, Maggie's not insecure."

"None of them are insecure until you bring it out of them," Thatcher said.

Vince slumped his shoulders. "You're right, Charlie. It's not going to work on her."

Thatcher slapped Vince on the shoulder. "It'll work. Believe me dude. I studied her. She knows she hot. You want her to open wide and let you in on command?"

The thought of having Maggie spread her legs on command made Vince's dick throb. "Fuck yes. So how should I do it?"

"Pull back. Make her earn every fuck and tit touch. Do you go down on her?" Thatcher asked.

"Every chance I get." Vince could see Thatcher fantasizing about tasting Maggie. It kind of bothered him.

"Then spoon-feed her that shit too. Take her to the edge, but don't let her come until she earns it."

Charlie burst into laughter, pounding the bar top. "If that shit works with Maggie, then dude, you are a god, and I will bow down like a heathen and worship you."

"What's the alternative?" Vince asked Charlie.

Charlie's laughter simmered. After pondering for a moment, he shrugged. "There isn't one. Unless Maggie changes, then brother, you have an expiration date."

That was Vince's thought exactly.

The first thing he'd done was refuse Maggie's calls. It wasn't easy. He missed the phone sex.

Maggie could get him so excited that he would finish before she reached the end of the scenario. But he was tired of making love to her only in the fantasies she fed him.

A couple of weeks passed, and he had gone so long without contacting Maggie that he began to feel free of the power she had over him. When he saw Emily at his sister Lexington's wedding, a flash of attraction made him do something stupid. He hadn't even known that Emily would be there.

He'd later learned that his sister Lexi had set them up. Vince's sisters hated Maggie. Lexi didn't like her because she said Maggie was rude to her once in high school, and Alexandria and Madison didn't like her because they had concluded that Maggie was crass, which made her unsuitable for him.

Emily was the opposite of Maggie. Emily was wide-eyed and affable. She laughed at all his jokes. She stared at him from across the room. On the day before the wedding, the two of them had gone to all their favorite spots in Denver, which included "The Watering Hole," a place where the kids used to make out and fuck. It was nighttime, and he and Emily stood on the edge of the polluted lake. Sunburned condoms and marijuana butts littered the ground.

They reminisced about their first time there and how he'd really had to work to get into her pants. The next thing he knew, they were kissing. Then they were fucking, and then they were fucking like rabbits.

He liked the way Emily always wanted to be around him. She'd even said something about them moving in together one day. Sure, it had made him squeamish, but it also made him wonder why it could never be that easy with Maggie. He didn't understand why Maggie had had to purchase that apartment in Lincoln Square when she could've just moved into his place, south of Central Park. He had the best pad in the building!

Then Robert, who had also been a guest at his mother's house for the wedding, caught him and Emily fucking behind the toolshed. When Vince lied and said it was their first time, Robert admitted that he'd seen them in the pool house as well. So Vince was forced to 'fess up. He also declared that he was done with Maggie, but Vince wanted to take it back as soon as he saw that look in Robert's eyes.

"Then she's fair game?" Robert asked.

Vince shrugged. He didn't know what to say. "Maggie's free to do whatever the hell she likes. She does what she wants anyway."

It was Robert who had asked Emily to work for them. Vince knew it was a calculated move on Robert's part. Vince's life was spiraling out of control—he was fucking Emily but missing the hell out of Maggie, who had no idea he was fucking another woman. He racked his brain for a way to dump Emily while making sure Maggie never learned about his indiscretion. The more he thought about it, the more he realized he was in too deep to come out unscathed.

Then Maggie had showed up at the office that morning. One look at her, and he realized that he'd definitely made the biggest mistake of his life. Vince didn't want to give her up, and Robert was already pouncing on her. However, Vince could look at Maggie and tell that she was still the same. If only she could be more like Emily and ache when she wasn't in his presence. It sure as hell made him ache not to be with her. So he'd decided to use the BDSM shit on her.

At the moment, he had to press his lips together to keep from suckling her nipples as he pulled her dress off. Her skin was so soft, ready for him to sink into. Their eyes met. He felt the pre-cum moistening the tip of his penis as he watched her crawl up against the headboard and part her milky thighs. His dick twitched, and he had to grab it to keep it from spraying.

"Touch yourself," he said, going against the BDSM handbook.

"Where?" she asked.

"Your pussy."

"How?"

Oh shit. He was ready to devour that swollen knot of hers. He wanted her sweet, slippery juices on his tongue, but he had to control himself. He had to make Maggie think that this was her only chance with him, and if she fucked it up, then that was it. He had to be prepared to leave that hot, dripping pussy on the bed, legs spread and untouched.

"Make it ready for me, baby," he said.

Maggie grinned naughtily and plunged two fingers inside her as she rounded her clit with her thumb. In and out, she finger-fucked herself. Vince's mouth watered, and he swallowed the extra fluid.

"Pull on your nipple, baby," he said.

He skipped a breath as Maggie tugged at the tip.

"Fuck," he muttered.

He dropped his pants and underwear and pulled off his shirt. His dick was so hard that the vein along his shaft wanted to pop out of his skin. It was too late to eat her out; he was too close to coming. Vince slammed his dick into her slippery caves. Oh shit, she was dripping wet and hot. He pounded the hell out of her, hitting bottom.

He clutched her ass, scooted her away from the headboard, and rammed his dick deeper inside her. He held still, warning himself not to come. Maggie tried to shift to chase her orgasm, but he held her hips. She moaned out of frustration. The blood in his dick settled. He was thankful for the reprieve. He pulled out of her and smashed his tongue against her swollen knot. It was soft and slippery and hard, all at the same time. She wriggled against his mouth.

"If you don't stay still, then I'm going to stop." He hoped she wouldn't call his bluff because there was no way in hell he would discontinue.

She nodded wildly. Her eyes were glazed. Hell, he was in complete control, which made the blood rush back to his penis. He plunged his tongue into her wetness, and then reattached his mouth to her clit, sucking and lapping. She struggled to stay still, and that turned him on even more. He was about to blow, and she hadn't even come yet. He slipped two fingers inside her. Maggie screamed with pleasure. She tried to grab the headboard, but her arms couldn't reach. If only he could eat those tits and stay where he was. He would have to wait.

"Oh, Vince," she cried, arching her back and tugging at the sheets.

He strained to hold in his orgasm. Finally her walls pulsated around his fingers, releasing the nectar he'd been milking her for. He slammed his erection deep inside her. One thrust. He shivered. Second thrust. His balls tightened, and he blasted his seed inside her, grunting at the top of his lungs.

Vince trembled until the sensation subsided. He pressed himself heavily upon her, and Maggie wrapped her arms around him. For a moment, he felt their souls merging. He wasn't done with her yet. In his mind, the last person who'd given her breasts a good go was Monroe. He had to take over. Vince kissed her sensual mouth and sucked his way down her neck to stroke her nipple with his tongue. He'd just learned that she loved it when he raked his teeth across the tip.

He kissed the tip of her damp nipple and looked her in the eyes. Maggie looked as if she didn't know what he would do next. He hoped he hadn't taken the BDSM tactics too far. He loved his feisty sex goddess who had started taking more initiative in the bedroom since they'd first gotten together. He didn't want to mind-fuck her away.

"So what's this talk about you quitting?" he asked.

"I think it's best I work with Monroe."

"Why?"

"At first it was because of what happened this morning, but now I'm kind of excited about the work." She raised her eyebrows when she said "work."

The way she said "work" pissed him off. Her tone exposed the fact that she still loved it more than him. His dick was still too soft to punish her with it. "You know what you need? Get back on your knees."

She grunted and rolled her eyes. "That again?"

Without saying a word, Vince slid out of her and off of her. He grabbed his pants.

"Okay," Maggie said.

He was relieved that that had worked. Perhaps he was actually getting somewhere. He dropped his pants the moment she got on her knees. But there was no way he was getting back up that night, and Maggie was settling back into satisfying her ambitions before him. Vince would have to make her feel something she would never forget—all pleasure, no pain.

He moved behind her and spread her ass cheeks. Starting from the bottom, he licked until his tongue plunged into her asshole. Maggie gasped and moaned to let him know how much she liked that.

He pinched her round ass then sucked the blushing flesh against his tongue. He had changed his mind. The principle of pleasure and pain excited him, and just like that, his dick was getting with the program.

MAGGIE

I turn to see how Vince is making all those delicious sensations happen at once, but he jams his cock into my slippery space. The way he's rimming me makes my legs quiver. I whimper, and Vince grips me around the belly to make sure I don't move.

"You like this, baby?" he grunts.

"Uh-hum."

He bobs me expertly against his cock. I get louder as each thrust spurs pleasurable sensations. Then Vince pulls out and springs to his feet. He snatches his pants off the floor and quickly puts them on.

"No…" I groan.

"Your car is parked out front." He takes the keys out of his pocket and hands them to me. "Here you go."

I hesitate. He's all business, but it's evident by the size of his bulge that he's still aroused. I take the keys, and he grabs my wrist and pulls. Our chests collide before our tongues explore each other's. My sex throbs for more.

"Um…" I lick his sweetness on my lips. "How about we go back to your place?"

Vince drops his head and sighs gravely. "I can't."

"Why not?" I pelt his chest with kisses.

"Stop…"

I grab his cock. "No."

"Mags." He removes my hand.

"Is it because she lives with you?"

He frowns, confused. "Oh, Emily? No. I live alone, thanks to you."

"Thanks to me?" I step back, looking in his eyes. I feel as if he's accusing me of something that's not my fault. "What is the fucking problem, Vince?"

"I told you already!"

"All you've told me was to get on my fucking knees."

"Maggie, you're the problem."

"Me?"

"Give up your business plans with Monroe. Decrease your workload with A&Rt and be with me every day. Can you do that?"

"Huh?" What he's asking is not only unreasonable but undoable.

He shakes his head and clears his throat. "Don't worry, I knew you wouldn't be able to do it. But a lot has to change before we can make another go at it."

Vince is giving me a headache. "Like what?"

He sighs as though I've asked him a difficult question. "Remember the wedding?"

"We've been going downhill since then."

"You left me there. I didn't even know the guy."

I rear back as if he's slapped me in the face. "But you were with Charlie and Jack. I thought you were having a good time."

"I was until you left!"

"I had to fly to London because—"

"You always have to fly some-fucking-where! You have a team for a reason. You should delegate more," he says.

I take a deep breath. Vince needn't say more. He has been dropping hints for a very long time regarding how he feels about how much I work, even if it's for *his* company. Yes, I have staff to deal with events, but I love the grunt work, not sitting behind a desk and calling the shots. "What do you want me to say?"

"What do I want you to say? Do you want to be in this with me?"

"In a relationship? Yes. I love you."

"Charlie thinks you're going to leave me one day."

"You're listening to Chuck?"

He shakes his head. "Forget it. I have to go. Are you still determined to work with Monroe?"

"Well, yeah, I guess so. Yes."

His expression goes stone cold. "Are you giving us two weeks' notice?"

"Are we breaking up?"

He lifts my hand and spreads his thumb over my ring. "Don't take this off." He kisses the ring. "I'll call you." He drops my hand and walks to the doorway.

"Vince?"

He turns and gives me a look.

"Should I do my last two weeks in L.A. instead of New York?"

His eyes fall down my body then go back up to my face. "Go to New York."

Ouch. "But Robert will be there."

"Is that a problem for you?" he asks.

I shrug. "Probably."

"Don't worry about it. Do what you want, Mags. You already let Monroe suck your tits—*my* tits."

For some strange reason, I'm compelled to look at my breasts. When I look up, Vince is already running up the stairs. I would follow, but I'm naked.

By the time I've dressed and rejoined the party,

Vince is gone. The music is louder, white lights are flashing, and people are smashed. I search for Monroe through the provocative dancing, face sucking, tit sucking, dick sucking, clit sucking, and old-fashioned fucking. This is so not my scene.

"There you are, sexy," someone behind me says in my ear.

The man's hands grip my torso and massage me. I turn my head to see Dash, and he nibbles on my neck. I'm supposed to have sex with him tonight. After the way Vince left things, it wouldn't be so bad to get banged by a newbie just to get back at him. But that's only spite talking, not my desire.

"Do you know where Monroe is?" I ask.

"She'll join in later."

The moment of truth has arrived. I take a deep sigh. "I'm not going with you, but thanks."

He chuckles. "I heard you required my services."

"Services? Are you a hooker?"

"No. I'm just good at fucking." He massages my muffin. I must've moaned or something because he asks, "You want more?"

I gulp. "No..."

He doesn't stop. "Come on. Let me fuck you sideways." He gently bites my shoulder and does exactly what Robert did in the elevator, except his dick strokes my ass with more vigor. He sinks his tongue in my ear. His hand slides up my thigh. "I could bend you over right here."

"That's okay," I say in a rush and shrug away from him. I run down the stairs and all the way to my room.

That was close. That was very close.

Three guys are in my room. One of them looks at me as if he's considering adding me to the madness. It's Delta Foster. The other two are engrossed in getting Delta off.

"Excuse me, but you're on my bed," I say, trying to keep my voice steady.

"You want to join us?" Delta's still getting his knob scrubbed and nipples sucked. "I like pussy too."

I squeeze my eyes shut and open them. I'm really seeing what I'm seeing. "No, I'm not feeling well. So could you take the orgy somewhere else?"

Delta chuckles. "You're hot, you know?"

"If you say so."

"I'll send these guys away, and it'll just be me and you." He closes his eyes and grunts.

I squint squeamishly. I mean, what the hell! "I just need to get some sleep."

"Fuck," he mutters and jerks as he shoots his load. The guy comes up for a kiss, but Delta pushes his mouth away. "Is that your phone?" he asks, breathing heavily.

What the hell? My eyes follow his gaze. "Yes."

"It's been ringing."

"Oh..."

"Whoever it is, you should call them back. Let's go. Maggie needs her beauty rest," Delta says.

The two guys obey on command.

I clear my throat nervously. He knows my name. "Thank you."

"I'll see you soon," he says on his way out.

I close the door and lock it. I can still hear the music, the rumbling of voices, and people splashing and frolicking in the pool. I'm from New York though, which means I can sleep through a hundred jackhammers pounding concrete. Hopefully when I wake up, my encounter with Robert in the elevator, Vince's insistence that I get on my knees, me quitting my job in a fit of jealous rage, the left turn I took onto the border of lesbianism, which culminated with my weird yet intriguing sex with Vince, and getting hit on by Dash—none of it will have ever happened.

4

A NEW LINE OF BUSINESS

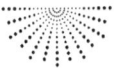

MAGGIE

*I*t's morning. I'm clearly aware that last night *did* happen as my pussy flexes with memories of Vince being inside me. I also remember Delta saying something about my phone ringing a lot. I check the messages. The first is from Jack. He wants me to look in on Daisy, and he heard that I'm leaving A&Rt, so he wants to talk about that. The others are from shocked colleagues and poachers who want to take me to lunch to talk about opportunities I might find interesting.

I'm still wearing the dress from last night. As soon as I sigh with dread at the thought of having to go to my car to get my suitcase, I see it tucked in the corner. I wonder if it was there last night. I fling the suitcase onto the bed, open it, and put on my white

V-neck T-shirt, stretchy miniskirt, and flip-flops. I want to make it easy to take off my clothes later and jump in the pool. I return Jack's call before I head out to see how Monroe is doing.

"Mags," he says.

"Did you call me last night?" I ask.

"What's this I hear about you leaving A&Rt?"

"Did you hear the whole story?"

"I probably did. I can make Emily go away if you want."

I smile. "I love you, Jack. It's always a comfort to know that I have you in my corner, but I don't know. I quit out of anger, but that made me really consider this new venture with Monroe."

"What venture is that?" There's a note of caution in his tone.

"Monroe thinks we should go into business together. I would be an image consultant." I wait for Jack to process that.

"What's Monroe's role in all of this?"

"I imagine she'll land the clients and help keep them in line."

"Are your clients famous?" he asks.

"Yes."

"I don't know about this, Mags. Shit can get hairy quickly."

I sigh, remembering Delta Foster and his fondness for dick—and not his own. He has a reputation as a ladies' man. I'm not one to keep up with celebrity gossip, but the fact that Monroe feels Delta needs an image consultant must mean that the smokescreen is fading and fans are wondering what team he plays on. "You're telling me."

"Whatever you decide, I'm in your corner. I didn't like you working around Vince and Robert anyway," he says.

Once, Robert referred to Jack as my bruiser, which made me question whether or not Jack had warned him against flirting with me. He once caught Robert discreetly squeezing my ass, and Robert often looks at me as if we're stranded on a deserted island and I just turned into a hot dog or something. I'm used to it. I've learned to ignore him. Yesterday was the first time he'd ever masturbated against my ass. I felt his dick twitching and everything. I think he had groomed me for that moment. I wasn't surprised and was slightly aroused.

"Yeah." I sigh. "I think it's run its course."

"If you need me for anything, let me know."

"I will."

"And, um…"

"And what?"

"Since you're in L.A., could you check on Daisy for me?" Jack asks.

"My pleasure, but I wish you two would just get back together already."

He's silent.

"Jack?"

"I'm here."

"Apparently you miss her, since you want me to check on her."

He's silent.

"Jack?" I ask again.

"Tell me how she's doing as soon as you find out."

I roll my eyes. "You guys could work through your issues better and faster if you lived together."

"If the fix was quick, then I would have fixed it already," he snaps.

"Then make me understand what she did so wrong? Tell me you're not mad at her because of Joella."

"Of course not," he hisses.

"Then what?"

"Daisy's…"

"She's what?"

"Too fluid."

I'm taken aback. "She likes chicks?"

"Is that what they're calling fluid these days?"

"That's what I call it. What do you mean by Daisy being too fluid?"

"She doesn't give a fuck about much unless you're her dead brother."

His words hit me like a two-ton steel beam. "But the operative word is 'dead.' You're still alive, and she married you."

"She hasn't called me."

"Have you called her? You're the one who left."

Silence.

"Jack?"

"I'm here," he snaps. "You know I'll never hang up on you."

"I know..." I sit on the bed and wait patiently through the rest of his silent spell.

"You'll check on her for me?" His tone indicates that he's wrapping up this conversation.

"Yes."

"Thanks. Call me as soon as you know something."

"I will. Love you, Jack."

"Love you too, Mags." He hangs up.

I think it's stupid they're apart. It makes no sense no matter how you slice it. I do believe that Jack has created the whole mess though.

I head out to find Monroe. She has a lot of house

73

for one person. I poke my head into her bedroom. "Roe?"

Her sheets are messy, but she's not on top of them. I look in the bathroom, and she's not in there either. I figure she's probably starving just as much as I am, so I head to the kitchen. The house is immaculate, as if the salacious night never happened. When I reach the kitchen, I see Delta at the oven, flipping pancakes.

He turns to look at me. "So you weren't a figment of my imagination?"

He's wearing a pair of sheer purple boxers. It's a cliché, but he does look better in person. Delta sports a crew cut, and he has light-brown eyes and a heart-shaped face. He reminds me of a female version of Jennifer Love Hewitt. That's how pretty he is, which is probably why he's used to getting plenty of whatever he wants.

"Where's Monroe?" I ask.

"Around. Are you a two-pancake woman, or one?" He gazes at my body. "Did I eat your pussy at any point during the night?"

"Um, no." I plop down on a stool at the island.

"Humph, maybe I wanted to eat your pussy. I was getting my dick waxed like a motherfucker." He shifts his hips. "It's sore as fuck."

I try to keep a straight face. "Right."

"The first time I saw you, I was like whoa. I tossed my head back and looked up, and there you were in that blue dress. You were wearing a blue dress, right?"

I narrow one eye. "Uh-hum."

"I was in your bedroom?"

"Fucking two men," I say.

He chuckles. "Don't let looks deceive you. I like pussy too."

"Yeah, you said that too."

"I meant it. I eat pussy. I don't fuck it. I don't fuck anything. I'm all about the oral."

"Yep," I say dismissively. The guy has issues, and I'm not a shrink.

"I don't know how it's going to work, you being my image consultant and me so turned on by you."

"Well, maybe we can find you a new image consultant." I'm ready to pass on this psycho.

He laughs and sets three pancakes in front of me. "You need to eat. I consider myself a bodiologist—"

"A bodiologist?"

"You're curvy slim. Your pussy's not snug, but it's tighter than average."

"I thought you didn't dip your dick in pussies."

"You would be the exception."

"How many exceptions have you made so far?"

He smirks. "I'm not done. Have you seen your ass?"

"It's behind me, so no."

"It's remarkable. And your breasts are too, but you're fifteen pounds skinnier than you should be. Did you just lose that weight?"

I frown. "Huh?"

"You look like you've dropped a lot of weight fast."

I glance uncomfortably over my shoulder. How the hell could he tell? I have lost weight. I've been too damn busy to eat.

"Well, I'm going to give you a little advice," Delta says. "Add fifteen pounds, and your pussy will be a fraction more snug as a bug in a rug."

"Monroe!" I shout at the top of my lungs.

"Maggie!" she replies from somewhere far away.

"Get the fuck in here!"

Delta sets a fork on my plate. "Not fucking yet!" he calls and squeezes syrup on the pancakes. "You said you saw me fucking two guys?"

I throw up my hands. "Don't care."

"Yeah, but you mention that to the wrong person and…" He makes the sound of an explosion and uses his hands to demonstrate. "My career in smoke.

Chicks don't want to think that their leading man likes dick."

"Delta, you're irritating me. What the hell is your point? And say it fast."

He smirks. "Once you're A-list in this town, you're trucking through a field of land mines. Everybody wants to take you down."

I nod. "Well, you're skipping through that field as though those land mines are lilies."

"It's time to… progress."

"Progress into what?"

"The family man."

"You want me to make the world believe you're a family man?" I ask.

He smiles as if the joke will be on every sucker who buys what he wants me to sell. Delta puts his face close to mine. We stare into each other's eyes. My mind is racing, figuring out how to make the lie reality.

"Do you have a family?" I ask.

"Could you get me one?"

I snort cynically. "Sure, I can just order one up in the family catalog."

"Humph…" He steps back and away from me. "Maybe you're not an image consultant."

I feel as though he's challenging me. I narrow my

eyes to think then throw up a hand. "Wait. Do you know any lesbian thespians?"

He smiles again and nods. "I do."

"Well, we can start there."

"Yes, we could. But, Maggie, I'm not gay."

"You would know."

"I like my dick waxed by a man. The lips are stronger, jaw tighter, and they can deep throat like a motherfucker."

Damn, TMI. I pick up the fork to dive into the pancakes. "That's your business."

Delta extends a hand. We shake on it, but he seizes my left hand.

"Are you engaged?" he asks.

I shrug.

"No? Yes?" he asks.

"I think so."

"Ah, fuck, because um…" He keeps my hand as he walks around the bar.

I ruffle my eyebrows.

"Maggie, you're going to have to let me eat you for breakfast."

"Um, nope." I clamp my legs together.

He nods. "Yeah, you will, because you're not going to make me keep wondering. It's not conducive for doing business together."

It happens so fast. He's on his knees, and his face is between my legs. My first inclination is to push his head away from my pussy, but his hot tongue has already slid up my slit, and my clit tingles as soon as he sucks it.

"Shit," I mutter, looking around wildly. I can't believe I'm letting Delta Foster eat me out.

He clamps down on my thighs so I can't shift my butt, but I haven't felt much after that first sensation. His tongue is all over the place, slurping and drenching me with saliva. I had higher hopes than this.

"Pancakes," Monroe says as she strolls into the kitchen.

I point downward as soon as she looks at me.

She rolls her eyes and mouths, "Just let him finish."

I shake my head. I could help him out a little if he stops holding me in place. If I just turn a little to the left, I could reach orgasm. He keeps slurping and licking me here and there and everywhere. Monroe and I widen our eyes at each other and laugh without making a sound.

"Ah," Delta cries as he quakes. He came before I could fake it!

Monroe and I laugh even harder.

After the sloppy vagina-bath Delta gave me, I need a shower. I laugh through it. That was so surreal. This time, I make sure my crotch is far less accessible by wearing panties under my cutoff shorts. I leave through the bay doors and drive down to Malibu to check on Daisy. On the way to her house, I'm bombarded by calls. My colleagues are panicking. I promise to work with each of them to wrap up our projects before I leave.

"Two weeks?" Linda, who used to be my assistant before Mavis, asks.

"Robert convinced me to follow protocol. Were you watching on videoconference?"

"I saw it," she says squeamishly. "But in your defense, Vincent Adams was acting like a jackass."

"I agree," I say, happy she and I have come to the same conclusion.

"That Emily woman, I was going to tell you to watch out for her. I've heard things."

"Shit!" I push on the brakes, and my tires screech. I almost ran a red light. "What have you heard?"

"Did you get into an accident?"

"No. What have you heard?" My blood is boiling.

"Janice saw them kissing."

I roll my eyes. "Janice is a shit-starter. Did anyone besides her see anything?"

"Everyone knows that they're always together. She's into him, and he doesn't seem uninterested. Everyone thought you and Vince had broken up about a month ago."

Oh damn, my heart hurts. "We weren't. He was just cheating on me."

"I'm so sorry, Maggie. I should've said something earlier. Shit, I'm your friend, and I dropped the ball."

"Don't beat yourself up about it."

"I'm going to knock myself out!"

I shake my head. "I guess I suck at relationships."

"No way. You do relationships well enough. Remember that woman he was seeing and was going to marry last year? What was her name?"

"Mariana, Vanessa, Gabrielle…"

"That's it Gabrielle! Well Emily and Gabrielle are the Bobbsey-Twins. He's a nice guy but you're too good for him.

I smile, appreciating the support, although I don't think Vince's complaint about me is invalid. " Perhaps but I'm sure going to miss you."

"I already miss you. Change your mind."

"I don't want to. But apply for my old position. You're the best replacement they could find. We work together on just about everything." I pull up onto the cement slab in front of Jack and Daisy's house.

"You think I should?"

"Hell yes."

"Will they hire me though?"

"If they know what's best. Just keep me in the loop. I'll let them make the right decision fair and square, but if Robert's dick gets in the way and he tries to hire his next fuck, then I'll talk to Jack."

"Oh my God, what is that you always call him?"

"A scoundrel."

"He's such a scoundrel."

"The king of them. But don't mind Robert Tango. Toss your name in the hat, and I'll make shit happen."

"Okay! I'll toss my name in the hat."

I smile. "Good."

"I'll see you in New York on Monday?" she asks.

"Bright and early."

We hang up. I sit for a while and stare at the ring on my finger. If Emily is Vince's new girlfriend, then why does he insist that I wear this? So I pissed him off because I work too much? That's not going to change, especially since I'm forming a new company. Perhaps he should be with a woman like Emily. She looks like the kind of woman who has no hopes or dreams to give up. Well, I have too many. If Vince is asking me to choose this ring over them, then he should definitely make a life with Emily.

I hop out of my SUV and gaze up at Daisy's house. It doesn't look as though anyone's home. The shutters are closed. Daisy usually keeps the sliding glass doors of the sun-room open, but they're closed. I decide to check out the house regardless. Daisy has a habit of wasting away in bed when she's depressed. It's heartbreaking to see her that way. I ring the doorbell three times then knock. After no one answers, I use my key and enter. The hallways are shadowy, but each room that I pass is unoccupied.

"Daisy?" I call as I go.

I check her office and then Belmont's. She's not in any of the bedrooms or bathrooms. I check the deck. She isn't there either. She's not in the kitchen or garage.

So I call Jack. "She's not here."

"Then where is she?" He sounds as though he's panicking.

"I don't know. I'll call her mother and Angelina."

"No, I'll call. Thanks for checking."

"Hey, no problem. Let me know where she is when you find her. I'm worried. I think you should come home."

"Later." He waits for my response.

"Later," I say.

He hangs up.

I shake my head. Since I'm done here, I drive back to Monroe's. She and Dash are in the swimming pool when I arrive. They're both naked, and her legs are wrapped around him. Either they're having sex or have just finished.

"Done?" I ask.

Monroe snickers. "We're done."

Although I'm hesitant to join them after what happened last night, I strip and dive in anyway. Monroe and I swim laps, then we stop in front of my bedroom to talk shop.

"Delta will pay us two hundred thousand, plus fees, up front. Once we land him the girl, he'll pay us four hundred thousand. We'll get six hundred thousand each following year for five years and a payoff of one million on the seventh and final year, contingent upon the relationship staying intact."

"Wow, we're expensive, aren't we?"

"Very expensive, and those are just Delta's fees. When we find the woman, we'll negotiate a contract with her and treat them as two separate clients."

I grin.

"What?" she asks.

"You've really chopped this up like an expert."

"Oh ye of little faith in Monroe Blanco."

"I have a lot of faith in you. I wouldn't go into business with you if I didn't."

Monroe nods as though she believes me. "Here's the deal though—no one can know what we really do for our clients."

"I get it."

"Technically, we're a public relations firm. What should we call ourselves?"

"How about Mo&Ma PR?"

Her face lights up. "I like it."

"Me too."

"I'll talk to our business advisor tomorrow. His name is Brent Sherman."

I nod.

"This is going to work, Mags."

"I know."

"I love you."

"I love you more."

We hug, then Monroe dunks me. Shit. I should've seen that coming.

LATER THAT EVENING, WE GO TO CASCADE'S FOR

dinner. Dash offers his services to me yet again, and Monroe tries to encourage me to take him up on his offer.

"It'll be the first time we've fucked the same guy," she says.

I'm *this* close to calling her insane, but I remember she doesn't like it when I say that. "I love you too much to have sex with your boyfriend. So how about we put this to rest once and for all?"

"But you're missing out," she says in a cautionary tone.

"We're all missing out on one thing or a million."

After dinner, we return to Monroe's house. I sleep in my bed alone, and they sleep together in Monroe's bed.

I fly back to New York on Sunday. My flight lands in the afternoon, and later that night, I have dinner at Cloud Rich in the Meatpacking District with Hannah and Cleo. I hadn't seen either of them in a while. The guy Hannah met last year at the pop-up bar is "so three guys ago," and she's moved on to love interest number four. This one is an investor who lives in the Financial District.

"You should meet him, Mags," Cleo says with her eyes widened eerily. "He reminds me of the American psycho."

"Well, my head is still attached, so he's not," Hannah says defensively.

"For now, that is."

"And will you please stop calling me every night?" Hannah says. "He's starting to wonder if there's something wrong with you."

"He's what's wrong with me! Just move on already, Han. He's a serial killer."

"How about we get Maggie all caught up on you and Perry? How often do you fuck now that you're married?"

"I'm actually curious to know the answer," I say.

Cleo scowls at Hannah. "What makes you think we don't hump every night?"

"Do you?"

"For us, there's no difference between being married and just being boyfriend and girlfriend other than the tax benefit for him."

"I'm calling bullshit on that," Hannah says. "Every married couple I know only fucks once a month."

"Perry and I fuck twice a day, every day." Cleo takes a drink of her cocktail and gives Hannah a "take that" look.

I've been studying Hannah since we sat. There's something different about her. "Did you cut your hair?" I think that's it.

"Yeah, I added some layers."

"It looks good."

She examines my hair. "You could use a haircut."

"I think so too," Cleo adds. "You're beautiful, Maggie. You've been going around looking like a cavewoman for too long."

I take the cocktail out of Cleo's hand before she takes another swig. She always gets very candid when liquor rushes to her head. "No more for you until after you've eaten something."

"I'm fine." She takes the drink back.

"You just called me a cavewoman. I haven't looked like a cavewoman in a long time. Give me credit for that."

"Well, we haven't seen you in a long time," Hannah says.

"I know."

"So how is Monroe?" Hannah asks.

"Oh shit, how could I not lead with this? She and I are business partners."

Cleo's eyes expand. "Are you kidding me?"

"Nope."

"Well, she's never failed at anything she's done," Cleo says.

"That's true," Hannah says. "Okay, now to the

good part. Vincent Adams. How's it going between you two?"

I groan and bury my face in my hands.

"Oh no," Cleo says.

I recount what happened between Vince and me and how I made an ass out of myself on Friday. They both laugh as if it's the funniest thing they've ever heard. We have more drinks, gossip about the people we know, and cab it home.

I moved into my apartment in Lincoln Square last year. Vince's pricier Central Park penthouse isn't that far away. He's asked me to move in with him so many times that I can't count them all, but I've always dreamed of being able to afford a nice apartment in this city. It was an aspiration that I needed to fulfill. I pay six thousand a month for a one-bedroom apartment with a den. I may not have the panoramic views of Central Park that Vince has, but I can see it from my living room window.

It's two a.m., and I check my emails before going to bed. Monroe sent me a list of names, all female, with an ambiguous message that says, "Per our discussion in the kitchen." Some of the women are actresses and models. She's put an asterisk next to the ones she really wants me to examine.

"Got it. Love you," I write back.

She answers immediately. *"Love you too. P.S. and your tits."*

"LOL, shaking my head and rolling my eyes," and not calling her crazy, which she clearly is.

We agree to speak on Wednesday after I narrow down the list and do more research on Delta Foster's career and life. Jack had mentioned that the woman he'd brought to Curtis's wedding was an investigator, so I'll call him tomorrow to ask if she provides services for someone with my kind of request. I want all the shit I can find on Delta Foster—the good, the bad, and the freaky.

I forgo breakfast so that I can make it to work by seven thirty a.m. The other early birds study me as I walk to my office. Mavis is already at her desk, and she stands as soon as she sees me. Her almond eyes are reddened and her expression dreary.

I point my head toward my office. "Join me in there."

Mavis is rigid when she sits in the chair in front of my desk. She's clenching my schedule and avoiding eye contact. I never took a moment to ponder how my leaving would affect her. I'm the one who asked Mavis to be my assistant. She had been working for the company as a marketing administrative assistant for three years, so one day, I asked her about her goals. She had said she wanted to be an executive assistant because her strengths were in handling details and keeping a very busy person on schedule. So after Linda was promoted, Mavis became my executive assistant. She has made my hectic life manageable.

I set my briefcase on my desk and settle into my chair. "I'm sure you've heard."

"That you're leaving? Yes. If the reason..." She ruffles her eyebrows as if she's reconsidering saying whatever she wants to say.

"It has nothing to do with the meeting. I mean, not anymore. I'm pursuing a new business venture." The look on her face says she doesn't believe me. "But I won't leave you hanging."

"But are you sure you want to leave? Maybe you should take some time to think about it. You're very important here. I've been receiving calls all morning and this weekend from concerned clients."

"Well, they shouldn't be concerned..." Robert says.

I look over Mavis's head at Robert standing in the doorway.

"Good morning, Maggie." Robert's smirk lingers on me for a few beats before he looks at Mavis. "Good morning, Mavis."

"Good morning, Mr. Tango."

"Maggie, we need to..." He points his head toward his office, which is next to Vince's.

"In a minute," I say. "I just want to finish up with Mavis."

He nods. "Are you running over your schedule for the day?"

"We're getting to that."

He walks in, takes a chair from the round table I use to hold small meetings, and sits next to Mavis. She and I are caught off guard. I was just about to invite her to come work with me, offering her the same salary and benefits. Of course, I'll have to hit Jack up for a loan to do that.

"Well, I'll wait until you get to that part," he says, making himself comfortable.

I glare at him. "How do you know I didn't want to speak to her in private?"

He throws up his hands nonchalantly. "About what? You're leaving."

"I'm still here now."

Robert clicks his tongue. "Now, now, Maggie. I only want to see how you work with Mavis since she'll be my assistant after you leave."

Mavis and I both look shocked.

"You can't take her from me," I whine. No one can make me regress like Robert. I focus on Mavis. "I was going to ask if you wanted to come work with me."

Finally, she smiles. "Well, of course!"

"I was going to double your salary if you come work for me," Robert says.

She slaps her hand on her chest and gasps.

I shoot to my feet. "Mavis, could you give us a moment please?"

Her eyes flicker between Robert and me. I can tell that she's already accepted Robert's offer because she's second-guessing my request.

"Yes, Maggie and I should talk alone," Robert says while wearing that naughty smirk.

I seethe as Mavis walks out the office. I don't like the way he looks at her ass. He's such a scoundrel. Robert shuts the door behind her. If looks could kill, he'd be six feet under.

"Alone at last," he says.

"Who are you fucking with, me or Mavis?"

Robert tilts his head as if he has to think about it. "Could I fuck you both? What is she? Latina? Black? A combination of the two?"

I take a deep breath and hold it to keep myself from exploding. "You are way out of line."

He nudges my shoulder. "It's just a joke. Lighten up. But I do want her to work for me.

She's better than every secretary in the company."

"She's an executive assistant," I snarl.

"Right. But since she's already an asset to our company, I want to *keep her.*"

"I think I'm the one you're fucking with," I say because of the suggestive way he spoke.

He smirks. "I'd like to *keep you* too."

"Okay, you win. If you double her salary, then I won't fight for her. But I want to see that offer in writing. And I want you to add an executive health package. And profit sharing."

"Is that all?"

"No. You know that fancy penthouse health club upstairs? I want her to have a full membership to that for as long as she works for your company."

"Done, done, done, done, and just to put you at ease, done again."

I sigh. "So is that it? Have you gotten your kicks for the morning?"

Robert's expression turns serious as he takes the seat Mavis abandoned. "I'll be shadowing you this week."

"Why?"

"You don't need to know why."

"I do if you're getting your kicks."

"What do you mean by 'kicks'?"

"Grinding my ass, declaring you're going to sleep with me, and looking at me like you're fucking me in your thoughts."

He sniffs. "You make it too easy. But I promise, no more funny business. You don't want me, I get it."

I narrow one eye. "Do you?"

He shakes his head. "Yes."

I laugh. He's impossible.

OUR FIRST MEETING IS WITH LINDA AND HER TEAM. We review the event schedule for the next three months as it applies to Prime D TV. Linda continually mentions the fact that I won't be available when things go wrong. We get through that meeting and the three more afterward.

At ten minutes until two, Robert asks, "Do you eat lunch?"

We're heading back to my office for our next meeting with the *Bugsy's Blue* miniseries international marketing team in London.

"You're hungry?" I ask.

"That's just too easy," he says.

"For food?"

"Yes. You haven't eaten all day. No wonder you're losing our hills."

"Our hills?"

He slides his hand down my hip.

I slap it away. "No touching."

"Okay, but you're going to have to let me take you to dinner tonight."

"Nope," I say as we walk past Mavis's desk. I catch the wink Robert gives her.

She accepts it with an obligatory smile.

"Is this how your schedule has been all along?" he asks as we enter my office.

I plop down in my chair and link into London. "Yes, boss."

"I have to eat. I'm going to ask our executive assistant to order lunch. What do you like?"

"Mavis knows," I say just before Rayford Riley says, "Hello, Maggie."

"Hello, Rayford, Betis, and Magnus."

"I hear you're leaving us, yes?" Betis, a pure redhead like Prince Harry, says.

"Unfortunately, I am. You shall be missed."

Robert walks out to have Mavis order lunch, and he closes the door behind him. He's back fifteen minutes later when we're almost finished solidifying the media strategy for the new show.

An hour later, Mavis lets in two men who set up sushi dishes on my small table. Robert digs in before we bring the meeting to an end.

Mavis knocks on the door. "Ten minutes before your next meeting with the print publications division."

"Cancel it," Robert says. "Maggie's done for the day."

"Tell them I'll be there," I say.

"Tell them that Robert Tango says the meeting and all meetings on Maggie's schedule for the remainder of the day are cancelled. She's worked her quota."

I'm too stunned to object again. Mavis looks at me to gauge my reaction. I just shrug. She nods and backs out of the office.

"What the hell was that?" I ask.

"Shit, I didn't know you worked this fucking hard."

"Vince knows how hard I work. If you were around more, you would too."

"Vince..." He closes one eye. "You haven't mentioned him all day."

I raise my hand and show him my ring. "The last I saw or heard from Vince, he fucked me and made me wear this."

He drops that smirk. "Your engagement ring?"

"Yes," I say, studying the pretty cluster of diamonds.

He snorts and sets a plate of food in front of a chair across from where he's sitting. "Eat now, Maggie."

The smell of Asian spices stimulates my appetite. I go right over and dig in.

"That's the first time you've ever done what I asked without me cajoling you," he says.

I roll my eyes and stuff shrimp on a bed of rice into my mouth. The taste hits me right away, and I close my eyes. "Yum."

"Again, too easy."

I roll my eyes. "Is there ever a moment when sex isn't on your brain?"

"Not around you."

"You can't stand it, can you?"

"No, I can't. Let's just do it tonight. My place. No one has to know but you and me."

I narrow my eyes. "Vince is your friend. Don't you love him?"

"Yeah, I love him, but if you remember, there was you and me before you and him."

"Do you mean eons ago back in high school?"

"It wasn't that long ago. I used to dream about you."

I can't help but laugh.

Robert looks amused but confused.

I say, "You dreamt about me? What did you dream?"

"Do you want me to show you?"

"Is it sexual in nature?"

"Let me show you, and you'll see."

"Nope." I shake my head. "It's sexual."

He chuckles. "It's sexual, but it's romantic too."

I laugh and cough, nearly choking on a scallop roll. "Romantic?"

"You and I were watching the sunset, making babies and shit."

I study him while chewing, searching for clues that he's pulling my leg. I swallow. "What if Jack had called you instead of Vince and asked if you could give me a job here? What would you have done?"

Robert nods as he ponders. "I would've asked you out for a drink."

"Basically you would've tried to get into my pants from day one."

"That's part of it."

I laugh. There are three knocks on the door, and I recognize the cadence. My jaw drops when Vince enters, but I frown when I see who's with him. Emily is wearing a tight, satiny emerald midi-dress. Robert looks just as surprised to see Vince and Emily as I am. Vince comes over to me and gives me a peck on the cheek.

"Did Robert tell you?" Vince says.

"He's told me a lot of things," I say.

Vince scowls. "Emily is going to take over your position."

Emily looks at me with a satisfied smile. "By the way, we never formally met, although we've met before."

"We've met before?" I ask, shaking her outstretched hand.

"In high school. Vince and I were dating," she says as if that's supposed to ring a bell.

I shake my head. "I barely noticed Vince in high school." I sneer at him.

His frown deepens.

"She only noticed me," Robert says.

Vince peels his glare off Robert and pins it on me. "You should show Emily what you do."

"Vince, we should discuss this before we make any final decisions," Robert says.

I wonder if Emily realizes she's staring at me. It's

uncomfortable. She's standing so close to Vince that she might as well cling to his ass.

"Is there a problem?" Vince asks Robert.

"A big one. We seriously underestimated Maggie's workload. We're going to have to perform a legitimate executive search to replace her."

I look at Emily, waiting for her to chime in and sell herself, but she just stands there looking pretty and protected by my beautiful ex-boyfriend, or perhaps now fiancé.

Vince checks his watch. "We'll discuss it tomorrow. We're going to attend the Guggenheim event tonight," Vince says, referring to Emily and him.

Maybe that explains why she looks as though she's on her way to a photo shoot.

"Oh?" Robert says as if he's intrigued. He shoots me a look.

"I think you should attend as well," Vince says to Robert. "You too, Maggie. A lot of clients will be there. You should smile and explain to them that you're leaving to pursue another business venture."

This alien Vince is certainly the same guy who insists I get on my knees whenever his dick gets hard. Although he's said he's not involved with Emily, I get a different vibe. I bet she gets on her knees whenever new Vince tells her to. Even though he's avoiding eye contact with me, I beam in on him as I slip that damn ten-thousand-pound ring off my finger. He looks at me when I drop it into the top drawer of my desk and slam the drawer closed. That felt better than flipping him off with both hands. Vince does an about-face, puts his hand on Emily's back, and they exit my office. I'm so pissed that I can feel my lips scrunch.

"So you're my date tonight, and she's his," Robert says, taunting me.

"Don't you have any compassion for my heart?"

He's about to make a snappy comeback, but instead, he uses his chopsticks to put another roll on my plate. "Eat that. It's a cucumber roll. It's good."

I slam my chopsticks on the table. "I know it's good, but I'm not hungry anymore."

"Oh, you're going to eat." He groans regretfully. "I can't believe I'm going to say this, but don't let him get to you. That's what he's trying to do."

"Is he fucking her?"

Robert shrugs. "Have you asked him that?"

"Yes."

"What did he say?"

"He said he wasn't."

"Do you believe him?"

"No."

Robert nods. "And what if they were fucking? Would that be the end?"

I take a moment to ponder the question. "Aren't we already at the end?"

He picks up another cucumber roll with his chopsticks and lifts it to my lips. "Eat it."

I eat the damn thing.

He winks. "So what time should I pick you up?"

5

CURIOSITY GETS THE SCOUNDREL

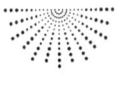

MAGGIE

*A*s soon as I'm home, I shower and wash my hair. Emily's thick, long hair puts my blond tresses to shame. That's why I call Hannah and ask if she could help make me over for tonight's event. I want Vince to regret ever making me feel second to another woman.

An hour later, there's a knock on my door. I open it wearing only a half slip and tank top.

"Is this she?" a seven-foot-tall man with a jet-black ponytail and accent that's between French and Italian asks.

"Maggie, meet Gianfranco," Hannah says. "When he's done with your hair, your life will never be the same."

"More than it already has?" I mumble sarcastically.

"But we can't talk as he works. Gianfranco requires complete silence."

I gesture zipping my lips and let them in. I sit on a stool in my kitchen before Gianfranco opens his kit and gets to work. My hair flies all over the place as he cuts. He's quick and thoughtful about what he's doing. He uses a big-barreled curling iron then combs his fingers through my hair when he's done.

"This?" he asks Hannah. It's the first word that has been spoken since he started.

Hannah kisses the tips of her fingers. "É bellissimo."

"É vero," he says to her. "I have finished. You are a lovely. I wish to change the teams." He laughs.

Hannah winks and hands me a mirror. I gasp at the woman staring back at me. My hair is layered with sexy waves. I look as if I wake up looking like a sex-goddess without any effort at all.

"And you didn't use any extensions, Gianfranco. You are a genius," Hannah says.

"This I know." He packs up his case. "I must go."

I study myself in the hand mirror as Hannah walks Gianfranco to the door. I'm not sure if the seductress I'm looking at is the real Maggie Conroy.

"What is it?" Hannah says when she returns.

"Look at me. I look…"

"Hot? And look at your graceful, milky neck, Mags. It's about time you embrace your sensuality. I've never understood why you insist on watering yourself down."

"I'm not watering myself down. I just think that the inside is more important than the outside."

"That's hogwash."

"Hogwash?"

Hannah laughs and kisses my forehead. "I have to go too. Enjoy your night. Let me know which one you end up fucking, Vince or Robert."

I playfully shake my fist at her, and she shakes hers at me on the way out.

"You're beautiful, Maggie, just face it. And hello, Robert Tango," she says extra loudly.

Robert catches the door before it closes. His eyes don't know what to focus on first: my face or my half-naked body.

"I'll be dressed in a few!" I dart off to my bedroom. My heart is beating out of my chest.

When he stared at me, I could feel his dick stab me. I think I've taken his breath away. I wonder if my new image will have the same effect on Vince. Since it's femme fatale night, I choose to wear royal blue, which is akin to smoldering red for a pale woman like me. The dress is silk and clings to my curves. It's also a midi like Emily's, only I look better in mine since I have a curvy and toned body like the actress Jessica Biel. That, I'll admit. I grab a clutch, put the things I need in it, and head to the living room to further test my appeal on Robert.

"Whoa," he says and throws up his hands. "What gives?"

"What do you mean?"

"Look at you." He walks up, turns me around, and pins his dick against my ass. "You feel that?"

"Yes, I feel that. You're grinding my ass after I told you not to."

He spins me around again, and we ram our tongues into each other's mouths. I feel as if I've stepped into my fantasy. Robert lays me on the black, furry rug and rubs his dick against my pubic bone. He's dry-humping me, and it feel so good. Robert pulls the material down from over my breasts. My nipples point at his face, and he devours one, then other. Oh, the way he's making my body feel...

"Are you feeling it?" he asks.

"Um-hum..." I moan.

His bulge is so damn solid. Back and forth, he

rubs me, brushing sensations deep inside the land of my pussy.

"Ah!" I cry extra loud when orgasm strikes me.

Robert nails my clit with his dick, and I continue to whimper as the tickling feeling ripples through my pussy. Robert jerks and grunts but doesn't loosen his grip. We look into each other's eyes as our sensations wither.

"Let's just get it out of us," he whispers.

I'm breathing heavily. "Get what out of us?"

Robert pulls up my dress and gazes at my vagina as if he's just found a pot of gold. "Maggie, may I?" His finger slides across my clit.

I close my eyes. "Yes, you may," I say with a whimper.

Robert lowers his face between my legs and sucks my clit against his tongue.

"Oh…" I dig into the rug.

He's amazing at this. I wish he weren't. I lift my head to see how he's doing that. I have no idea how he keeps the sensation going. It's like a never-ceasing tingle bolting from my clit into the depths of my pussy. The sensation gets more and more intense. I suck air and try to squirm away, but he's clamped down on me. I whimper and wince to bear it.

"Oh shit," I squeal when that powerful sensation

explodes and refuses to simmer. I feel my walls pulsate. I grab his hair, and it goes on and on. "Robert…"

As soon as my orgasm subsides, he kicks his pants off. His curved penis springs forward. I'm mesmerized by the girth and length. He drapes my legs across his shoulders but comes to a complete halt before slamming his dick inside me. "Fuck!"

He falls on his back. We're both staring at the ceiling. That was close. He couldn't go through with it, but I certainly can. The only thing I regret is not insisting he wrap up that glorious dick first. Robert's not the kind of guy I'd fuck without a condom.

"You're going to have to break up with Vince before we go all the way," he says.

I can't take my eyes off his dick. It glistens, coated with his cream. I can't believe I'm this turned on by Robert Tango. At the moment, I want him more than I do Vince. "Do you have a condom?"

"I was snipped before Vince got snipped."

"Impregnation is the least of my worries. Do you have condoms or not?" I hold my breath. His answer will determine whether we go through with it or not.

He smirks. "Condoms? How many do I need?"

"You tell me."

"I have condoms."

I let out a sigh of relief.

Robert's expression turns serious. "So you really want this?"

"I want this."

Just to test my claim, his fingers dip into my pussy. "You taste like I thought you would."

"And I was hoping you wouldn't be as good as you are."

He chuckles as we stare into each other's eyes. "I'm still in love with you, Maggie, and that's the truth. Vince has had sex with Emily. More than once."

I roll my eyes at the ceiling. "You're just saying that."

"I would lie but not about that. I don't want you to feel guilty about what we just did and what we're going to do."

I sigh gravely. I believe him. Plus, Robert's already told me in his cryptic little ways.

Here I am, lying on the floor of my apartment with my pussy exposed and soaking for Robert's luscious dick. He was so good at going down on me that I can't feel the depths of my despair. Am I furious? Yes. Is my anger enough to make me want to rush out and confront Vince about his lies?

I rest on my side and wrap my hand around Robert's cock. "Let's just get this over with." I slide my hand up and down his shaft. Goodness, the girth of it.

Robert sucks air between his teeth. "Once we do this, there's no taking it back."

"I've always been curious, and you've opened me up." I run my finger around his tip and use the stickiness to moisten his shaft.

"You said you weren't curious," he says.

"I lied."

Robert reaches for his pants and takes out his wallet and a strip of condoms. I watch impatiently as he tears one off, rips the packet open, and slides the rubber over his erection. We lock eyes. My breaths come quicker. He lifts me, and my legs wrap around him as he carries me to my bedroom. We kiss passionately. I feel as if I have so much desire for him stored up inside me, and now it's all gushing out. He lays me on the bed and drapes my legs back over his shoulders. He slams his dick into my pussy. He's so damn wide, and we cry out in unison.

"Does it hurt?" he asks.

"A little," I whisper. But it hurts so good.

Robert's dick strokes me slowly. His tongue is like a feather fluttering down the side of my neck. I never thought Robert Tango would be this sort of careful lover. His mouth feels so sensual. His breath makes my nipple warm before he chews it tenderly. Then he bites hard, and I gasp. His tongue soothes the stinging. He does it again and again, jabbing me harder with his dick whenever I tense. I feel orgasmic traces every time he does it. *Damn it, Robert Tango! Why do you have to be so skilled?*

"Look at me," he says.

I open my eyes. We pant against each other's mouths. I wonder what he's thinking, because something inside me just clicked. I'm not in love with him. I am in lust with him, but what we're doing right now is quenching it.

"You know how to tighten your pussy?" he asks.

I Kegel his pole. "Like this?"

He grins. "Like that. Hold it."

Robert grabs my headboard and rams his dick in and out of me. No thrust is wasted. This man has bags of tricks hidden inside his bag of tricks. He's going so fast that his dick feels like a mechanical device.

"Oh shit!" I shout as I blast off. The sensation is so intense that I white out.

Robert shouts and quivers as he ejaculates into

the condom. He collapses on top of me, breathing heavily. "How did you like it?"

"What do you think?"

He chuckles.

"So… it doesn't look like we'll be going to the Guggenheim," I say.

"Then you want more?" he asks.

"A little more, or maybe a lot."

"Same here. But first…" Robert slides his dick out of me.

My eyes widen at the amount of cream soaking the condom.

He winks. "Over-excited."

I reach up and pull him back onto the bed. We roll around on the covers as our tongues explore each other's mouths. Robert Tango is so damn hot, and at the moment, I just can't get enough of him.

VINCENT ADAMS

As the night wore on, Vince had come to the conclusion that neither Maggie nor Robert would show up. He tried calling them both but was unable to reach them. Vince didn't have to be a brain surgeon to figure out what was going on. When he saw Maggie in the office with Robert, his mind had made wild accusations against them. Robert had made it clear to him that as long as Vince was stringing Emily along and not being honest with Maggie, then Maggie was fair game.

Vince stood beside Emily, who was talking to Burt Tolken, one of their top advertisers, about the work she had done with a charity organization. The more she spoke, the more faith clients lost in her ability. Maggie always shined in those settings. She knew how to ask the right questions, and before the conversation ended, A&Rt would have a new client or someone they could call on when needed. On top of that, Emily was snubbing the other women, which was something Maggie never did, even if the other woman snubbed her first.

Vince gave the room another once-over. Maybe Maggie was mingling in the crowds and he'd failed to see her. There were a lot of people present, standing around with cocktails in hand, chitchatting to unearth what the next person could do for him or her.

"Well, I'm sorry to hear Maggie's moving on," Burt said loudly enough to reclaim Vince's attention.

Vince felt Emily tense up beside him. She was jealous of Maggie, and she had every reason to be.

"We are too," he replied bitterly.

"Is she on the market?"

Wasn't that a loaded question? Vince narrowed his eyes at Burt. Of course Burt wanted to schmooze Maggie; they all did. All night, it had been the same thing. He'd introduce Emily as their new Maggie, whomever he was talking to tested Emily's ability, she failed royally, and they tried to seize the opportunity to bring Maggie into their fold. Business was always so fucking cutthroat.

"No, she isn't," Vince replied.

"I see," Burt said as if he didn't believe him.

"She's working on a new venture."

"Is that so?"

"She's going into business for herself as an image consultant."

Burt lifted a finger. "But she's a consultant."

"You need some image consulting, Burt?" Vince couldn't control his snarl.

"I need the sort of consulting that Maggie provides. After all she's proven to be able to put sinking ships back on the ocean."

Vince snorted. Hell if Burt didn't just take a shot at him.

"Excuse me," Emily said and backed out of the conversation.

Burt watched her leave. He didn't have to say a word. Vince already knew Burt was thinking Vince was a fool to separate himself from Maggie in more ways than one.

Burt bowed his head. "Excuse me."

Vince took his cell phone out of his pocket and tried Maggie once again. The call went straight to voicemail. He listened to her say, "You've reached Maggie Conroy. Leave your name and your number, and I'll return your call as soon as I can." She always kept it professional.

He placed a call to Robert. He didn't answer either. The question was where were they: his place or hers? He waited until he saw Emily walk out of the restroom. She grinned as she approached him. The way she strolled when she walked made her appealing. Maggie didn't stroll, although she did walk with confidence. Emily, however, had a goal in mind. She liked to make dicks hard, but she didn't really like sex. Just to test how much power he had over her, he told her to get on her knees. Emily complied, but she didn't enjoy the pounding. Not only was it torture for her, but it took him forever to come. Emily enjoyed a missionary fuck, and she still hadn't sucked his dick, although he knew she did suck dick. She had been dropping more hints about how convenient it would be if they moved in together. She'd also called Lexi and made plans for them to travel to Colorado together for the annual family Fourth of July picnic. He was drowning in Emily, and for the life of him, he couldn't understand why he hadn't already come up for air.

"Are you ready to leave?" Emily asked in a singsong tone.

Vince examined her for the longest moment, and the answer to the million-dollar question came raining down like dew from heaven. He was no different than from whence he came and neither was Emily, but Maggie wasn't made from that mold. Fear pumped through his heart. He had made a mistake trying to "get her in line" and pushed her right on top of Robert's dick.

"We're done here," he said.

Emily hooked her arm around his, and they strolled out of the museum. They slid into the backseat of his chauffeured car, and he instructed the driver to take them home.

"That was fun tonight," Emily said.

"Yes," Vince said with a stoic look.

"But I can't wait until we get back to Colorado. I miss home, don't you?"

"Not really."

She turned silent, which was what Vince wanted.

"I'll drop you off at my place. Ask Raymond the concierge to let you in with the spare."

"You're going to drop me off? Where are you going?"

"To take care of some business."

"It's awfully late for business."

"Yes, it is."

Emily shook her head as though she was frustrated. "Are you going to see Maggie?"

Vince glared out the window, refusing to answer.

"What are we doing, Vince? I need to know if I'm wasting my time."

"Wasting your time? Are you expecting a result?"

"Aren't you?"

"No, I'm not."

Emily cozied up to him, rubbing his soft dick through his pants. She unzipped him as she kissed his neck.

He grabbed her wrist. "Don't."

She looked at him as though he had just punched her in the jaw.

It would take a miracle for her to make him grow a boner. "Later. We're almost there."

"Later?" she asked.

"Just go to the apartment and get some sleep. We'll talk later."

Emily rested her head on his shoulder the rest of the way and talked about all the things that were wrong about her apartment in Studio City. Vince couldn't wait to dump her at the building. No matter what happened between him and Maggie, his relationship with Emily had to end. Not only that, but Robert was right—they would have to do a proper executive search to replace Maggie. Emily looked the part, but she sure as hell wasn't the person for the job.

MAGGIE

I'm on all fours, and Robert is behind me. One of his hands is around me, gripping my pussy with a finger pinned against my clit and the grips my hip. He's banging me at an angle. Orgasmic sunbursts explode inside me with every crash of his dick. He must feel my pussy twitch, because he nails me in a spot and stimulates my clit. My entire body quivers as the tingling fills my groin. Robert flips me onto my side, stretches one leg out in front of me, and slams his dick back into my pussy.

"Oh!" he says and speed humps me.

This is a different feeling. It's like a pussy massage, but I can tell his dick is searching for a live spot. When he finds one, he stabs it like Norman Bates with a knife. I hear myself make gurgling sounds. Just like that, another orgasm takes form.

"Do it, Maggie, baby," Robert says, gritting his teeth.

I squint to bear the pleasure. He goes faster. I'm about to blow, and he goes even faster. I scream, and Robert grunts and quakes. After he's milked, he shifts my legs and lies on top of me.

"Fucking fantastic," he says.

"Tell me about it…"

"Now I'm ready to get stoned."

He slides his softened but not dead dick out of me, trots to the bathroom, and comes back with a towel to wipe me dry.

"Did you actually say you're ready to get stoned?" I ask.

"Yep." He retrieves his pants off the floor, digs his cell phone out of the pocket, and goes into the living room to make a call. I curl up in a fetal position and will my body to stop stirring orgasmic vibrations.

When he returns, he parts my legs and slides his face near my pussy. "I'm going to make you come seven times back to back."

"Wait! What about your drugs?"

"It's marijuana not drugs. My order is on the way."

"Your order?"

"Hey I'm a legal citizen of Colorado and a card carrier in California. It's all legal baby."

"But we're in New York."

"That doesn't change my circumstances."

I shake my head and his tongue works its magic on my clit before I can respond to his stupid claim. I pin my head to the pillow and grab his shoulders. I'm sucking air again. Damn it. He's an expert at this.

One. I cry out.

Two. I scream.

Three. I shiver.

Four. I grit my teeth and white out.

Five. I gasp.

Six. I whimper.

There's a knock at my door. My body is as limp as a rag doll.

Robert jumps up. "I haven't forgotten number seven," he says as he shuffles out of the bedroom.

I curl up in a ball and try to calm myself. Robert has turned the nerves in my body all the way up. I'm still feeling orgasmic sparks even though he's not touching me. Whenever Vince's face rises to the surface of my mind, I push it back down. I refuse to consider him. He sure as hell hasn't considered me. Banging Robert is pure fun. No wonder he fucks a lot of women. Every girl on the planet should bang Robert Tango at least once in her life. He just may be the greatest fuck on Earth.

He's back and shakes a plastic bag, which contains marijuana and squares of paper to roll it into joints.

"I haven't smoked that shit since eleventh grade," I say.

"Then get ready for a sweet little buzz tonight."

"You mean this morning." It's after midnight. "And I never said I wanted to smoke marijuana."

"Oh come on, Mags. You can't let me hit this shit alone."

He sits beside me to roll the joints.

"I can't believe you have a dealer on speed dial. What else do you partake in besides marijuana?" I ask.

"I do a little blow here and there."

"Cocaine?" I'm shocked.

"Every now and then."

"Are you going to get addicted and bankrupt A&Rt?"

He snickers. "I don't get addicted to drugs or pussy."

I smirk. "Is that your way of telling me that my pussy has no power over you?"

"Oh, Mags… You have a powerful pussy. I've dreamt of your pussy. I've fantasized about your pussy. You did not disappoint."

I kick him playfully on the back. Robert is such a smartass.

"You first." He hands me the joint.

I sigh. "All right but only one."

He winks. "One is all you need." He retrieves a lighter from his pocket, and ignites the stick.

I take a puff. "You keep a lighter in your pocket?" I wheeze and cough.

"No, Donnie just gave me one."

"Is that your dealer's name."

"Yes."

"That's so cliché."

He crawls between my legs. "Enough talking. You smoke, and I'll finish what I started. I'm starting from number one since we were interrupted." He pulls my pussy to his face.

"I don't know, Robert," I say squeamishly. "I think I may have had too many orgasms already."

"You can never have too many. Now you do that." He points his head at the joint. "And I'll do this. If you stop, then I'll have to start back at one."

"Games, games, games... You're always playing games."

He winks at me, and his tongue flicks my clit. Then he does that thing that he does.

I cough to keep myself from choking. "Shit! How in the hell are you doing that!"

He stops, and the sensation subsides. "If you're talking, then you're not smoking."

"No, really, how do you do that?"

"Do you think I'm going to let you take my secrets back to Vince? If you want your pussy eaten my way, then you're going to have to come to me. Now smoke." He waits for me to take a puff.

I roll my eyes and suck on the joint. He winks and goes back to work. I release the smoke as the sensations whirl in the depths of my pussy. I moan and shake, trying to smoke. Robert watches me, and he lifts his eyebrows, warning me not to stop. My pussy is sparking. My head is spinning. If I'm going to get high, then this is the only way to do it.

VINCENT ADAMS

Vince used his key to let himself inside Maggie's apartment. He kept her spare with him at all times; it made him feel closer to her. He heard Maggie moaning, yelping, and calling Robert's name. His instinct was to race into her bedroom and bring an end to whatever they were doing, but he wondered if what he smelled was marijuana.

"What the fuck?" He tiptoed to the bedroom.

He didn't have to reveal himself to see what was taking place. Maggie was going crazy. A joint was on the sheets, burning the fabric. She was squinting and making a lot of noise. Robert offered no reprieve as he ate her pussy.

Maggie screamed and clung to Robert's scalp. "Fuck! You're a fucking genius!"

Robert grabbed his dick. He was getting ready to fuck her. It was time to step in.

"You decided to stay in for the night?" Vince said, walking into view.

Maggie and Robert pasted their shocked gazes on him. She and Robert scrambled away from each other.

"Vince?" Maggie said.

"Your sheets are smoking," Vince said and walked away.

"Shit," Robert said.

Vince heard something beat against the mattress.

Maggie chased after him. "Vince!"

He stopped at the door, mustered every ounce of self-control he had, and turned to face her. "What?"

Maggie looked lost, standing there in the buff. "I'm sorry. How did you? But..." She sighed resignedly and threw up her hands as if she had no defense. "You were fucking Emily."

"Is that the best you can do?" he snarled.

"I didn't think you cared anymore."

He stomped over and gripped her by the back of her neck. "I care." Vince looked toward her bedroom. "Robert, get your ass out of there." Vince waited, glaring into Maggie's eyes until Robert came out of the bedroom with his clothes on. "Get the fuck out."

"Maggie?" Robert said, as if he were asking her permission to leave.

"Get the fuck out!" Vince shouted.

"Not until Maggie feels safe."

He glowered at Robert. "You think I'm going to hurt her?"

"You already have."

Vince laughed cynically.

"I'm okay," Maggie said. "You can leave."

"You sure?"

"I'm sure."

"What the fuck?" Vince growled. The way they were speaking to each other as though both of them hadn't just broken his heart infuriated him.

"See you tomorrow then," Robert said.

"No, you won't," Vince said. "Maggie's not coming in tomorrow. She's officially terminated."

"You can't make that decision on your own."

Vince sniffed with disdain. "You know what, Rob? If I had the money, I would buy you out and let you wither by the roadside, you fucking loser."

"Vince," Maggie said, scolding him.

Vince glared into her eyes. How dare she defend Robert? "You guys can fuck until the cows come home, but I want to have a heart-to-heart with Maggie first."

"Just go," Maggie said to Robert.

"Call you later?" Robert asked.

Again, Vince sniffed disdainfully. Maggie didn't dare answer him. Robert closed the door behind him, and Vince and Maggie stared into each other's eyes.

"How long have you wanted to fuck him?" Vince asked.

Maggie shrugged. "Never, actually."

Vince took his hand off the back of his neck to scratch his temple. "What was the tipping point?"

"You were the tipping point. You know this was your fault, not mine."

"But with Rob?"

Vince took the ring Maggie had dropped in the desk out of his pocket. "Don't you *fucking* take this off again." He grabbed her hand and shoved the ring on her finger.

"You still want to marry me after that?"

"I don't know what I want. I want you to wear this until I figure us out."

Maggie stared at him with her mouth open...

MAGGIE

I close my eyes and try to digest everything Vince just said. Why is he always trying to brand me with that ring? It's weird.

Vince's gaze rolls up and down my naked body. "Could you put something on? I'll wait for you."

I nod and go into my room then into the bathroom. My head is light. My eyelids are heavy. The marijuana is wreaking havoc on my brain. I wet a washcloth and rid my skin of traces of Robert Tango. It's easy to get him off the outside of me, but my insides are screaming for more of him. I slip into an oversized T-shirt. Vince stands as I walk into the living room. He sits as I take a seat on the opposite end of the sofa.

"Now what?" I ask.

Vince closes his eyes and massages his temples. "You smoke marijuana?"

I shake my head. "Not since high school. Robert, he's..."

"He's what?" Vince snaps.

"Nothing, forget it."

"Let's not forget it. I want to know why you let him have you."

I sigh. "He's been seducing me. One circumstance led to another, and here we were."

Vince stands.

"So are we officially over?" I ask.

"Maggie..." He closes his eyes. "My heart is fucking broken. You can't ask me that right now."

"You've been having sex with Emily though, and you lied to me about it."

"Who told you that? Robert?"

"Is it true?"

He runs his hands nervously through his hair. "It's true."

"Then the question is why would you make love to another woman?" I sigh resignedly. "Maybe we're just not meant for each other." Vince's glare sends chills down my spine.

"Maybe," he says. "But I'm not ready to live without you yet."

"You've already chosen to live without me."

Vince holds up his arms. "Come here."

I slowly stand and go to him. He puts his arms around me, and we embrace. His chest feels so familiar against my face. Unlike Robert, I feel safe in Vince's arms. He kisses the top of my head.

"You changed your hair?" he asks.

I nod.

"I like it. Your neck is beautiful."

"Thank you."

"Maggie, I'm going to work some shit out, and I'll be in touch. We're going to start from scratch, you and I. We're never coming back to this place ever again. Is that okay with you?"

"It is." I squeeze him tighter. "I'm sorry." My voice cracks.

He looks at the door. "I'm going to lie down with you because I can't leave you right now."

"Okay…"

Vince walks me to my bedroom. He takes off his shoes and jacket. We lay on the part of my bed that's not burned, and he holds me. He doesn't massage my nipples or grind my ass as he usually does. He's not even hard. We're too hurt to have sex. Our souls need time and space to cleanse themselves of the traces of other lovers. So I fall asleep in Vince's arms, but when I wake up in the early afternoon, I'm alone.

LONDON BOUND

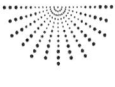

MAGGIE

$\mathcal{I}$f what has happened in the last four days of my life was an event, then how would I assess it? Have I gained anything from the experience, and how much have I lost? I study the ring on my finger. When I first took it off, I'd explained to Vince that the ring is wrapped around my heart, not my finger. All he'd said was "right," and then he kissed me. Maybe he should've said "bullshit" so that I knew he didn't accept the concept.

I shake away all my thoughts about Vince and turn to Monroe. We're on our way to London to chat with Francesca Bell.

On Tuesday, I'd called Jack and asked if I could be put in contact with the woman who'd accompanied him to the wedding. He was adamant about me not having any contact with her. Instead he asked for my list of names and promised to get back to me as soon as possible with any information he found. Four hours later, he'd faxed me a three-hundred-page report. I have no idea how Jack can be so resourceful. He's so secretive about his business contacts. Regardless, I was thankful for what he gave me.

Angelina called before I could start combing through the information. She wanted me to sit down with her and Charlie and devise a plan to get Jack and Daisy back together. I told her I'd fly out to New Orleans on Saturday. Ten hours later, after reading every word on every page, I concluded that Francesca's popularity and Delta's meshed the best. She's a twenty-six-year-old blockbuster film star. Hair: Brown. Eyes: Blue. Height: 5'4". Face: Standard Hollywood beauty. Acting Abilities: Questionable. She hasn't been linked to any men who are in the public eye, only men who are considered "ordinary." However, there were rumors that her last boyfriend was bisexual and the one before that was married. The London tabloids loved to eat her alive and doused in ketchup. Monroe and I held a conference call with her manager, Aiden Marlowe. He thinks it's time to kill two birds with one stone—settle her down with an A-list actor and move her to the United States.

So I called Jack and asked if we could use his jet to fly across the Atlantic. He said yes, Monroe flew to Manhattan, and we boarded our flight at midnight so that we could arrive at Biggin Hill Airport in the morning.

"But you just skipped over the best part. You banged the scoundrel?" Monroe asks.

I flash back to being with Robert. I'm on my knees, one leg up, the other leg up, both legs up, and sitting on his face. "Yeah," I say with a sigh. "I did."

"And?"

I nod. "He has to be the best fuck on the planet. I don't know how a man gets so skilled at it, but OMG."

Monroe claps and laughs. "Shit, I knew it!"

"I would totally recommend him. You should try him. He'll certainly oblige you," I say.

She narrows one eye. "You have no feelings for him?"

Those images replay in my head. "Oh, what fun we had, but alas, it was only fun. He's... Robert is... scary."

"Elaborate, please."

"He's unpredictable, but not in a good way. When

he's coming on to me, he can make me think I'm the only one he wants, but I know better."

"That's rule number one in the scoundrel handbook."

"Exactly. I'm pretty sure Robert Tango has already moved on now that he's finally fucked me. Good for him that I'm not going to go all psycho, 'you fucked me like you loved me' on him."

Monroe has a good laugh. "Boy, have you been having a time. I eat your tits, my boyfriend tries to fuck you on my request, Delta gives your pussy a slob job—"

"Oh my goodness, what was that all about?"

"He's done it to me three times. I just let him. It's like going to the spa."

I chuckle. "Sorry, I know you don't like me saying this, but you *are* crazy."

"And you're about to hop into my crazy world. Hear me good, Mags, Delta's only the beginning. Most of our clients will want to fuck and eat your pussy. That little cute mouth of yours? They're going to picture it going up and down their dicks. The all have God syndromes, so they'll believe you want them to do the shit they want to do to you. Get out now if you can't handle it."

"I can handle it," I say.

"Are you sure?"

"Are *you* sure?"

The flight attendant brings us blankets. She announces the lights will dim shortly and asks if we would like anything else. Monroe requests two glasses of brandy to help us sleep better.

"Listen," I say, "I've been off my A-game ever since Friday morning, but I can handle Delta the next time he wants to go down on me or you when you want to bite my nipples. I only have a problem with lying to the world."

"Well, if that's your only quarrel, then we're going to do just fine, because we're in the business of making lies the truth."

I shake my head gravely. "I don't know... What happens when our clients are tired of living a lie?"

"Anything can happen, but we'll cross that road *if* we get to it."

I let out an extended sigh. After we're given our drinks, we outline our immediate plans for Delta and Francesca then grab as much sleep as we can.

Robert Tango wrecks my dreams. His mouth is clamped on my clit. We stare at each other. My thighs shiver and tingle like the rest of my groin. Suddenly it stops, and he's on top of me, thrusting into me nice and slow. I should wake up, but I'm refusing to do it. It's so real—maybe it's happening all over again.

"Do you really want me to fuck your friend like this?" he asks.

"No." I'm emphatic about that.

"Am I out of your system?"

"No."

"You're out of mine," he says.

I feel as though I'm diving off a cliff. I'm falling fast and far. I try to open my eyes before hitting bottom, which I'm approaching quickly. I wake with a stop.

I look at Monroe, who's snoring lightly with a mask over her eyes. I curl up on my side and stare at the frame in front of my face. I have too many thoughts to go back to sleep. Why did I have that dream about Robert when I'm a hundred and ninety-nine percent clear that I'm done with him? And what are my true feelings about Emily and Vince? Then there's the thousand-pound ring on my finger. Why does he insist that I wear it, even after he caught Robert going down on me while I smoked pot? I shake my head at how crazy that was. Was my behavior beneath me? No way. I never restrict myself. If it appeals to me, I try it. If I don't like it, I move on. I'm still not a fan of marijuana. It stinks like chicken shit. It also puts me in a deep sleep, which was why I didn't hear Vince leave.

I don't have to ask if I'm the kind of wife he wants—the answer is weighing on my finger. But why do we need to get married? We're not having children. Neither of us needs a green card. There's no one pressuring me to tie the knot. He's the one who stands to lose the most if we end up divorcing, because I'm not signing a prenuptial agreement. Really, I just don't get it. I thought most men would love a woman like me, one who doesn't pressure him into marrying her. I guess I was wrong.

The airplane soars over England's plush grasslands. I never miss this part of the flight. Every view looks like the spread on a postcard. Monroe and I freshen up before we deplane.

We load my one suitcase and Monroe's three pieces of luggage into the cab and ride to the hotel, which is settled along the banks of the River Thames. I travel to London so often that it feels as though I already live here. I've even considered buying an apartment near the Tape Museum. Usually in the mornings I walk the span of the river. I'm fond of the Tower of London, which housed many of history's most famous prisoners right before the executioner went off with their heads. I love the narrow cobblestone alleyways—which are swallowed up by Victorian-age architecture—the old tower bridge, and the way they've tastefully inserted the new with the old. This won't be a long trip, and I probably won't return to London for a while. I'll try to wake up early tomorrow morning to walk a lap before we fly back to L.A. at ten a.m.

The hotel is five stars at its finest. The hotel's structure is contemporary, made mostly of glass, and shoots into the sky like a phallic wet dream. We check in, and the bellhop takes our luggage to our room on the fifty-first floor. The room is actually a suite. It has three bedrooms, all the bells and whistles, and amazing views of the city.

"Did we pay for this out of our budget?" I ask Monroe.

"No way. This grand suite comes courtesy of Delta Foster."

"Oh, wow. I didn't know he had an ounce of class."

"He has at least ten ounces."

I snicker.

There's a knock on the door. Monroe and I look at each other, puzzled.

I count the number of rooms again. "Is that...?"

Delta opens the door. "Honeys, I'm home!"

He has a leather duffel bag slung across his body. He bear-hugs Monroe and gropes her ass, and I brace myself for impact. His hands are like tentacles fondling me. I give Monroe a look as he squeezes my pussy.

"Tonight, I'm feasting on you," he says and kisses my cheek. He gazes out of the window then flops down on the sofa in front of it and kicks up his feet. "So when do we meet my future wife?"

He's either high or drunk.

Monroe rolls her eyes and sets her laptop on the desk. "You know the paparazzi are ferocious here."

"Yes, indeed," he sings, making light of it.

"Then where have you been and why are you coked up?"

"I've been to the den of sin."

Monroe kicks his feet off the arm of the sofa. "Sit up!"

"Why don't you sit on my face? Looking at the two of you has put me in the mood for pussy."

Monroe looks as if she's chewing lemons. "What the fuck happened to you when you were growing up?"

Delta gazes at the ceiling as though he's having a religious experience. "When do we meet Francesca?"

"Sorbet, tonight at eleven," Monroe says.

"Wait, I thought we were meeting her at her manager's office at three?" I say.

She scowls at Delta. "I was just about to tell you before our client showed up unannounced and high as a kite. Aiden sent me a text. Francesca doesn't want our meeting to be so formal."

Delta looks at the watch. "That's nine hours from now."

"Which gives you nine hours to sleep it off," Monroe says.

"You don't sleep off a bump. You fuck it off."

"I thought you went to the den of sin?" she says.

"I just got blown. I need a fuck. Maggie, are you into anal?"

I blink, taken aback. If it weren't for that look on his face, I would think he was fucking with me. "No, I am not into anal."

"All right, Monroe, then I need your ass, although Maggie has a better one."

I shake my head at Monroe. My expression is asking her why we're dealing with this clown.

Delta says, "I think we should write me having the right to fuck the both of you whenever and wherever I want into our contract."

I've reached my limit. "Listen, Delta, you can fuck

whomever the fuck you want to fuck. Hell, you can fuck a peach for all I'm concerned. But Monroe and I, we're asexual to you. We have no pussies, no dicks, and no mouths or asses for you to stick it in. *Capisce?*"

He smirks. "I'm going to keep trying, Maggie. One day, you're going to say yes."

I fold my arms and widen my stance. "You see, that answer doesn't work for me. *Capisce* means—"

"I understand." He sits up. "I tell you what. Get in the bedroom, strip, and let me have my way with you."

I go stand right in front of his face. My pussy is *this* close to his mouth. "Touch it, and I'm out of here. You don't know my work very well, but I'm a fucking genius at making audiences believe what I want them to believe. You're not going to get better than me. But my pussy belongs to Vincent Adams." *I think.* "Now, feel free to call him and ask if you can lick it, fuck it, do whatever you want to do to it, but without his permission, it's off-limits. Now. *Capisce?*"

"What's his number?"

I toss him my cell phone. "It's in the contacts."

Delta looks at me askew. "He your fiancé?"

"Yes." No need to tell him that I hope so. We've

taken a free fall after he caught Robert assaulting me with orgasms.

Delta twists his mouth as he ponders. "Fuck it." He hands me back my phone. "I can respect that."

Monroe and I look at each other, shocked and relieved that he didn't call my bluff. I was half hoping he would call Vince. I want to hear his voice. I want him to know that I've rededicated myself to him. I sit beside Delta, and Monroe goes back to working on her laptop. She's letting me handle him.

"Everyone already sees you as the all-American boy," I say. "You've dated enough actresses not to arouse any suspicions about the kind of shit you're really into. Why change it?"

It appears that my question sobers him up. "The person sitting in front of you right now is the only Delta I want you to sell to the public, not that boring-ass fuck that Lou made me into. Maybe one day I'll settle down with someone seriously—man, woman, dog—but that won't be for a long while, and I'm tired of getting involved with a bunch of anorexic, psychotic bitches. I want a fake thing that's going to last a long time so that I can fuck what I want and when I want without destroying my box-office take."

He has a wayward dick, but he's kind of smart.

"Monroe and I can get you the bells and whistles; just stop trying to have sex with us. We're not your muses. We're the professionals you've hired to keep your career afloat."

Delta studies me then looks across the floor at Monroe, who keeps her eyes on her computer. "Okay, deal. Now let's go eat. *Food*."

"Let's," I say.

Monroe finally looks up. "Yes, let's."

On the way to the hotel restaurant, Monroe slaps my ass in appreciation of how I handled our spoiled boy/man actor. I slap her back because I'm proud of myself too.

Vincent Adams

VINCE HAD JUST ENDED A CALL WITH CHARLIE. Charlie had asked if Vince had heard about the plan to get Belmont and Daisy back together. For some stupid reason, Vince didn't want Charlie to think there was trouble in their paradise, so he'd lied and said that not only had he heard, but he planned to accompany Maggie to New Orleans on Saturday. Lying and spending the last two days without Maggie had given him a headache. But nothing was worse than the email he had read before Charlie's call. It was a picture of Maggie, Monroe, and the actor Delta Foster.

"Is that even his real fucking name?" he had muttered bitterly.

They were in London. Maggie had been identified as the cousin of billionaire Jack Lord and Monroe as the daughter of the late Clara Richardson. The tabloid couldn't distinguish which woman was Delta's new fling, but that wasn't what had pissed off Vince. He figured Delta Foster was probably their new client.

Robert had flown to London on Tuesday morning. He and Maggie were now in the same city. It was as if the universe and Vince's bonehead decisions were trying to pull him and Maggie apart and put Robert and Maggie together. If only he had talked to Maggie about his issues with her before fucking Emily and trying to make Maggie submit. He could've saved them both a ton of grief.

Vince's calendar was jam-packed for the day, and it would take upward of three hours to arrange a flight and then ten hours to arrive in London. But at least he didn't have Emily hanging on him. To say that she had been furious he'd spent Monday night with Maggie would've been an understatement.

He'd taken every accusation Emily had flung at him like a champ. He was a selfish jerk who didn't know what he wanted. He'd strung her along. He'd misled her on purpose. He would be old and alone. She was better than Maggie. Then her eyes had turned soft, and she'd begged him to give her another try. They could be happy.

There had been no need to say what he was thinking. It would've been cruel to reveal that he could never be happy without Maggie. It was the little things about Maggie that took up so much space in his heart. He loved her honest reactions. She had the best rants. She had a great head on her shoulders, and he found her "I don't give a damn" attitude about all the shit that didn't matter, which meant she wasn't a nag, sexier than sexy. Although he hated how hard she worked, he loved that she was so damn good at her job. She could smile through a verbal assault without taking it personally. He had never met a woman more secure than Maggie Conroy.

His sisters hated the fact that Maggie drew breath, but they could stand to learn a hell of a lot from her. Vince also liked her family. He and Maggie, Jack and Daisy, and Charlie and Angelina were becoming as thick as thieves. Never in a million years would he have guessed that he and Charlie would become good friends, but Charlie was becoming a better friend to him than Robert had ever been. Robert had been riding his coattails since high school. It was time Vince shook him off and crushed him under his heel.

Emily wanted to stay with the company. She was fine with being the director of corporate PR, which was more her speed, so he'd recommended she fly back to L.A. as soon as possible. The air he breathed felt fresher after she was gone.

Vince had a lot of interviews lined up. He couldn't cancel them all. He shuffled through the resumes and saw that Linda was the last candidate of the day. For some reason, her name stood out. She was Maggie's protégé. They always traveled together. Linda knew how Maggie thought and how she worked, and they shared a lot of the traits he liked about Maggie. He tapped the butt of his pen on the desktop. Why waste his time interviewing a bunch of people he knew he wouldn't hire? The job would be Linda's if she wanted it, and apparently she did.

Vince called Linda into his office before the next candidate arrived, then he called the charter company to schedule the quickest flight to London. Perhaps luck was in his court; they could have him speeding down the runway in an hour and a half.

Linda was visibly nervous when she walked into his office. "You wanted to see me?"

He smiled to put her at ease. It didn't work. "Have a seat."

She sat.

"I'm going to get this over with so you can relax. You applied for Maggie's position, and it's yours."

She gasped. "The job is mine?"

"If Maggie puts her trust in you, then so will I. Your new position starts effective immediately. I'll message Lena." He was already putting his computer in his bag. "I'm supposed to interview six candidates today. You'll interview them. If there's any talent you want to explore, then find a place for them on your team. If not, tell them thank you and we'll call them next week to inform them of our decision." He winked.

Linda had turned red, although she remained as cool as a cucumber. "Yes, I will." She stood. "Thank you, Mr. Adams."

He hung his bag on his shoulder. "Can you not call me Mr. Adams anymore? I'm Vince."

She beamed. "Yes, Vince. I'll call you Vince."

Vince grinned. It felt good to make a woman that happy. "Good. See you soon." He bolted toward the door.

"Oh, Vince?" Linda said.

He turned to face her. "Yes."

"Do you mind if I call Maggie and share the good news?"

Just hearing Maggie's name made his pulse race. "No, I don't mind."

Linda frowned as if it took her a moment to realize he had given her permission to inform Maggie. "Thank you—for everything."

He winked and went on his way. He couldn't wait until Maggie heard the news. Maybe hiring her protégé would benefit him in more ways than one.

Maggie

IT'S TIME TO GO TO WORK, AND BOY, HAS MY WORK

attire changed. I'm wearing a white tank top, black leather miniskirt, and silver pumps. Monroe's boyfriend, Dash, has shown up. I finally know what he does for a living. He's our personal paparazzo.

Dash opens a suitcase and shows Delta and me his collection of cameras. He takes out the smallest one. "This baby is compact but powerful. I can get a good shot, hook it into my phone, load the images, and you'll be on everyone's radar within the hour."

"Not before we have a verbal agreement on the contract with Francesca. We want to capitalize on this opportunity, but we don't want to start something we won't be able to finish," I say.

"She's not going to say no to me," Delta says.

I study how self-assured he seems and hope he's right. "Francesca will be five minutes behind us."

"I know the drill, Maggie." Delta tilts his head. "You're uptight, but I like that about you. It's sexy. And you look sexy tonight."

I frown. "I'm not uptight."

He nods. "Oh yeah, you are."

"You're uptight," Dash says, pointing his camera at me.

"Whatever…" If that's how they perceive me, so be it.

"What about you, Dash? What are you into?" Delta asks, staring at Dash's package.

Dash snaps pictures of me. "Pussy."

"Only?"

"Only."

"Your loss," Delta says.

Monroe struts out of the bedroom in a red bandage dress that's only an inch away from showing her snatch. Her long hair is bone straight, and her eyelashes are longer and thicker than usual. Dash whistles his approval. Monroe poses as he snaps shots of her. I'm waiting for Delta to invite Monroe to sit on his face or something.

Instead, he points his hand toward the door and says, "Let's hit the road."

Monroe takes my arm. "Let's go get her. Client number two."

We get into the elevator, and Monroe and Dash start kissing. Delta looks at my legs. I frown at him inquisitively.

"A miniskirt?" he asks.

"What's wrong with a miniskirt?"

"If you want me to respect your lines, then you can't make it so fucking easy to get to."

I look down at myself. "Shit, I didn't even consider the fact that you're like a spoiled child who lacks self-control when I dressed myself for the night."

Monroe chuckles into Dash's mouth. Delta snorts and shakes his head, apparently appreciating my sarcasm.

The hotel has a subterranean level, and our car waits for us there. We load up. Delta pours us a drink, and we toast to his forthcoming trans-formation.

7

FRESH CONTRACTS

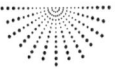

MAGGIE

*S*orbet is a club located in an eighteenth-century row house with six floors. The club is trendy, busy, and loud. We take the stairs to the top level, which is by invitation only, so that fans can stroke Delta's inflated ego along the way. He waves, takes photos, blows kisses, and winks, eating up the attention. The racket his presence stirs is rivaled by the buzzing coming from the lower floors. Francesca must've arrived.

We make it to the top floor, and Delta gawks at the four scantily clad women performing on a stage in the middle of the room. They're rapping in French, and their music is just as sensual as the dim lighting and red-velvet ottomans, sofas, and booths set up throughout the room. There are a lot of people up here, and Delta greets those he knows with a kiss on the lips. One guy wearing full eye makeup whispers in Delta's ear.

"You've had your turn, bro!" Delta says without braking. He likes being the big man on campus, and he's basking in the attention.

We arrive at our reserved booth and take seats around a white table that changes colors. Delta turns to the server and places an order. I can't hear what he's saying over the music, but the guy nods and scurries away.

Delta puts his face too close to mine and rubs my thigh. "Are you still uptight?"

I'm monitoring how close he gets to my goods. "What if I am, and what if I'm not?"

He sneers, studying me. "What was that? A riddle?"

"It's just a question. My answer depends on the result."

Delta laughs and shakes his finger. "Right..."

I lean toward Monroe. "What's taking Francesca so long to get up here?"

In my mind, the night will be short and to the point. We'll have a drink or two, ask Francesca a couple of questions to make sure she isn't a psycho, and see if there's marketable chemistry between her and Delta. If they have enough of a connection, then we take the next step. If they revile each other, then we'll move on to the next candidate—although I'm positive Francesca is the one.

"Patience," Monroe says. "It can't look like we set this up, Mags."

I try to relax and appear as though I'm here for pleasure and not for business. Delta is doing a lot of talking, but I can only make out parts of what he's saying. He's telling us about the first time he visited this nightclub. He mentions the band, and, if I'm not mistaken, he says, "Mounds of blow."

"What did you just say?" I shout.

Delta doesn't hear me. The waiter is back with a cart loaded with bottles of alcohol on racks, and he gives Delta a metal plate. Delta takes a small bag of coke out of his pocket and sweeps the substance into the indentations on the plate. He prepares his servings with the ease of pouring a glass of water. Then he sniffs one line, two, then three.

Delta hands the plate to Monroe. "Dig in."

She pinches one nostril and inhales a white line with the other. I'm not shocked that she sniffs coke. Delta gives me an impish look. I'm waiting for him to pressure me to take a hit, but he doesn't.

The girl band brings their song to an end, and "Let's Dance" by David Bowie cuts on.

"Let's dance," Monroe says and grabs Delta's hand.

Buzzed, they prance their way to the dance floor. I lose sight of them in the crowd, so I check my phone to see if Vince has called or texted me. Instead there's a message from "the Scoundrel."

"Where r u," it says.

I'm hesitant about replying. I want to put distance between us, but sitting alone in a noisy nightclub waiting for shit to happen makes me restless.

"I'm in London," I write.

"Me too. Where?"

I roll my eyes. Robert is clearly screwing with me. *"Sorbet."*

"Only a few blocks away. Meet me outside."

My eyes expand. *"Don't believe you."*

"Believe me and meet me."

I scratch my forehead. Is this really happening? *"Why?"*

"To talk."

I'm on the verge of writing, *"About what?"* but I already know the answer. Yes, we need to talk.

"Ok. Will meet u," I write.

. . .

I HUG MYSELF BECAUSE IT'S CHILLY OUTSIDE. ROBERT is already out here, leaning against the wall and puffing on a cigarette. The collar of his black leather jacket is flipped up. He's a long, lean drink of something addictive. He smirks at me upon eye contact, drops his cigarette, and smashes it with his foot. One look at him, and I remember the other night. His skills in the bedroom are unmatched, even by Vince.

"What are you doing in London?" I ask.

He smirks. "No small talk first?"

Due to our recent encounter, I'm not as repulsed by his smirk as I used to be. It's suggestive but honest. He is the embodiment of sensual sex.

"How are you?" I say brusquely.

"I've been better. I'm in London because no one knows what the hell to do without you."

I grimace as I hug myself tighter. "And they called *you* to the rescue?" My tone is sarcastic.

"Are you cold?" he asks.

"That's obvious."

"My room isn't too far from here."

I snort. "I'm not going to your room."

He laughs. "I'd be lying if I said I wouldn't try

anything. I have a confession." He pauses and waits for my reaction.

I crumple my eyebrows.

"I can't stop thinking about what we did—all of it."

"So how long are you going to stand there with your jacket on while I'm freezing?" I shake a finger at him. "That's my number-one issue with you. You aren't chivalrous."

Robert takes off his jacket and drapes it around my shoulders. "Now do you want to go back to my room?"

"You're also impossible, and look at this…" I raise my ring finger. At the moment, the beautiful jewelry is as light as an eyelash on my finger.

"I thought I saw you take that off."

"Vince put it back on."

"He personally put it on your finger?"

I nod.

Robert tosses his head back and yells, "Fuck! Fucking Vince!"

I'm pretty surprised by his reaction.

"Am I supposed to be in love with you for the rest of my life?"

"You don't love me. You were coming on to my assistant right in front of me," I say.

"Then you don't trust me? Is that why you're choosing Vince?"

"No, I don't trust you, but that's not why I'm choosing to do whatever the hell I have to do to keep Vince. I just love him, that's all."

"But you and me, we have chemistry. You really don't want more of the other night?"

I laugh bitterly. "That's what you were counting on?"

He shrugs.

"Yeah, you are an amazing lay. I climaxed so much I probably would've gone blind if you'd kept it up. But Robert, I'm not the kind of woman who chases after a prime fuck. Vince is in my heart. He's in my pores. I can't breathe without him."

Robert and I turn at the same time to look at a group of people who are huddled together and smoking about five feet away.

He puts an arm around me. "Let's walk."

We're moving along before I can acquiesce, which is something else about him that makes my panties dry. We pass a pub that I've been to before. They have the tastiest "chips," which are french fries in American-speak. I'm hungry again.

"If I ask you a question, would you answer honestly?" he asks.

"I always do."

"There's not even a tiny bit of you that wants more of Monday night?" He measures a small amount of air with two fingers. "Just this much?"

I glance at him sideways. "You know what I think?"

"Is this the part where you try to tell me what's wrong with me?"

"I think you're like a child surrounded by all of your toys. They're piled up to the ceiling. But all you want is Vince's rattle because it's his favorite thing to play with. Monroe has the same problem, except she loves me way too much to make a pass at my boyfriend."

We listen to our feet shuffling up the sidewalk. Horns honk. People pass us.

"He said he and I are finished," Robert says.

"Vince said you and him are done?"

"Yeah," he barely says.

I picture what we were doing when he walked in on us. "I'm surprised he hasn't left me out in the rain. Gosh, you were… And I was…" I shake my head, trying to rid myself of the memory.

Robert draws me against his hard body. "It'll be worth it if you come back to my room with me."

"And then what?"

"Let's do it differently. Let's make love."

"And then what?"

He sighs. "What the fuck?"

I grunt. "It doesn't matter anyway. I don't want ever to put that look on Vince's face again."

Robert stares into my eyes as if he trying to change my mind. Finally he nods. "All right. Me neither."

"Good. We're on the same page."

"Well, do you want to go grab a drink, at least?"

"I'm working."

"Are you really going through with this quitting shit?"

"Yes, I am."

"Then I'll be seeing a lot less of you."

"No one else to mind-fuck?" I ask.

He chuckles. "There's Mavis."

I lean back to make sure he sees the warning in my expression. "If you screw with her, I'll hang you by your balls and throw hot coals at you."

He flexes his eyebrows. "Promise?"

"You're impossible."

His body shakes when he laughs, and it dawns on me that we're still embracing.

"Plus as soon as we become profitable, I'm going to make her an offer she can't refuse," I say.

"Then I'll double your offer."

I feel my face crumple. "You suck."

"Oh, that's way too easy."

We look into each other's eyes, smiling.

"A kiss before we say good-bye?" he asks.

"What the hell," I say.

Robert comes in slowly as if he's savoring the moment. Our lips lock. His tongue tastes like whisky and cigarettes. I don't feel weak in the knees, and my head doesn't swim. I like Robert more than I did before we smashed, but I just don't love him. We step away from each other, I undrape his jacket from around me, and hand it back.

"Do you want to come in and join us? Monroe's upstairs. I think it's about time you two get better acquainted."

He takes his jacket. "I'm not interested in your friend, Maggie." He sounds as though I've insulted him.

"I'm not offering her as a consolation prize."

"She's not my type."

"No? I think you two are perfect for each other."

"Then you're wrong. Plus I have something brewing at Hokey-Pokey around the corner." He points his thumb over his shoulder.

I'm not surprised that he was trying to catch one fish while having another on the line.

"Well…" I say.

"Okay…"

There's nothing more to say but good-bye. I feel as though I've got this part of my life under control for the time being. Vince can trust that Robert is completely out of my system.

I skip up all six flights of stairs, and I'm only slightly winded when I reach the top. Francesca and her manager, Aiden, are seated around the table. Her thin legs, which are confined by tight blue jeans, are draped over Delta's lap. An attractive young man wearing a black business suit sits close to Delta. The guy's hair is slicked back, and he's talking and gesturing wildly. Whatever he's saying must be pretty interesting because he has the attention of everyone except the two dark-haired, slender girls with super-red lipstick who are standing near Aiden's shoulder and humping the air out of rhythm. The girls appear to be identical twins. Monroe sits in the middle of the group. The key people turn their attention toward me when I sit next to the guy in the suit. I'm momentarily caught off guard by how good he smells.

"Where the hell did you go?" Monroe asks.

"I had to take care of something."

Her eyes narrow curiously. I can tell that she wants to ask a follow-up question, but now isn't the time or place.

"Did you take care of it?" Delta asks.

"I did. It looks like the two of you have gotten better acquainted. Are we ready to move forward?" I ask.

Monroe rolls her eyes, which is a clue that there's a bump in the road.

Delta slides Francesca off his lap. "Time to unclench those ass cheeks of yours, Maggie." He gestures to the server. "The special brew!"

The server glances at me then brings a bottle of wine from under his cart. It's already uncapped, and white vapor snakes out of the neck.

"I'll loosen up when I know we have a deal," I say.

Francesca studies my chest as though she can see right through my shirt. "So you're Maggie?"

I glance at my tits to make sure they're still covered. "I am."

"I didn't know you were so…" She chews on her bottom lip and finishes undressing me with her eyes. Francesca is wearing a see-through blouse with no bra, and her nipples are right in Delta's face.

I shift uncomfortably. "Did Monroe explain—"

"Get a drink in her mouth now!" Delta says.

The server hands me a glass filled with clear, greenish liquid. I set it on the table. People like Delta and Francesca are used to others jumping through hoops, but I'm not their trained monkey.

"I'm not drinking this until our deal is done." My tone says that I mean business.

Delta motions to the server. The guy pulls out another silver tray.

Francesca recoils as Delta fills the indentations and sniffs two lines of white powder. "You're a fucking junkie?"

"No," he says as though he's not sure.

"The fuck you're not. No way am I getting involved with a junkie."

Monroe and I are shocked. We would've never guessed Francesca has such an aversion to blow. I figure it's a common practice in the thespian culture.

"Hey, I can attest that he only does it when he parties," Monroe says.

"How often does he party?" Francesca's English accent isn't very strong, since she was born and raised in Connecticut, but it's pronounced enough to make her sound condescending. When Monroe doesn't answer, Francesca says, "Right... I want to improve my image, not flush it down the loo."

I raise a hand to halt Monroe from saying whatever she was going to say. "You have a valid point," I say to Francesca.

"Don't call me a fucking junkie!" Delta says.

"But coke up your nose is so nineteen-seventy done," I say. "Marijuana is legal in two U.S. states, and it doesn't bake your brain the same way other narcotics do." I focus on Francesca. "What if he replaced one with the other?"

"I can handle my shit," Delta says, sniffing and wiping his nose.

"For now, you can," I say before Monroe can respond. "See that's the thing about 'junkies.' You have it under control until one day it controls you. I know you feel invincible and shit, but you're a fucking human being. Just like me." I point at the twins. "Just like them. You will fall. How far is up to you. So if you want me to change your fucking image, then you're going to do what I say next... rehab."

Monroe is speechless. We're very different in that I'm ready to walk. For so many reasons, I want Delta to get over himself and follow the program. We cannot begin to change his image if he's calling the shots and telling us what he will and won't do. I've gotten to him. I can tell because I've never seen him look so angry.

"Then it's a fucking negative," he says. "I'm not going to fucking rehab."

I down the drink in the glass. The contents are so strong that it stings my brain. My eyes water and my nose burns, but I show no signs of that. I stand up, and my head is spinning. "We'll annul the contract," I say to Monroe.

"Where are you going?" Francesca asks.

"Back to the hotel. I'm wasting my time here." I feel the air dancing on my skin.

Delta has gone from frowning to smirking. "Sit your ass down, Maggie. I'll give you one stint in rehab. I pick the place." He turns to Francesca. "How does that sound?"

She points her chin at me. "Throw in a night with her, and you have a deal."

"There will be no nights with me. Tell her, Delta." The look on my face dares her to object.

Delta turns the corners of his mouth down and shakes his head. "She's asexual."

Francesca studies me intensely. "He goes to rehab in Newport. It's where I went." She lifts two fingers. "Two years sober."

I blink slowly. "Then we have a deal?"

Delta whispers something to Francesca, and they grin at me.

"I'm in," Francesca says.

The room is spinning. Delta and Francesca engage in a slobbery kiss to seal the deal. My head is spiraling up a vortex, and I'm flooded by happy feelings. We're signing our second client, I've resolved my issues with Robert, and I'm ready to…

Francesca takes my hand. "I want to dance!"

I'm ready to dance! I'm splitting the crowd. I can't feel my feet hit the floor. Perhaps I'm walking on air. Disco lights spray my face. Vince is my partner. His smile is made of diamonds, and his eyes are like emeralds.

I beam. "You're here."

He's shirtless. I rest my cheek on his chest. His skin feels like velvet.

"Didn't I promise that I'd never leave you?" he says.

"Yes, you did, and I always believed you."

We shuffle to a slow, rhythmic, sexy song. Our eyes are fastened on each other. His hands are like vines caressing my waist. They grow up to my breasts and down to my hips. I close my eyes as the vines sweep around my thighs and my clit. I fall into him. Wetness and warmth covers my nipples. I moan.

"Vince…" I sigh.

"No, no, no…" Monroe's voice fills my head. "Not like this."

The sensations dissolve. I'm sitting, and the world is moving in slow motion. Where did Vince go? The spotlight illuminates a single glass of wine.

"Open your eyes, Mags!" Monroe says.

It's time to toast to success. Liquid warms my throat. The dark-haired twins grind on each other. A head bobs against Delta's lap. It's the man with the slick hair. Delta is panting, his eyes are hooded, and he's staring at me. A Marilyn Monroe lookalike plays with the hem of her dress as she changes poses.

"Are you okay?" Monroe asks me.

I grin and signal with my fingers that I'm "A-OK." I close my eyes. I open them.

Delta is reciting a scene from *Romeo and Juliet*. He slides his thumb across my lip. "Is crimson in thy lips and in thy cheeks?"

"Suck, Maggie," he says.

I suck his thumb. He grunts then sucks his thumb after me.

Francesca leaps in front of him. She pretends to swallow poison. "O true apothecary," she yells as if she's playing a scene in a rock drama. "Thy drugs are quick. Thus with a kiss, I die."

Her face moves toward mine. Teeth nibble on my lower lip, and a tongue sinks into my mouth.

"Back off," Monroe says. "Not when she's like this."

I close my eyes. When I open them, Francesca and four other men are singing in Italian.

"*C'é un concerto*," the good-looking guy in the red silk shirt says.

"I want to see!" I say.

"We can go then," Monroe says.

"*Andiamo!*" he shouts.

My arms and legs are buoyant. I'm dancing, surrounded by a sea of crying, singing, moving bodies. It's raining. The sounds are bold. The man's voice is passionate. My heart swells with love.

"I love you, Vince!" *Ti amo, mio amore... Solo te. Solo me.* I sway with my hands over my head. My limbs are as light as feather. "I do!"

I'm seized from behind. Something wet and soft slides up the side of my neck. My breasts are groped.

"Hands off!" Monroe shouts.

I shut my eyes. I open them. The space is constricted and dim. I'm sitting on a leather reclining chair. Marilyn Monroe is riding the cock of one of the Italian singers. The twins are entangled with Francesca. The man with the slicked-back hair is blowing Delta.

"Are you sure she doesn't need a doctor?" Aiden asks.

"Drink this, Mags," Monroe says.

I must've swallowed whatever Monroe gave me because liquid slides down my throat and satisfies my stomach. I can't move my arms or legs, and my eyes won't stay open.

I SCRAMBLE TO SIT UP ON THE KING-SIZE BED. I LOOK down at myself. "What the hell…"

I'm wearing a blue leather minidress. The last I remember, we drank to Francesca signing on with us. Where am I, and when did I put on this dress? My head feels funny. My nausea passes.

"Shit." I slip my fingers up and down my slit. No stickiness, dampness, or soreness. No sex. I sigh with relief.

I make a feeble attempt to call for Monroe. My throat is too dry to compete with the blaring music. I stand up too fast, and dizziness makes me sit. I try again, this time much slower. *That's better.*

"Cell phone." I look around the room for my

purse or anything else I can recognize. My suitcase is against the wall, so I rush over to unzip it. My purse is on top of my other things. I search through it and find my phone, but it's out of power. "Shit. Monroe, where the fuck are we!"

The floor is shifting. I'm not on solid ground. I climb a short flight of steps, which lands me on the deck of a yacht. Sun stabs my eyes. I squint as the achy feeling in my head settles. The atmosphere is too bright for London. The sea is aqua and holds clusters of coral reefs. Trees blossom on an island in the not-so-far distance.

"Am I…"

"You're up from the dead?" Monroe says.

I grab my head and spin around. Monroe is standing in the doorway I just walked out of. She's wearing a tiny white lace bikini, and her hair is messy. She looks as though she's had a lot of sex.

I point at the grassy islands around us. "Are we in Australia?"

"I knew you were as high the Milky Way. You don't remember a thing, do you?"

"Not if we're in Australia."

Monroe shakes her head. "Delta had the waiter mix you a cocktail. I've never seen you have such a good time. I got a kick out of it."

I frown as she chuckles. "How the hell did I get into this dress?"

"You wanted to wear it to the concert."

I get a flash of a sea of people clapping their hands above their heads to a quick beat. "I think I remember."

"Marco Santi."

"The Italian singer?"

"We were invited backstage to meet him." She grins. "And you hugged him and kept repeating, 'Ti amo, Vince.'" She chuckles.

I gasp, embarrassed.

"Don't worry. I explained your situation to him."

I'm mortified. "What did you say?"

"Don't worry about it, Mags. He understood. He even kissed you on the forehead and said that he loves you too."

"Fuck," I whisper.

"Believe me, I tried to shut you down plenty, but you refused to sleep it off. You were going with the flow. But I kept an eye on you. I also kept Delta and Francesca from fucking you."

I shake my head. "Wait? What day is it?"

"It's Friday."

I slap my hand over my mouth and gasp. "I have

to be in New Orleans by tomorrow evening! I need to catch the first flight out of here!"

"We're almost done here."

Her nonchalance annoys me. "What are we doing in Australia in the first fucking place?"

She points. "Because of them."

My glare follows her finger. Delta is on the bow of the yacht, rolling around with Francesca, who's topless.

Monroe points in the opposite direction. "Dash is on that yacht taking pictures. By ten a.m., people will know that Delta Foster and Francesca Bell are in a hot and heavy relationship."

I sigh gravely. "And you arranged all of this while I was out of it?" I feel as though I've dropped the ball.

"Mags, we're a team. I had your back."

"But we're going to have to get this shit under control. I let myself be dragged down a fucking rabbit hole. I'm never doing that again."

"Get a grip, Mags—"

"No! I'm not getting a fucking grip. And you know what? The fact that *you* know what my pussy feels like and my tits taste like still doesn't sit well with me. I mean…" I look up to stop my tears from falling. "Damn it, where's Vince? I want Vince."

She grunts and rolls her eyes. "Goddamn it, I knew it. You're looking for excuses to walk."

"I'm not finding excuses. It's just *this,* on top of you masturbating me and sucking my tits, and then me fucking Robert... I'm losing control. How long have we been friends? Too long to count, and you've never done anything like that before."

Monroe wipes my tears with her thumbs. "Calm down, Mags. You've known me to do plenty of stupid shit."

"Yes."

"If you would go there, then hell yes, I'd go there."

"You know me well enough to know that I would never go there, especially with you. You're like my sister, Roe."

"I'm sorry. You're right. It's just..." She walks over to the rail and gazes over the aqua sea. "Sometimes I think that if I could wrap myself in your skin, I'd be perfect."

I shake my head and join her. "Is that your roundabout way of saying that eating my pussy would neutralize your envy?"

"Always getting straight to the point."

"That's what sorority girls do to make themselves feel less insecure about the airhead clone they're jealous of." A wave of nausea grips me, and I clutch my stomach. "Grow the fuck up, please."

"I think I've just aged five years after that."

"I'm serious."

"I know you are. Maybe we should get a contract drawn up. If I don't grow the fuck up, then you can toss my ass overboard."

I almost dry heave. "We don't need a contract. Just do it."

Monroe takes my elbow. "Are you going to be okay?"

"I will be. I just need to get back to Vince, or I'm going to lose it."

"I knew you were going to say that. Our flight leaves in an hour."

"Thank you. By the way, did I see you snort cocaine?"

She rolls her eyes. "Yes, but don't worry. That was me taking one for our team."

I look at her askew. "I don't need you taking one for the team. Leave that shit alone."

"If you're worried I'll get addicted, then don't. I hate bumping that shit. I just did it so Delta wouldn't feel awkward."

"He should feel awkward!"

"Maggie…"

I bend over to clutch my cramping stomach. "I'm going to make sure his stint in rehab works."

"I believe you, but first, let's get you to the bathroom. It's a good one. You'll like the toilet, and it won't try to fuck you either."

I elbow her playfully in the ribs, and she laughs as she leads me to the white porcelain throne.

8
LOST IN LONDON

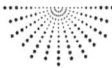

VINCENT ADAMS

YESTERDAY, THURSDAY

*V*ince's airplane touched down late in the afternoon. London had never been his favorite city. It reminded him of amusement park towns that tried to recapture a time period that was long gone and would never return, except London was the real thing. He could never take the city seriously.

Vince had two goals. He wanted to find Maggie and get them the hell out of town. He had already tried to call her six times, but the calls went straight to voicemail. Her phone was either unplugged or out of power, and Maggie was far too responsible to let her cell phone fall into either state. That was why his worry was off the charts. Vince made a seventh call after he settled into the black cab he had ordered to usher him around for the day. No one knew how to navigate the city better than the drivers of black cabs, and he hated London traffic more than L.A. and Manhattan combined. So their expertise of evading the insanity was much appreciated.

Langley had confirmed the hotel Maggie was staying in. It was along the River Thames, and Langley had even managed to get him the room number. Vince frowned when Maggie's voicemail picked up again. He was beyond frustrated and had to beat back the thought that she was somewhere banging Robert. Vince placed another call.

"Hello," Robert said chummily.

"Have you seen Maggie?" Vince asked rather coldly.

"I saw her last night."

Vince clenched his jaw. "Did you fuck her?"

"Damn it, Vince, no, I didn't fuck her. That's done."

Robert's ego made Vince seethe. "It can't be *done* because you never had her to begin with."

"You're right. I didn't mean it that way. She was signing a new client."

Vince sighed with relief. He couldn't forgive Maggie for sleeping with Robert twice. "Thanks. That's all."

"Hey, Vince?" Robert asked.

"What?"

"I'm sorry, brother. I didn't meant to… I'm sorry."

Vince hesitated. "By the way, I hired Linda Matthews for Maggie's position."

"Oh, her. She's hot."

"She's a solid replacement."

"Right," Robert said.

Vince ended the call. He and Robert had been friends for far too long to terminate their relationship, but in order for them to move forward, Robert would have to look into his bag of shit and figure out why he did the things he did. Vince thought about the first time they'd met Lena Chance. It was their senior year in college, and Vince and Robert had been selected to attend the Future Business Leaders of the World conference in San Francisco. The first night, there was a mixer, and Lena had accidentally bumped into Vince. Her cascading black hair, which contrasted with her light brown eyes, captivated him instantly.

She'd smiled and said, "Oh, please excuse me."

From that moment on, Vince had wanted to know more about her. They carried on an interesting conversation. She was representing the University of Oxford. She was enjoying San Francisco, and the cloudiness felt like home. She had no boyfriend, but she had a dry sense of humor and a sexy way of flickering her eyebrows after saying the punch line.

Then Robert had joined them, and before Vince knew it, Lena and Robert had made plans to have dinner alone later that night. The next morning, the two of them were fucking like nymphomaniacs. It was just another example of Robert taking a shot at the woman Vince was interested in. Robert had a ninety percent success rate at winning them over.

Vince had never stopped Robert from coming on to Maggie because she consistently shut him down, crucifying Robert's ego. She was the one he couldn't steal. So when Vince had seen them together on Maggie's bed, he'd felt defeated. Maggie used to be his champion. He didn't know what she was to him anymore. But he would be dead and in a coffin before he let Robert win her.

Vince's cab dodged down streets. Vince would never get used to riding on the wrong side of the road. It was impractical. All the street signs and stoplights were ass-backward. Man, did he hate London. He was relieved when the car pulled up to his hotel.

"Here we are, mate," the driver said.

"I'll be back," Vince said and bolted out of the back seat.

As instructed, he gave the concierge his name. The concierge was supposed to escort him to the restricted floor where Maggie and Monroe were staying. However, after Vince gave his name, he was informed that the party had checked out in the wee hours of the morning.

"But they were checked in until tomorrow morning. Where the hell did they go?" Vince knew the stress he felt was written all over his face.

"I'm sorry, sir, but the party did not leave word of their destination."

Vince cursed under his breath. "You said the party? There should've been just two women."

"According to the night shift, there was a large group, and they were in quite *jovial* spirits."

Vince looked at him askew. He'd picked up on what the concierge was insinuating. "Were they drunk?"

"I do believe so."

"Even the blonde?"

"Especially the blondes."

Vince was rendered speechless. He wondered what the hell was going on. Maggie had always been way too serious to participate in drunken nonsense. She had changed, and not in a good way.

"Thank you," Vince grumbled and trotted back to the cab.

Once he was tucked in the back seat, he placed calls to Maggie's friends and former colleagues who lived in London. None of them had seen or heard from her. He tried Monroe, but she didn't answer her phone either. Maggie was lost in London. Vince considered driving around until he found her, but that would be like searching for a needle in a haystack. He remembered that she planned to be in New Orleans on Saturday night. The impulsive lie he'd told Charlie was now the truth.

Vince asked the driver to take him back to the airport. As soon as Vince rested his aching head on the seat, his cell phone rang. His heart raced because he hoped it was Maggie. "Hello?"

"Did you find her?" Robert asked.

Vince grunted and clenched his lips. "No."

"Are you sticking around?"

"No. What the hell do you want, Rob?"

"Can I catch a ride back to the States with you?"

Vince massaged the corners of his eyes. He really wanted to say no, but he didn't know how to punish Robert for crossing him. "Sure. The plane takes off in an hour. If you're late, I'm leaving without you."

"Aye, aye, captain."

Vince grimaced and ended the call.

VINCE WAS ALREADY SEATED WHEN ROBERT ARRIVED with five minutes to spare.

Robert plopped into the seat beside Vince, wearing that silly grin. "Were you really going to take off without me?"

Vince's expression remained stone cold. "Yes."

Robert clipped on his seatbelt. Vince avoided eye contact, but he felt Robert's gaze upon him.

"What?" Vince snapped.

"So where the hell is Maggie?"

Vince didn't look up from the first-quarter reports he was reading. He couldn't believe Robert asked about her.

"You're still angry," Robert said.

Vince snorted. That was an understatement.

"She and I had a long conversation last night."

That got Vince's eyes off his papers.

"I tried to fuck her again," Robert said. "She's not having anything to do with me. It's all you, brother."

"Why in the hell would you try to fuck her *again?*"

Robert furrowed his eyebrows. "She said I'm a kid who wants to play with your favorite rattle even though I've got my own toys. That's been fucking with my head."

Vince took a moment to absorb what Robert had just said. He'd never thought of it that way, but hell if Maggie hadn't hit the nail on the head.

"I gave her my best work," Robert said, referring to the sex. "I did something that drove her crazy, and I'll tell you how I did it. It'll be my apology, my gift from me to you to her."

Vince frowned. "What the fuck are you talking about?"

"The way I…" Robert shifted his tongue from left to right.

Robert was lucky that the flight attendant had told them to remain in their seats for takeoff because Vince knew exactly what Robert was referring to. Maggie had nearly climbed the walls while Robert was going down on her.

"I don't need you to teach me how to eat pussy," Vince said, although he was curious as hell.

The plane raced down the runway, and Vince tried to concentrate on his work. All he could see was Maggie sucking the air and pulling on the sheets. She looked so sexy with her legs spread and nipples erect. He wanted to pull Robert off her and take over.

"A microscopic speck," Robert said, interrupting Vince's flashback.

Vince looked at him with his eyes narrowed.

Robert took a sheet of paper and brushed the edge. "About that much packs a powerful punch. They can hardly contain themselves. Just that much is all you need. She bursts, and you go around the globe, speck by speck."

Vince squinted at the speck of corner Robert was referring to. "You know you're a bastard, right?"

"That was a real apology I gave you. If I could go back and do it differently, then I would. That's how much you and I—"

"It's over," Vince said. "We'll take it one day at a time."

"I can handle one day at a time," Robert said.

Vince nodded and put his focus back on his work. Two hours later, Robert was talking about the silver Maserati a guy they knew wanted to sell him. Robert explained how smoothly the test drive went, but said the thing was just ugly. He thought it looked like a spoon. Vince laughed, and that broke the ice. They talked about Emily and whether or not they should keep her after all that had happened.

"I'm fine with it," Vince said.

"She's not going to stop trying to get you," Robert said.

Vince watched Robert intensely. "I'm marrying Maggie. That'll bring her back to reality."

Robert narrowed his eyes. "What the hell are you looking for? You think I want to stop you?"

"Just like that, you're over her?"

"Sometimes it takes hearing the right words. I'm just glad you're still in love with her. I could've fucked it up for the both of you."

"Yeah, you could've, but you didn't."

"Then are you ready to buy her a Maserati, a silver one that looks like a spoon?" Robert asked.

Vince laughed. "You let him talk you into buying the car?"

"Yeah…" Robert said with sigh of regret.

Vince laughed louder.

"It's parked in my garage in Laurel Canyon."

Vince laughed even louder.

ROBERT DEPLANED AT TETERBORO IN NEW YORK, AND Vince flew on to New Orleans. He got a suite at the Westport Continental Hotel. Vince wanted to call Maggie, but he also wanted to surprise her. So he got some sleep and woke up on Saturday morning ready to work.

His first meeting was a three-hour videoconference with their accountant and lawyer. Then he met with the vice president of development for three more hours to talk about shows that needed to be cancelled on Prime D TV because they were losing so much money. If Vince had allowed it, the stress of keeping A&Rt afloat would've taken him out a long time ago. After ordering breakfast, lunch, and a steady flow of coffee, it dawned on Vince that Maggie wasn't the only workaholic in their relationship. He fought the urge to call her. What if she hadn't made it to New Orleans? What if she'd run off with some other guy and said sayonara to him? He would burst into a million pieces if that had happened.

Finally, eight thirty p.m. arrived. He took a shower and put on a dark pair of jeans, his burgundy suede tennis shoes with the white stripe on the sides, and a white shirt. Maggie liked when he dressed casual. She'd said it made him look delicious, like a bag of chocolate chip cookies that she wanted to devour. He would be the one doing the devouring tonight. *A microscopic speck*, Vince thought as he headed one floor up to the penthouse lounge.

9

CONTINGENCY PLANS

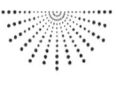

MAGGIE

I already know I look like shit. I don't need Charlie harping on it. I feel like shit too. I try to straighten myself up, but my temples throb as Angelina sells me on the brilliance of Dr. Luc Calvet. My eyes burn like crazy. I just want Angelina to get to the point already. I shift uncomfortably as I'm served crawfish étouffée. Charlie's given his shrimp po-boy, and Angelina gets gumbo.

I hold up a hand to stop her talking. "I think we all know we're here to strengthen the contingency plan, so let's just get to it." I yawn.

"But where the hell is Vince, Mags?" Charlie says, glaring at me.

"You've asked that already."

"You haven't answered."

"Hell, I don't know! I was in London."

"What were you doing in London?"

"Are you the Spanish Inquisition?"

He grunts.

"Leave me alone, Chuck. Let's get down to fucking business."

He looks at Angelina as if I've just slapped him in the face.

"Problem number one," I say forcefully. "Getting them alone and isolated in a place they can't escape."

Charlie sighs as if he's going to let it drop. I think Angelina just kicked him under the table again.

"I've been thinking about the island," Charlie says.

"Martha's Vineyard?" I shake my head. "That won't work. He knows just about everyone who lives there."

"Not the Vineyard. Jack owns a private island in the Bahamas. His closest neighbors are thirty miles away."

I aim the butt of my pen at Charlie. "Now that's a good idea. So how does he normally get to, from, and around that island?"

"He flies into Nassau, that's where he keeps his yacht docked. Then he boats over to the island. He keeps two speedboats and two sets of jet skis there…" The skin between Charlie's eyes puckers as he ponders. "That's it."

I write that on my pad. "What about telecommunications?"

"He has phones and… He has a whole communications room just in case he's caught in a hurricane."

I cross *Private Island* off my list. "Well, there goes that idea."

"Nah, I have some engineers who can rewire shit."

"Oh, great," I say. I'm a tiny bit sobered by Charlie's newfound capabilities. I've never subscribed to the idea that a woman can change a man, so I don't know what came first: him finally growing up or his love for Angelina making him evolve. Regardless, I sure as hell don't miss the old lazy, philandering drunkard who could barely tie his own shoes.

"Luc is also going to hold daily sessions with them," Angelina says.

Charlie pecks her tenderly on the lips. "I'm going to have it all set up, babe."

Seeing them together makes me miss Vince. "Okay, what about the fucking?"

Charlie and Angelina look confused.

"That's their major problem. Instead of talking, they fuck their way to a temporary resolution. Put them together on a deserted island, and Daisy will be pregnant again by sundown."

"That's true," Angelina says thoughtfully. "I forgot to mention that to Luc. I'll let him know that as long as they're having sex, they're stable."

I instinctively study Charlie's body language. Wow, he no longer cringes at the idea of Jack and Daisy doing it. He used to want her so badly that I thought he would murder Jack or something to get him out of the way. But hell, he really is over Daisy.

"I wouldn't call it stable," Charlie says.

"It makes them numb to their shit," I say.

"That's more like it."

"Jack and Daisy and a deserted island…"

"They're going to fuck," Charlie says.

"A lot," I say.

"Maybe we can put ankle bracelets on them or something," Angelina says.

"Like what prisoners wear?" I ask.

She shrugs. "At least we can have Luc look into it."

Charlie snorts and smirks. "Daisy… She's not going to like that shit. It's going to feel like a shackle."

"Oh, you mean with her issues of being tied-down," Angelina says.

Charlie nods.

"So ankle bracelets or not?" I ask.

"Maybe," Angelina says. "If it can be done, then yes."

I write *ankle bracelets?* on my pad. "Okay. So… how do we get them there?"

"We'll drug them," Angelina says so nonchalantly that I wonder if I heard her wrong.

"Drug them? I don't know about that." I think about what I just went through—over twenty-four hours of my life lost, and now my head is paying for it. "Is it ethical to drug someone without their knowledge? Especially if we don't know if there are side effects? And then they'll just lose all that time and wake up in a fucking stupor without knowing what the hell happened… It's just not fair."

Charlie looks at me cockeyed.

"What?" I snap.

"Someone drug you, Mags?"

"No!" *Fuck, how did he guess?*

He looks as if he doesn't believe me.

"Well, Charlie has a friend who's an anesthesiologist. He's already agreed to help however he can," Angelina says.

I snicker. "Engineers and anesthesiologists? Did you dump all the losers you used to hang around?"

"I never hung around losers," he says, still studying me suspiciously.

I feel like hiding inside my skin. He knows something's off about me. If anyone could tell, it would be Charlie. I'm on the verge of spilling the beans about the rift between Vince and me and my last couple days. I feel like a hypocrite.

However—and it's possible I'm experiencing an aftereffect of whatever the hell Delta gave me—I lock eyes with Vince, who's walking in our direction. I shut my eyes tightly. When I reopen them, he's hugging Angelina. Then he shakes Charlie's hand, which means he's not an apparition.

"How are you, babe?" he says.

His lips meet mine, and I indulge in their brief collision. Vince and I stare into each other's eyes.

"Fine," I mutter.

"I didn't think you would show up," Charlie says.

"Sorry I'm late," Vince says. "I was on a call. I'm staying here in the hotel, so I should've been on time."

"You're staying in a hotel? You guys can stay in our guest room," Angelina says.

"Unless you're not sleeping together," Charlie says.

Vince and I stare into each other's eyes. I'm still

surprised he's here. I thought I'd have to find him and beg him to love me.

"We're going to stay here tonight. Tomorrow we'll stay at your house," Vince says. "How's the remodeling going?"

Water rushes to my eyes. I love the way his hands feel massaging my shoulders and neck. I could fall into him and never come out.

"It's going fine. But why not just come over tonight? The guest room is on the other side of the house. You'll have your privacy," Charlie says.

"I'm already dug in here for the night."

Charlie looks at Angelina, who shrugs. "Okay, but will you be okay, Maggie?"

It dawns on me that Charlie is spooked by my appearance. I'm not willing to tell him that I've spent the last day and a half as high as Mars and can't remember a thing about it. "I'm okay, Chuck. I'm just tired. The sooner we're done here, the sooner I can remedy that."

Charlie nods and gets Vince up-to-date about what we've discussed so far.

"Daisy will be easy," Angelina says. "We'll do a spa day with her, and Stanley, the anesthesiologist, will be her 'masseuse.'" Angelina draws air quotes.

I have a question, but I can't form it because my

focus has left the room. Vince is surprisingly frisky. We lock eyes. I can't believe he's here and touching me. His body heat and the energy emanating from him make me feel so secure.

Vince looks away to ask, "Charlie, you want me to help you subdue Jack?"

"Unless we hire someone to kick his ass."

"Are you out of your mind?" I say. "It's bad enough that we're sitting here casually planning kidnappings and druggings."

"But for a good cause," Angelina interjects.

"It is a good cause, but I don't want Jack hurt," I say. "Take him down yourselves or not at all. Maybe I can convince Jack to take a spa day with me. He's gone with me before."

"You'll be with me, Maggie." Angelina lifts a finger. "Wait, I think we have a problem…"

"What is it?" Charlie asks.

"It all has to happen simultaneously. We're going to need two anesthesiologists."

Charlie winks at her. "I've got it covered."

Angelina bats her eyelashes at him as if he'd just agreed to save her life.

"Are we done?" Vince asks impatiently. He squeezes my left hand and slides his thumb over my ring.

"You just got here, bro," Charlie says.

A guy with ginger hair and an instrument case strapped on his back puts his hand on Charlie's shoulder. "Y'all going down to Frenchman tonight?"

A fresh group of musicians start playing.

Charlie bounces enthusiastically in his chair. "Where you going to be?"

I've never heard him sound so Southern.

"We playing on the Pit," the redhead says.

"Hot shit! Who's on bass?"

"You are if you come on now."

Charlie and Angelina spring out of their chairs.

"You don't want to come, do you?" Charlie asks Vince and me.

We shake our heads. Vince's thumb is massaging my palm.

Charlie is overexcited. "See you tomorrow then?"

Angelina and I kiss each other good-bye on the cheek. Charlie waves as he walks away backward. Vince and I face each other as if time has stopped—we have a billion options, and we don't know what to choose first.

His lips are on my ear. "Hey."

I turn to face him, and our cheeks brush. "Hey."

My head climbs up to cloud nine. A magnetic force fuses our lips. Our tongues get reacquainted.

The taste of his mouth makes me moan. This still feels like a dream, except it's come true.

"My luggage is with the concierge," I say.

Vince guides me to my feet, and we walk out of the restaurant. He asks a bellhop to bring my luggage to his room. The young man remembers me and says he'll take it up right away.

Vince rubs my shoulders as we enter the elevator. "You're shivering. Are you cold?"

"I'm just nervous and tired," I say.

Our tongues plunge into each other's mouths. Our kissing is so sensual. When the doors open, he takes my hand and leads me down the long hallway. He pulls his key from his pocket, and once we're inside, Vince pins me against the wall. The only sounds in the room are our moans and whimpers. Our lips separate as he pulls my dress over my head.

He looks at my crotch. "You wore panties?"

I smile slightly and nod. He traces my bottom lip with his thumb then sucks my lip into his mouth. He unhooks my bra, and it drops onto the carpet. His tongue draws circles on my collarbone, then he draws my nipple into his mouth. I fall against his chest and sip air between my teeth as he stimulates the tip. His fingers slide up and down my creamy slit. Our breaths come quicker.

He picks me up, and we kiss as he carries me to the bed and spreads me on it. Our eyes stay locked on each other as he snatches off my panties. He smirks and lowers his face between my legs. He licks my juicy pussy twice then covers my clit with his mouth.

"Whoa!" I pin my head against the mattress. My cry gathers steam and pounds the air on release.

My pussy clenches. Orgasms blast off like firecrackers, and he keeps me from squirming away from his mouth. The sensations are unrelenting. I try to hitch myself up on my elbows to see how he's doing that, but it starts all over again.

I fall back down. "Vince... please..." I'm moaning and squealing and gritting my teeth.

The firecrackers-orgasm punches me deep in my pussy. I can hardly bear it. I suck like a fish out of water. Sensations are building upward and outward. I tense, grit my teeth, and screams when it happens.

"Mm..." Vince's tongue slides in and out of my hole. He sucks the lips of my pussy.

"Oh my God," I pant.

"You liked that?" he asks, grinning proudly.

I fall back on the mattress and cover my eyes with my forearm. "That was intense. How in the world?"

Then I remember what Robert did to me. Oh my God! I stare at Vince as he unzips his pants. I dare not ask if Robert taught him how to do that. He takes off his shirt and steps out of his underwear. He slips between my legs and easily into my creamy pussy. Our breaths collide, and our lips enfold. We stay like this, staring into each other's eyes. I can't keep tears from forming.

"I love you," I whisper.

"I will always love you more, baby."

"I still want to marry you."

"Me too," he says.

"But let's love each other for a while. Let me try to give you what you want first."

Vince shifts his hips slowly. "Mags—"

"No." I sigh from the massaging his dick is giving my pussy. "Charlie was right. I'm a runner. I want to try to be normal first."

"Baby, you're the normal one." He rams his dick deep inside me. "Do you promise to have me? To hold me and the rest of that shit until death do us part?"

I make a noise that's somewhere between a laugh and a gasp. "I do."

"I do too." He picks up the pace.

My hips are in his grip. Every inch of him rides

my pussy. With one more hard slam, he jerks and grunts as he comes.

"I now pronounce us husband and wife. I'm going kiss my bride."

We roll around the bed, kissing. My eyes are closed and it's hard to open them again.

"Vince?" I ask.

"Yes," he says, dry humping me.

"Can we sleep now, please?"

"How about you sleep and I play with you?" He moans as he sucks a mouthful of my tit.

I sigh from pleasure and exhaustion. "Deal."

Vince spoons me and gropes my breasts, hips and thighs. As time passes, I fall asleep, wake up to satisfy the needs of his erection and then fall back to sleep.

ONE MONTH LATER....

Call it luck, fate, or divine intervention, but it's all in Jack and Daisy's corner. Last week, all hell broke loose in their relationship. Daisy and Jack were on the verge of fucking their way to a resolution when the investigator chick, Stacy Pruitt, sent Daisy a string of pics of Stacy and Jack in compromising positions. Angelina had called Vince and me to say that the contingency plan was in play. It took two days and a gang-load of Charlie's buddies to prepare the private island. Angelina readied Dr. Luc Calvet, who is going to orchestrate their therapy from his home in Paris.

On Monday morning, Angelina received a phone call from Heloise, asking if she could fly to Chicago and check on Daisy. We were going to wait until Charlie and Angelina's fake engagement party to separate them, have them knocked out, and transport them to the private island, but we've decided to take advantage of this fortunate, unfortunate situation.

Since we could only secure one anesthesiologist, Charlie and Vince hopped a flight to Chicago and managed to subdue Jack after he left a meeting. I haven't seen Charlie, but Vince said he's nursing a black eye. Regardless, they accompanied a transport team on four-hour flight from Chicago to Nassau and then a fifteen-minute helicopter ride to the island.

When Jack woke this morning, he found himself locked in his safe room. It has a bedroom, bathroom and is stocked with plenty of food. When Daisy arrives tomorrow, Dr. Calvet will unlock the door remotely so that Jack can find Daisy. They'll both be outfitted with ankle bracelets that will shock them if they get too close to each other. Dr. Calvet agreed with outfitting them with the devices as a solution for keeping them from having sex before they get to the core of their issues.

Today is Daisy's turn. I'm driving a van with tinted windows and a hospital bed in the back to Daisy's place. Angelina is in the passenger seat. Stanley Roswell, the anesthesiologist, and two attendants will meet us at Daisy's.

"You seriously consider yourselves married?" Angelina asks.

"Why not? We made vows to each other," I say.

"I'm not knocking it, but it's bold as hell."

"Maybe you and Charlie should try it. I can be your witness."

"No way. Charlie and I are going to spend the rest of our lives together just as we are."

"I actually believe you. My cousin's a bonehead, and I'm surprised he was able to stop screwing whichever chick fell on his dick because he loves you."

"Was he really a man whore?"

"The king, supreme man whore." Angelina is so quiet that I glance at her to make sure I haven't upset her.

"I trust him so much," she says.

"As you should. Plus, I overexaggerated things. He wasn't the king, supreme man whore. That would be Robert Tango."

"Who's Robert Tango?"

"Vince's business partner. My ex-boss."

"Oh…"

She's quiet again.

"I can't believe we've actually gone through with all this," I say, purposely changing the subject.

"I know you're a wee bit uncomfortable with the whole ordeal, but once it's over and it works, then you'll see that it was worth it. Belmont and Daisy are the glue that holds us all together. If they fall apart, we fall apart."

I stop at the light on Wabash and study her long enough to catch a glimpse of her soul. I can see why Jack and Daisy's relationship is so important to her. She thinks if they break up, then she won't see as much of Daisy, and their relationship will disappear. I wonder why everyone who loves Daisy is afraid of losing her. I've been on Daisy's side since the beginning, but perhaps I've chosen wrong.

I squeeze Angelina's hand. "We'll never fall apart, Angel. You can't get rid of me so easily, or your sister."

She squeezes my hand in response.

We're just around the corner from Daisy's apartment. I follow the GPS and make a left onto Wacker, right on Columbus, left on Randolph, left onto Field, and then an immediate right. The building is to my right. I stop in front of a young, short guy and two taller females. They're all wearing green hospital scrubs.

"Keys?" I ask Angelina.

She reaches into her purse, takes out a set of keys, and holds them up. "Here."

"Let's not delay!"

She takes a calming breath before getting out of the van. The two women take the hospital bed out of the back, and they and Stanley follow Angelina and me into the townhouse, which is large and beautiful.

"Who's there?" a man with an English accent calls.

"It's Angelina, Daisy's sister! Is she here?"

A good-looking man blessed with height walks out of the kitchen. His sleeves are rolled up to his elbows. He looks as though he's been here for a while.

Angelina walks toward him with an outstretched hand. "You must be Javar Les?"

He raises his eyebrows in admiration. "You're Daisy's sister?"

"Yes, I'm Angelina."

He looks at me. "And may I ask, who are you?"

I hold out my hand. "I'm Maggie, Daisy's cousin-in-law."

"Ah… right. You're related to Jack Lord?"

"We have to get this show on the road," Stanley says.

"We're taking Daisy home," Angelina says.

Javar flinches. "Is that right?"

"Is she upstairs?" Angelina asks.

"Why, yes." Javar's behavior is pretty spastic.

Angelina looks away from the kitchen. "Look, there's an elevator." She turns to me. "We'll be back down with Daisy."

I nod. It's my job to stay with the attractive "friend" who has spent the last twenty-four hours nursing Daisy. No guy does that for a woman unless he's in love with her.

"Well, I was making myself some tea. Would you like a cup?" Javar asks.

"You don't look like the tea type," I say.

"Of course I'll spike it with a wee bit of brandy."

I shrug. "I'll just take my tea plain. I'm driving."

He grunts thoughtfully, and I follow him into the kitchen. The television mounted on the wall is showing the local news.

Javar takes a box of Earl Grey tea from a cabinet. "So where are you taking her?"

"You really know your way around this kitchen," I say.

"Well, I've been here for some time."

"Over twenty-four hours."

He glances at me with a lopsided smile. "And you're the relative of Belmont Lord."

"Yes."

"I see… Daisy's working on a television program. She's expected to join the crew as soon as she's better." He fills the teakettle with tap water.

I'm just about to tell him I don't drink tap water when I hear…

"Billionaire Jack Lord has been accused of allegedly offering sexual favors in exchange for purchasing coveted Chicago Riverfront property…"

I look up at the television.

A grumpy looking man stomping away from the cameras, which are chasing him says, "It's unfortunate he brings these kinds of practices into a city like ours…"

My mouth hangs open. Did I just hear what I thought I heard? I look at Javar Les. We share the same expression.

"Speaking of the devil…" he says.

"Holy shit..."

Angelina rushes into the kitchen. "Okay we're loading up!"

I point up at the TV.

"How Jack Lord's bid to own one of the most prestigious landmarks in Chicago is tied to his questionable past, coming up in the next hour," the anchorwoman says, concluding the news-bite.

Angelina looks stunned. "What questionable past?"

"It's a long, dead and buried story. Can you go without me?" I ask.

She nods emphatically. "Yes, yes... Absolutely."

I fumble my cell phone out of my purse and call Monroe. Two rings and she answers. "Guess what?"

"What?" she says.

"We have ourselves a new client."

PART II
AND HE LIKES ME

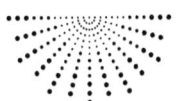

SIX MONTHS LATER

20 HOURS BEFORE TAKEOFF

onroe and I flew into Manhattan on the red-eye this morning. Now we're in a lunch meeting with Lolita Best, a scorned pageant winner. Two months ago, she was stripped of her crown after officials discovered she worked as a stripper when she was eighteen. Monroe and I took up the task of repairing Lolita's reputation, and I think her case is the straw that broke my back. I can't remember how I cleaned up her mess, but I got it done. That's how my job has been for the longest time now. I've just been going through the motions. I have no love and no passion for what I do. Even now, instead of listening to my client, I'm staring out the window, watching New Yorkers trample the sidewalk.

A lot has gone wrong in my life since I left A&Rt Media Group. The worst of it hit six months ago when Vince asked me to meet him at his office in Century City. I asked if he could wait until I returned from a two-week press tour with an actress named Connie Limon. She had a movie coming out on the heels of her getting a DUI from the Highway Patrol in Malibu. Anyway, he said no, so three hours before my flight, I rushed over to see what was so urgent. I never expected Vince's stern expression. He said that he'd tried to ignore the fact that I had fucked Robert Tango, his best friend. Vince said that he still loved me when he should hate me, but he couldn't find what he needed inside himself to forgive me. He broke up with me, and my heart was pulverized.

Monroe snaps her fingers. "Maggie."

I face her grimace.

"Well, I was saying that I don't think we should end our relationship now, especially when I kicked their asses and I'm back on top," Lolita says.

She kicked their asses? "I kicked their asses," I snarl.

Monroe chastises me by widening her eyes.

Lolita claps her hands and rubs them together.

"The point is that I'm back on top. I think we should spread the steam while it's hot."

Lolita has a black mark above her top lip on the right corner. I think she accidentally poked herself with the tip of a pen or a marker or something. I want to tell her, but I don't want to be responsible for her anymore.

"I think what Maggie wants to say is that we accepted you on our acute client list, and at the moment, we don't have an opening in our P&A list," I say.

"What's that?" Lolita asks.

Monroe ruffles her eyebrows when she looks at me. "P&A is perception and acceptance."

I take a drink of my pink butterfly cocktail. It's sweet and delicious. Normally I'm the one who directs these sorts of meetings, but I can't think of anything to say. I try really hard to listen and be in the moment as Monroe talks to Lolita about how Monroe just sold Clara Richardson's, Monroe's late mother, condo on the Upper East Side. The new owners will take ownership of the famous actress' digs on Monday morning. That's why we flew to New York to have our wrap meeting with her instead of the other way around.

Lolita's eyes shine in that gratifying way they do

just before she's about to give or receive gossip. "Didn't she die in an airplane crash with her lover?"

"But Maggie's flying to Louisiana tomorrow. Her cousin is throwing an engagement hoedown," Monroe says.

Lolita points at me. "Wait. Isn't Jack Lord your cousin?"

I snort at how easy it was for Monroe to divert Lolita's attention away from the scandal surrounding her mother's death. "Yes, but she's referring to Jack's brother—"

"Charles Lord," Lolita says.

I narrow one eye. Like the average gold-digger she is, she's done her homework. To those who aren't familiar with her kind, Lolita Best is beauty incarnate. She has long dark hair and deep-green eyes, the skin of a baby's bottom, and a body that most women covet. For those of the masses who haven't developed my sort of lenses to see the shit past the shinola, Lolita Best is exquisite. But when I look at her, I see an opportunist who would fuck the bus driver to get from one block to the next for free. She uses her pussy as cash, and it's worked for her for far too long to believe there are more effective methods to obtain success. Deep down, I'm sick of Lolita Best and the ten other clients we have who are just like her.

Monroe looks at me with concern and starts a conversation about introducing Lolita to some people who can help her career. Monroe calls these services a la carte. I've never heard of us offering those services, but I'm not interested enough to question her. I sigh, and again, Monroe frowns. I think I'm dead inside. If I don't love my job and I can't love Vince, then I don't know who or what to love.

14 HOURS BEFORE TAKEOFF...

Monroe didn't say anything during our cab ride back to her mother's apartment. I think she doesn't want to have the conversation that we need to have because she thinks I might confess something neither of us is ready to deal with. When we got home, she retreated to the master bedroom to pack her mother's things, and I helped the maid pack up the kitchen. Everything in the apartment is being donated to charity.

At ten p.m., a king-sized harvest moon lords over us. An old bottle of sherry sits on the round metal table between Monroe and me.

Monroe takes a sip of wine from her glass and grimaces. "It's so sweet."

I take a sip. "It's so terrible."

Monroe holds up her glass. "But in honor of the fur goddess…"

I hold up my glass. "The silk goddess."

"The three-thousand-sixty-second worst mother on the planet."

"Sixty-three. Give her some credit."

Monroe turns the sides of her mouth down to ponder. "You're right. The three-thousand-sixty-third worst mother on the planet."

I shake my finger. "Wait. Universe. You have to at least expand it to the universe."

"Is there a difference?"

"Sure!"

"Then the universe."

On that note, we take a large guzzle of the sweet wine. We scrunch up our faces and cough to get the liquid down our throats.

"That's terrible," I say.

"I think it's spoiled." Monroe sets her glass on the table. "Anyway. How do you feel about seeing Vince tomorrow?"

I'm slightly taken aback by the sudden change of topic. "Okay, I guess."

She eyes me suspiciously. "You guess? Do you miss him?"

"Yeah—I mean no. He broke up with me so…"

She casually pulls the quilt over her bare legs. It's getting chilly. "That's because you fucked him over, Mags."

I grunt, insulted. "Monroe, really?" Who is *she* to judge me?

"What if Vince had fucked me while you two were on a break? Would you forgive him? Or me?"

"No and no."

"See? I know he started it, but you sure as hell finished it. But…" She gazes at the moon as she muses.

"But what?"

"But Vincent Adams is in love with you."

I snort. "He has a funny way of showing it."

Monroe chuckles. "I'm positive at some point tomorrow, he'll be showing you his long pink pole and you'll be the horn."

"So vulgar…"

She nudges my arm. "And you love it!"

Someone howls at the moon I'm thoughtfully gazing at. Nothing's changed about the moon. Not the patterns, the variations of light, or its shape. The sight isn't enough to make the heavy feeling inside me go away.

"I haven't cried over our breakup," I whisper. "Which is odd because I love—loved Vince."

"Then you do still love him?" she asks.

I shrug. I really don't feel ready to answer that question. My thoughts take a turn. I picture Vince and his model girlfriend, Cindy O'Lay, walking in a space with no background or foreground—possibly in a universe that doesn't exist. Cindy O'Lay is known for her cinnamon-colored hair, flawless tanned skin, and ice-blue eyes. I've successfully avoided seeing them in tabloid photos together. I don't think I'm jealous, because the thought of Vince being happy, with or without me, makes me happy.

I flex my eyebrows excitedly. "Why don't you just come with me?"

Monroe lets out a harsh laugh. "No fucking way. I can't believe you asked me that. Forgive me if I don't want to celebrate Charlie and his chick's engagement."

"I thought you were over him."

"I am. I tell you what, when Vince asks that malnourished model to marry him, why don't *you* go to *their* engagement party?"

"That's a false equivalency."

"I beg to differ, Magnolia."

I gasp emphatically. "Magnolia? You're really going there?"

"You've just pissed me off, so yes, you're Magnolia."

I chuckle. "Okay. I get your point. I can't believe Charlie invited Vince after I asked him not to. What an asshole."

Monroe tops off my glass of wine. "Just have another of this horrible-tasting shit and forget tomorrow's coming, because tonight is all about that thing up there, baby." She points at the moon. "Ain't she pretty?"

I lift my glass. "Very."

We toast to the here and now and guzzle our wine. I let the sweet, syrupy liquid deaden my thoughts and any latent feelings of love that I might have for Vincent Adams.

6 HOURS BEFORE TAKEOFF...

What's that buzzing noise?

I open one eye. A heavy brown duvet covers me. My cell phone and an empty wine bottle sit on the tiny round table between the empty lounge chair and me. My cell phone is doing the buzzing, and I turn it off. It's seven thirty in the morning. Monroe must've set my alarm before she headed out for an early run. In a lot of ways, she's the most disciplined person I know. After her run, she'll go to the gym to lift weights for an hour with her trainer, take a shower, then take a cab to Mesa in Chelsea to have brunch with our friend Hannah.

I stretch and yawn and get a whiff of fumes, greasy food, and rat piss. The invigorating scent makes me hungry. I call J Bistro, the café on the corner, and Clarissa, the hostess, says she can have a table for one available for me in twenty minutes. I thank her. Walking into a restaurant and grabbing a quick sit-down breakfast is never easy on the week-ends in this city. Monroe and I eat at J Bistro so often that we're like family, which is why they give us special treatment.

Now that that's settled, I dash inside, strip out of my pajamas, and hop into the shower. Anxiety won't leave me. I can't forget that I'm going to see Vince today. What will I do when we see each other? What will I say? I have this random thought of Vince sitting at the table, shirtless, while reading *Digital Dial* magazine and munching on toast that's slathered with butter and strawberry jam. I'm sitting across the table from him, reading a client's profile. I feel him watching me, so I look up. We lock eyes. Love inflates my heart until it feels as if it just might burst.

"What's new?" I ask him,

Vince commences to describe in detail a new app that will help media outlets track exponentially more viewers and therefore change the entire method of how ratings are calculated. He speaks with such enthusiasm and intelligence that all I want to do is jump his bones. There were so many moments like that that I now miss. He was always such a sexy nerd.

"Damn it," I mutter as I rub the loofah across my thigh. I just realized that I can't cry because I haven't accepted that Vince and I are truly broken up. I need a hefty dose of reality. Perhaps seeing him in love with Cindy O'Lay tonight will give me that.

I get out of the shower, dry off, and moisturize. I put on a little mascara and lip gloss, and I throw on a pair of skinny jeans and a blue cashmere sweater that matches my ankle boots. I pack my bag, lock the apartment, and hightail it to J Bistro. The line extends all the way to the end of the block, and I thank my lucky stars that I don't have to stand in it. I walk to the front of the line and wave at Clarissa. She waves me inside and escorts me to a small table near the window, which happens to be the quietest part of the café.

"It's always busy on Saturdays," I say as I take my seat.

Clarissa rolls her eyes. "It's crazy. Can't these people fucking stay home and cook some fucking eggs and toast and have some fucking orange juice?"

"You know I would if I didn't have a fucking flight to catch in..." I check my watch. "Two and a half hours."

Clarissa scowls at the line on the other side of the window. "Maggie, you can eat here twenty-four, seven as far as I'm concerned. It's the rest of those fucking people I'm talking about. Someone posts a fucking review on *Dining Dot,* and here the fuck they come. Fucking sheep."

"You're referring to the paying customers, I presume?"

"Yes. Those fucking people."

I laugh because she's not joking, that's how she really feels. Before the review, they were less popular. If Dale, the manager, and the rest of the crew here had a choice, they would turn away half of the customers.

"Eggs and bacon in a basket, topped with savory white cream sauce?" she asks.

"That's it," I say as I take off my jacket.

"Coming right up."

I watch her slog off with her shoulders slumped. I'm sort of surprised the customer service here hasn't deterred diners. I guess the food is too good. That's one thing they refuse to do—sacrifice taste in order to evade popularity.

After a moment, the thought hits me again. "Shit," I mutter. I'm going to see Vince today!

I feel like bailing on tonight's party. I could tell Charlie and Angelina that I caught a stomach virus. But do I want to miss their engagement celebration because my ex-boyfriend will be there? Plus, the bashes in Iberia are always extraordinary. I live for them. I could just avoid Vince. There should be enough people and space to do that.

I make a final decision as Paul, the waiter, sets my plate on the table, and my appetite returns with a vengeance. I thank Paul and dig in. With one bite, I take a moment to thank the food gods for this delicious meal. It's official. Their customer base will never decrease as long as they keep making food that tastes this tasty. I go in for the second delectable bite.

VINCE ADAMS

Vince studied his image in the bathroom mirror. He had failed to get enough sleep last night, which was why he felt as if a freight train had crushed his skull. Six months ago, he'd made a pact with himself to forget that Maggie Conroy ever existed. He hadn't made the decision out of spite. He toiled over it, envisioning his life without Maggie. Boy did he misconstrue how much he would miss everything about her.

Vince splashed water over his face as he thought about how successful Maggie and Monroe had made Mo&Ma PR. He'd had his doubts in the beginning. He'd pegged Monroe for being the same unstable bloodsucker that Robert was. But her reputation for image fixing was equal to, if not better than, Maggie's. Maggie and Monroe had become known as the dynamic duo. When Vince last saw Maggie, she was stressing out over the list of people requesting their services. The list was long, and they only represented ten clients per service list. Once word got out that there was an opening, people did whatever it took to fill that slot. So Maggie had left A&Rt Media Group and become more successful than she ever could imagine. Vince hoped she'd finally gotten what she'd been working so hard to obtain.

Vince had tried many times to forget the fact that Maggie had fucked Robert. He truly wanted to forgive her. He'd spent so many nights in the last six months wanting to spoon her naked body and listen to her sleep as his dick hardened and softened against her ass. At one point, he almost succeeded in forgiving her by telling himself that they had been on a break and he'd started the cheating by getting involved with Emily. Of course Maggie had already argued that point. Vince thought he could accept most of the blame.

Then Robert had walked into his office and asked for the financial status report. He'd studied Robert's face and couldn't escape the memory of seeing Robert munching on Maggie's clit. He hadn't caught them in the act of fucking, but he knew they had done it before he'd walked in on them. He could smell the scent of sex in the air.

That night, he'd bawled like a baby as Maggie slept. The marijuana she'd smoked put her in a deep sleep. In the morning, he left, feeling as though he couldn't break up with her because he loved her too much. He figured the way Robert kept chiseling at Maggie, he was bound to strike gold. Vince accepted that he had made Maggie vulnerable to Robert's relentless pursuit. However, Vince couldn't shake the belief that Maggie had wanted to fuck Robert from the start. If she hadn't taken the opportunity then, then she would've taken the opportunity later. Vince was sure of it.

Vince blinked a couple of times. He didn't want to think about Maggie and Robert at the moment. No, he had one goal in mind. He wanted to get Maggie to represent his client, and he would do whatever it took to get her to say yes. Vince wiped his face with a fresh towel. He was lodging in the guest room in the basement of Angelina's house in New Iberia, Louisiana.

He had arrived a day before the party to hang out with Charlie and their buddy Thatcher, and they'd spent most of the night at Belly's in New Orleans. Charlie played the trumpet with the band for most of the evening. Jacques Blanchard, Charlie's future father-in-law and a famous musician, had been giving Charlie some pointers, and he'd wanted to try them out on a live audience. Vince had to admit that Charlie played the trumpet like a pro. Vince had danced with a few pretty girls and drank bourbon with Thatcher until Angelina and Cindy arrived. He studied Cindy as she sashayed behind Angelina through the admiring crowd.

Vince had been dating the beautiful model for two months. He had been fucking Cindy, kissing her, and even sharing pretty good conversations from time to time, but he felt as if he were watching from an observation room as some part of himself carried on a relationship with her. He observed that she flipped her hair whenever she reached the end of whatever point she was making. The action seemed to be her way of swaying whoever she was talking to to see things her way. Cindy wasn't big on drinking either. She would sip on one glass of wine all night long.

At one point last night, she'd gotten into a discussion with Thatcher about running with the bulls in Pamplona. Thatcher had been partaking in the event every year since he was seventeen. Cindy had gone twice to watch from a balcony along the route but had never run through the galleys with the bulls. Thatcher invited her to run with him next year and promised to keep her safe.

For a second, Vince thought Cindy and Thatcher had shared a moment. Vince was surprised by the way he felt about it. He could've let her go. The idea of not having to initiate a breakup with Cindy gave him relief. But she had broken eye contact with Thatcher and smiled at Vince. The look on her face asked him to say something to confirm that they were in a full-blown relationship and she and Thatcher had crossed a line. Instead, Vince raised his hand and motioned the bartender over. He ordered another round of bourbon, and that was that.

Vince looked away from the mirror and at Cindy as she hugged him from behind.

"Hey, you," she said.

Vince kissed her cheek. "Hey, you."

Cindy pressed her forehead against his nose. He sniffed her skin, hoping that her scent would stimulate him as it had when they first met. But her scent did nothing for him. Maggie Conroy was coming to town, which made him feel both excitement and anxiety.

Cindy squeezed his cock and sighed with disappointment. "Too much bourbon last night?"

Vince snickered. Of course she would put the blame on him. She was a fashion model, for goodness' sake. Most men fantasized about fucking her. She surely thought he couldn't possibly be turned off by her.

"Well, he can't stand on command," Vince said.

Cindy chuckled. She stepped beside him and

jockeyed for space at the sink. "We had a late night." She grabbed her toothbrush. "Or should I say an early morning?" She raised her eyebrows flirtatiously.

"Depends on how you look at it," Vince said.

Cindy laid toothpaste on her toothbrush and started scrubbing her teeth. Only once or twice had Maggie brushed her teeth in front of him. Maggie liked her own bathroom space. She used to say that it was imperative if she was going to stay attracted to him. It was just another one of her odd quirks.

Maggie seemed to have a million quirks. She didn't want to hear him fart or burp. He had always been on guard with Maggie, trying to be whatever she needed him to be so she wouldn't dump him. Vince's sisters had told him that he had changed since dating Maggie, that he had become more anxious and less carefree. Perhaps Maggie did change him for the worse, but he couldn't ignore the fact that he couldn't wait to see her in the flesh.

Cindy rinsed the toothpaste out of her mouth, and Vince guided her in front of him. He needed to convince himself that Maggie didn't possess a place in his heart.

He stared into Cindy's ice-blue eyes. He'd found

them more mesmerizing when they started dating two months ago. "Hey."

Cindy beamed, digging his affectionate tone. "Hey back at you."

They kissed until his instrument rose to the occasion and his mind followed. Vince could finally give Cindy what she earlier sought.

*A*ngelina is waiting for me near the carousel in baggage claim. I never check luggage for domestic flights, but this area is our usual meeting point. As soon as I step off the escalator, I see her standing in front of a bench, talking on her cell phone. She's wearing skintight jeans and a blouse that resembles a handkerchief. Angelina has a superior physique and she's always showing it off. The intimate way she cradles the phone against her ear tells me she's talking to Charlie. As if she can feel my energy, she turns to look at me. I read her lips as she says, "She's here," and, "See you later, babe."

Finally I get Angelina's full attention. Her smile is as bright as fluorescent light and as affecting as the glare from an angel's halo. I'm forced to pretend that

I'm just as happy as she is. I'm not unhappy, but I'm not as happy as she is either.

She wraps her arms around me. "Guess what?"

I hug her tightly, resting against her soft but hard dancer's body. All my anxiety melts away. This trip is all about Angelina and Charlie deciding to tie the knot, and I don't want to make it about the impending doom of seeing Vince for the first time since our breakup.

"What?" I say, matching her level of excitement.

Angelina takes my shoulders and looks me dead in the eyes. Her expression turns serious.

Now I'm worried. "What is it?"

"Okay, this is supposed to be a surprise so Charlie told me not to say anything to you about it, but my instincts tell me I shouldn't let you walk in on what you might consider a pile of dung."

I'm worried. The first thing that comes to mind is Vince and Cindy have eloped. "What's the pile of shit, Angel?"

"Your mother's here."

It never takes much coaxing to convince Angel to spill the beans. She's the worst when it comes to keeping secrets. However, I'm relieved but confused. I feel as if I'm having an out-of-body experience.

Angelina looks me straight in the eyes as if she's

trying to steady me. "Maggie, take a few deep breaths, because I don't think you're breathing."

"Leah?" I strain to say. Hell, I'm not breathing. I take one deep breath then another.

"Yes," she replies.

"Conroy?"

Angelina nods. "Yes, your mother."

I search for the nearest empty bench and find it about five feet away. I rush to sit before my legs give out. I can't remember the last time I saw or spoke to my mother. We have an unspoken understanding that she lives on one side of the universe and I live on the other.

Angelina sits beside me. "Is it really that bad?" She frowns nervously.

I grab my knees and take deep, steadying breaths. "I don't know. It's just the sky fell six months ago, and now all of a sudden, I feel the weight of it."

Angelina's eyebrows furrow. "Oh... you're referring to your breakup with Vince?"

I set my tired gaze on her. "Has he arrived?"

She nods.

"But he didn't come alone, did he?"

The answer is written all over her face. My heart takes a nosedive, but I recover before it hits rock bottom.

"Cindy O'Lay," she says. "She's nice, but I don't know if Vince is all that into her."

I blink, taken aback. "Why do you say that?"

"He respects her. Vince is always the gentleman, right?"

"Right." He's such a gentlemen, which is one of many reasons why I fell for him.

"But they have no real chemistry. They're like a plastic couple."

"Hey, Angel!" someone calls.

Angelina and I look toward the sliding glass doors. It's a man from airport security.

"You ain't supposed to park out here like it's the lot," he whines.

She pats my thigh, signaling me to get up. "All right, Duncan. Damn."

I grab my bag, and we walk out.

Duncan grins at Angelina as we walk past. "I'm a see you tonight?"

Angelina narrows an eye. "Were you invited?"

Duncan throws up his arms. "Ah, come on, Angel!"

Her chuckle is airy. "Of course you were invited. Just don't come and hit on all the beautiful women, like Maggie here." She thumbs in my direction.

Duncan glances at me as if he's just noticing me.

"I want to hit on you." He's practically salivating at Angelina's physique.

Angelina swings open the back door of her black Jeep. "Later, Duncan." Her tone is dismissive.

He tosses his head back and laughs. "I know Chuck L got you locked up. But if he fucks it up, I'm coming to get you."

Angelina points her head toward the backseat. "Put your bag in, Mags." She says to him, "There's nothing Charlie would do to fuck us up, so stop hitting on me or I'll have him fuck you up."

Duncan chuckles nervously. "Nah, I'm just playing, baby. Let Chuck L know I'm playing first set with Jacques."

I toss my bag in the backseat, and Angelina closes the door.

"I'm not sure Jacques will make it tonight," she says as we both get in.

Duncan balks. "What the hell are you telling me?"

Angelina rolls down my window. "Are you coming to lick my dad's ass or celebrate our engagement?"

His smile expands. "Both, baby."

Angelina rolls her eyes, and my window rolls up. I buckle up, and Angelina drives away from the curb.

"Damn musicians. They're like hardcore drug

addicts except they're addicted to picking, plugging or beating some instrument other than their dicks." She glances at me. "Shoot, Maggie. I hadn't taken into account how heavy all of this must be for you."

I wonder why she said that. Do I still look stressed? "No, I'm okay," I say in the most agreeable tone I can find.

She turns down the volume of some jazzy number I've never heard. "But really, Maggie, how have you been since the breakup?"

I'm still baffled by how Angelina can look a person in the eyes while driving and keep the car steady. I keep my eyes forward in hopes that she'll get the hint. "It's been okay."

"Have you dated anyone else?"

"Who has time for that?" I snort facetiously. "Other than Vince."

"Ah! So you do care?"

"Care about what?"

"Vince."

"Of course I care about Vince. But he broke up with *me*, remember?"

"What about his friend, the one you—you know? Has he called you?" she asks.

"You mean Robert Tango?"

"Is that his name?"

"If you're referring to the friend I had—you know, then yes, that is his name."

"Well, have you gotten involved with him?"

I shift uncomfortably. "No. Why do you ask?"

"I was just curious. I thought you and Vince were in it for the long run."

"I did too."

"Then why did you do it?"

I feel as if she just lowered the boom. I take off my leather jacket when my skin runs hot. "I don't know," I mutter.

"Bullshit. Dig deep. Why did you do it?"

Thank God we're stopped at a light because she's looking me dead in the eyes. The light turns green, and she's still looking at me.

I point ahead. "You should go."

Cars honk behind us.

"Okay!" Angelina shouts and creeps across the intersection.

My heart is pounding from my fear of her driving. "You should pay a little more attention to the road."

She waves dismissively. "Okay, so I'll help you."

"You'll help me make you drive better?" I grin, hoping my joke will make her change this silly line of questioning.

"I drive fine."

I snort. "You don't drive fine."

She wiggles her finger. "I know what you're doing, and it's not working." She gets comfortable in her seat. "Okay, how did you feel when you were doing it?"

"Doing what?"

"Having sex with Vince's business partner."

I snarl. Hell, did she have to put it that way? "He wasn't just Vince's business partner."

"No, they were best friends too."

I detect a cynical, judgmental air in her tone. All I can do is glare at her pretty face. I feel as if she's blaming me for the breakup. Perhaps I did commit the worst offense. Emily didn't mean much to Vince, but Robert is like a brother to him, albeit a very toxic brother.

"Come on, Maggie. These are the facts, and you're going to have to swallow them."

"I know the facts," I snap.

"Then answer the question."

I take a steadying breath. "I don't know how I felt. I can't remember."

"Did you feel love?"

"Hell no, I could never love Robert Tango!"

"Then you felt lust?"

I shrink in my seat. My answer came too quickly, and I'm ashamed of it. I shrug.

Angelina's mouth falls open. "Did you just shrug?"

"Yes. Why?"

"Because that means you were definitely sexually attracted to him."

"Probably. Yes."

There she goes again, looking at me instead of the highway. "Good! We're getting somewhere."

I point forward with one hand and grab the door handle with the other. "Can you please look at the road? Could you do that for me? Please?"

Angelina rolls her eyes as if I'm overreacting, but I'm relieved when she does as I ask. "I can see through my peripheral vision, Maggie. I'm not going to kill us." She shakes her head. "But anyway, getting back to the subject at hand. You being attracted to that guy—what's his name again?"

"Robert Tango."

"You being attracted to Robert Tango is normal. He's prime rib. I saw him at A&Rt's Spring Gala last year. The problem is that your emergency reset system didn't kick in."

"My emergency reset system?"

"It's the part of your brain that tells you he's hot

but he's not Vince. His touch, his kiss, the emotional connection won't be as gratifying as it is with Vince, so why even go there?"

Now I'm angry. "No way. There's no way I'm going to let you put this on me. Vince was fucking Emily way before I fucked Robert. Did you ask *him* why the hell *he* did that?" She moves her lips to speak, but I raise a finger to stop her. "And we were still together when he fucked her, because he hadn't told me he was done with me. I found out in a meeting where I made a complete ass out of myself because of him. So this is not my fault, and don't make it my fault. I would've never gone there if Vince hadn't started all that shit in the first place. It's like that book *The Scarlet Letter*. She wore the fucking A, but where the fuck was his fucking A?"

"You can't draw any correlations from that screwed-up story and cheating-gate."

My eyes expand. "Cheating-gate?"

"That's what Charlie and I call the situation."

"The situation?"

She shakes her head dismissively. "Anyway, Hester wouldn't out the hypocritical bastard who fucked her. So—"

"Who's Hester?"

"The main character in *The Scarlet Letter*."

I'm lost, which is normal when having these sorts of conversations with Angelina. "Well, I didn't read the book, but I heard about it."

"It's not your cup of tea." Angelina pats my thigh. "The thing is, I care more about you than I do Vince. He's a good guy, but you're the one I love. I just want you to figure out your life because you're great, Mags. You deserve to feel love and be loved."

I rub her hand. "Thank you. I love you too."

Angelina informs me that she has to make a number of stops along the way to her house. She tells me how excited she is about marrying Charlie. She says she's marrying him because she hates to go an hour without speaking to him, kissing him, or smelling him. As Angelina pulls off the main highway and drives down an isolated road flanked by grassy fields, I push back the thought that I've been feeling that way about Vince lately, which is very dumb of me. He's moved on, and I haven't.

Angelina turns off the main road into the muddy driveway of a dilapidated house. We hop out of her car, and a man with flawless blue-black skin, wearing blue jean coveralls with a plaid shirt, walks out of the screen door. He's carrying a large aluminum pan covered with foil. Angelina calls him Mr. Tompkins, and she interacts with him as though he's a long-time friend. The fact that Mr. Tompkins smells like smoked meat clues me in to what's in the pan. Angelina patiently listens as he explains how prime the beef is since he went to the stockyard to choose the cows. We end up loading ten pans of barbecue into the back of the jeep.

Forty-five minutes later, we're back on the road. The next house we visit is on the edge of a murky swamp complete with weeping willows, cypress knees, and fibrous moss. I'm alarmed at first. The place looks like a cliché voodoo witch's house. Angelina knocks, and I put on my brave face. The sweetest-looking white-haired woman answers the door, and my senses are stimulated by a heavenly scent of caramel, brown sugar, and pecans. Her name is Ms. Fanny, and Angelina buys seven pans of freshly made pralines from her.

We hit the road again, and it soon becomes clear that we're going to stop every ten miles or so. I have a good time munching as we go though. Angelina stops for crawfish, fresh mint, and boxes of steamed and seasoned Gulf shrimp.

It's twilight by the time we make it to Iberia. Charlie and Angelina have done substantial work on the property. They've added two guesthouses because they're known to have fifteen to twenty guests staying on the estate at one time. There used to be a murky lake with strange microbes growing inside it, but they've made it swimmable—at least for me. They've expanded the basement and built a bridge to their neighbor Karina's house because guests often shuttle between both estates.

I'm rubbing my belly after downing my fourth praline. I swear I could eat those until I throw up or pass out from sugar shock. Angelina is telling me about how she's taking a break from dancing for a while. She and Charlie are trying to get pregnant.

"Oh," is all I have to say. I've never thought about Charlie being some kid's father, but I've also never pictured him as someone's husband.

Angelina smiles as she drives under the carport and around to the back of the house. They've poured more concrete out back. As soon as the Jeep comes to a stop, Charlie opens the sliding glass door to the kitchen.

She shuts off the engine, we get out, and I reacquaint myself with the feathery trees and the sound of crickets. I let the environment encapsulate me. It's always so perfect and still on this estate.

Charlie skips down the porch steps. "Magnolia!"

I smile. "Chuck!"

His hair has grown, and he's sporting a full beard

like Jesus. The tiny bit of weight he's gained looks really good on him. We hug and kiss each other on the cheek.

"Why the hell did you invite Leah?" I ask.

"Where's your suitcase?" he asks.

"In the backseat."

He opens the door and retrieves my bag. "Leah called to check up on you, and I mentioned our engagement party. It's no big deal, Mags. She's your fucking mother, for goodness' sake."

"I know who she is," I snarl.

"Good, then it shouldn't be a problem."

Charlie and I glare at each other.

"You two stop that," Angelina says.

Charlie looks away first, rolling his eyes.

Angelina takes a box of shrimp out of the back of the Jeep. "Maggie, everything will be okay. Your mother's a sweet woman."

Charlie rushes over to take the shrimp from Angelina. "Baby, leave everything in the back. I'll take it all out after I get Mags settled into her house."

I point at myself. "My house?"

"Yeah," Charlie says, sounding proud of himself. "I made it just for you."

I elbow him. "Are you trying to keep me out the main house?"

"Fuck no. I have a room inside for you, but…" He lifts his full hands cautiously. "I didn't think you'd want to stay in the big house this time around."

I snatch my bag out of his hand. "You're right. I don't. Help Angel get the food out the car. I'll find my way."

Charlie jerks the bag out of my hand. "But I can't gloat the way I dreamed it if I don't give you the personal tour."

I snatch the bag back. "No need to gloat. I concede to the fact that you're not a shiftless bastard anymore." He reaches for the bag, but I pull it away. "And I hope you understand how much I mean that. I'm proud of you, Chuck."

We grace each other with appreciative smiles. I truly used to believe Charlie would never find his way off his path of self-destruction. I always thought he felt entitled to be bitter since his father was a jackass and his mother was perpetually depressed. There was something extra strange about Uncle Charles and Aunt Carlotta. They were like stuffed people who never allowed themselves to be guided by their heart or soul.

"That's a beautiful moment," Angelina says, beaming at us.

Charlie and I come to our senses. I nudge his

shoulder, and he falls back as if that little shove knocked him off balance.

I look at him askew. "Don't tell Leah I'm here."

"Don't worry, she's otherwise occupied," he says.

My frown intensifies. Do I really want to know what he meant by that? Instead I inquire about Jack and Daisy. Charlie tells me that they're arriving late from San Francisco, where they've been for a while. Jack has business there, and they've been inseparable since learning that Daisy is pregnant. I can't wait to see their faces. I wish they would spend more time in L.A. I need them nearer as I go through whatever the hell I'm going through at the moment.

Angelina takes the boxes of fresh mint out of the back of the Jeep. "Charlie, I can't wait for you. I need to get this stuff out now."

I lift a hand. "Charlie, really, help her. I can find my way to the cottage."

Charlie stutter-steps as if he's torn between escorting me and helping Angelina. "Are you sure, Mags?"

"Positive," I say.

"Okay…" He hikes the box of shrimp onto his shoulder. "It's the cottage with the red door."

I salute him and walk off.

I KNOW MY WAY AROUND THE PROPERTY WELL ENOUGH to find the guesthouse. Angelina told me that the two bungalows were once part of a community of slave quarters. The rest burned down in the 1970s after Benny Michaels threw a lit cigarette butt on the dry hedges. Angelina and her neighbors refer to the incident as the Destruction of Bad Luck Benny. They do so with laughs and headshakes and relaying other stories of how folly followed their friend Benjamin Michaels.

Madame Beauchamp, Angelina's mother, refused to renovate the two remaining slave quarters. A psychic had told her that the souls of her ancestors were happy that she owned the land and they still lived in the quarters, finally free from servitude. So Madame Beauchamp gave those spirits access to her land and home.

"You don't believe that, do you?" I asked Angelina the night she told us the story.

We were picnicking around the murky lake before it was overhauled. Daisy and Jack had just returned from France with news to share, so we'd gathered at the estate to hear it. Daisy announced she was pregnant, and she was over the moon about it.

Angelina had gazed off dreamily. "I guess so. It's a beautiful fantasy, and I would wish it were true."

I wished I hadn't understood what she'd meant. As fickle as her answer was, it felt true to life.

I look up at the sky. The early part of the evening has already fallen. I don't spend much time in places with natural surroundings, so I stop to admire the abundance of trees on the property.

"No, no!" a woman cries then giggles. There's a loud splash, then the sound of limbs beating the water.

"Go faster," Vince says and laughs. "You're too slow!"

The woman giggles even louder.

The strangest emotions surge through me. I look across the courtyard and see the cottage with the red door. The woman I hear must be Cindy O'Lay. I clutch my stomach because her giggling is making me nauseated. Suddenly they stop making noise. *Oh shit.* I pick up my pace. I do believe that Vince has made his move, and I can't keep myself from picturing them. Their kissing is deep and passionate, as our kissing used to be. Her legs are wrapped around his waist. He caresses the nape of her neck with one hand and massages her waist with the other. He can't wait to lay her flat on the grass, kiss her lips some more, spread her legs, and thrust his erection deep inside her.

I run up the steps to the cottage. The door is unlocked, so I rush inside and slam the door closed. My back is plastered against the wood. I squeeze my eyes shut to try to erase the image I conjured of Vince and Cindy O'Lay. I take a deep breath, and the smell of new everything fills my head. I open one eye. The room is dusky, but I can see how nicely decorated the cottage is. I turn on the light.

That did it. I force myself to not give further thought to Vince and his new girlfriend. The living room is cozy and has an L-shaped cream leather sofa, an iron coffee table, and a furry ottoman. The area rug's pattern has multiple shapes and colors. If Charlie had me in mind when furnishing this little place, then he knows me better than I thought. I turn toward the kitchen. It's ultra-modern. The refrigerator has frosted- glass doors, the oven is red fiberglass, and the counters are speckled-white quartz.

I'm about to drop my bag by the door before I remember that I need it. I have to get dressed for the party. Running around with Angelina all day has made us late. The flight from New York to New

Orleans made my skin sticky. I hightail it into the bedroom and turn on the light. This room is just as nice as the living room. I stomp out of my jeans and pull off my shirt.

I catch sight of floor-to-ceiling windows in my peripheral vision. "Shit," I mutter.

The curtains are open, and I have a wide-open view of the lake. Purple underwater lights illuminate the water. Just as I blink, the lights turn red then yellow. Apparently Vince and his new girlfriend have taken their fun inside. Part of me wishes I had caught them having sex. Then I'd really be convinced that we're over.

I keep the curtains open. Everyone should be heading over to Karina's by now, so no one should be hanging out by the lake, and the view reminds me that I'm away from my stressful job. I don't know if I like what I do anymore. I'm tolerant and open-minded, but the majority of our clients are just pure assholes. Sometimes I think that I may have been too hasty when I left A&Rt Media. I used to love that job. Perhaps I left because I was hurt and embarrassed. It's too late to go back now.

I faintly hear the music coming from Karina's. It's not a band. The band won't start up until the shindig officially begins. I'm excited about the dancing, the bourbon, the good food, and the exquisite music. And shit! Charlie did it! He managed to get Angelina to say yes. I smile, and just as I'm about to head to the bathroom to take a shower, I catch sight of a person standing by the edge of the lake. I want to run and hide, but I recognize his figure. Vince is shirtless and wearing swimming shorts.

I blink to make sure my eyes aren't deceiving me. But it's him all right. I'm like a deer trapped in head-lights. My skin runs hot. He's just standing there, staring at me. Then he picks something up off the grass and casually walks away. I'm stunned, wondering what in the world just happened. Was that really our first sighting of each other? I thought it would be more remarkable. Nervous energy shoots through my body. I forget what I was doing before I saw him.

"Take a shower," I whisper and rush into the bathroom.

The shower is gigantic with no doors, just an entrance at the back. Once I'm naked, I turn on the water and let it spray my face. Ceremoniously, I wash Vince out of my memory. The times we spent jogging down trails in Martha's Vineyard—gone.

The time we used to…

When we used to…

I open my eyes and take my face out of the water. Shit, Vince and I never made any special memories outside of work and sex. This revelation makes me feel as if I've just awakened from a long winter's nap. Charlie and Angelina have traveled around the world together, experiencing historical landmarks and eating delicious food. They've flown to Rome, Paris, Berlin, and Dublin for concerts. Whenever the feeling hits, they head to New Orleans in Charlie's vintage convertible Mustang and find their friends and paint the town colors that don't even exist. I can say the same for Daisy and Jack. They've made lasting memories together. But Vince and I have zilch.

My heart hurts as if a strong hand is squeezing the blood from it. The pain hinders my breathing, and I gasp for air. I want to wail. The sound wants to rise from the pit of my belly and crash against the atmosphere, but when I open my mouth, nothing comes out. I slap my palms against the wet wall. My legs grow weak, and I struggle to keep them from buckling.

Admit it, a voice says from deep inside me.

I fight the truth as much as I can, but it over-whelms me.

Admit it!

"No," I manage to say.

I can breathe again. I pull my hands off the wall. Strength returns to my legs. I finish my shower, dry off, and moisturize, putting that little breakdown behind me.

"Magnolia?" my mom calls.

I stop slathering cream on my right arm. "Mom?" I want to make sure my mind isn't playing a bad trick on me.

"Yes! Where are you, lovely?"

"Shit," I mouth. I'm not ready to come face-to-face with her. "I'm getting dressed! And I'm running late! I'll talk to you later!" I cross my fingers, hoping that's enough to make her go away.

"I'm not leaving!" she calls.

I grumble a bunch of bad words as I open the wardrobe and yank a robe off the hanger. I put it on and stomp toward the living room. Leah has made herself comfortable on the sofa. A cloud of cigarette smoke engulfs her face.

I flop down on the sofa beside her. "Mom, you're still smoking?" I over-exaggerate coughing.

She kisses my forehead. "What do you care? I could die for all you're concerned."

"That's not true." My throat itches. "Could you put that out please?"

"No, I cannot." She takes another puff.

I roll my eyes. She's still impossible. "What do you want, Mom?"

She pinches my lips. "You always had a lot of sass."

I grunt and turn my face to free my lips. "What do you want, Mom?"

Leah chuckles. "I stopped by because I want to get it over with."

"Get what over with?"

She slides her thumb across one of my eyebrows. "Stop frowning."

I take the wrinkles out of my eyebrows. "Get what over with?"

"This inevitable meeting. When was the last time we saw each other? Seven, eight years ago?"

"Six."

"Oh… forgive my tone. That one year makes a big difference."

I roll my eyes. "Well, don't put the blame all on me, Leah." Blame Maggie seems to be the running theme in my life.

My mom shakes her finger. "Nope. You don't get to call me Leah to my face."

I leap to my feet. "You know what? I don't have time for this, Mom. Can you please leave?"

"Sit down," she says sternly then looks around the room anxiously. "I need an ashtray… does anyone smoke anymore?"

I cross my arms. "It's a dying habit."

She smashes the cigarette out on the bottom of her strappy shoe and puts the unused portion of the cigarette in a small metal case. "I said sit." She pats the empty space beside her.

I decide to stop regressing back to some stupid rebellious teenager and take the seat.

"How have you been?" she asks.

I put my feet up on the coffee table. "Good."

She pets the side of my face. "You look good."

"You look good too," I say.

She really does. My mom's skin isn't as fair as mine. She has a golden tint, but her cheeks have always been perpetually rosy. No matter what, her pale-blue eyes sparkle. Tiny lines are etched on her face, but they just make her look sexier. I can honestly say that I want to look just like my mom when I'm fifty-eight.

A face comes to my mind. "So where's Cobey Miller?"

Her smile turns upside down. "Cobey Miller?"

"Isn't that his name?"

"You're being cheeky."

"Perhaps."

She gives me a look of warning. "You're not too big, young lady. And where do you expect him to be?"

The way I shrug might clue her in that I'm about to spout some smart-ass remark. "Perhaps in the gym—lifting weights—admiring himself in the mirror. Perhaps married to some asinine chick his own age, which would be my age actually."

"He's alive," my mom says.

"Then you're still married?"

Leah takes her cigarette case off the table. "I have something to tell you." She takes out another cigarette. "I'm going to need one these though."

"Mom, you know those things will kill you, right?"

She studies me then turns her body toward me. "Does my smoking truly worry you?"

"Truly it does."

Leah grunts thoughtfully. After a moment, she puts the cigarette back in the case and hands it to me. "Take it."

I hesitate. "Is this a trick?"

"Take it. You win." I take the other end of the metal box, but she doesn't let go. "But only if we change the nature of our association."

I look at her cockeyed and let go of the case. "I don't follow."

"We should see more of each other."

"Why? Are you dying?"

She rolls her eyes. "No…"

"Mom, you know we work better when we're apart. Together…" I shake my head. "You'll tell me all the shit that's wrong with me."

"Stuff," she says.

"See, you're already doing it. I say shit because shit makes a greater impact than stuff."

"But I'm your mother, and you're in my presence."

"Mom, I curse like a fucking sailor."

Leah puts the cigarette case on the table, sits up straight, and massages her temples. She does that when I stress her out. "Well, perhaps you shouldn't."

"They're just words."

She furrows her eyebrows, studying my expression. After a moment, she brushes my eyebrows with the backs of her fingers. "Words are an expression of the soul, lovely. How about this? You choose every word you speak wisely, and I'll give up cigarettes."

"Elaborate on 'wisely' because I think a solid curse word gets the job done better than those sugary ones."

"Cursing is for the feeble, and I raised you to be resilient. I'm not a fucking Puritan, as you know."

I snort sarcastically. "I know."

"But don't make profanity your go-to language. Being able to express myself strongly without cursing has been one of the many great lessons I've learned."

She gives me a moment to ponder that. With all the great life lessons I've taken from my mother, I would think we would be closer. Perhaps we're too much alike. She loved her work until she met and married Cobey Miller. I figured she was having a psychotic break or something. He was such a meathead. When she married him, I lost faith in her level-headedness.

Leah waits for my answer. I can smell her cigarettes in her hair and on her breath.

"Okay," I say. "But what were you going to say that you needed a cigarette to tell me?"

"Oh." She stands. "Cobey and I were never married."

My mouth falls open. "Get the fuck out of here!" Shit, I wasn't supposed to say that. "I take the f-word back. I meant, get out!"

Leah shrugs, smiling. "We weren't."

I stand. "Then why did you say you were married to him?"

She takes me by the shoulders. "Because I got caught up in the moment." I must look confused because she continues. "Just know that the same could happen to you. I've heard how hard you work. My career was so important to me for so many years. Nurturing a career is important, but it's not the only part of us."

"Elaborate, please," I say.

"Well, when I got a little taste of something that felt like love, it felt so freeing. I wish I loved Cobey! But at least he taught me that true love was more important than all the things I was putting first in my life."

"Like your career?"

"Like my career." She tucks a stray lock of hair behind my ear. "Don't keep depriving yourself. I'm extremely proud of your accomplishments, but there's more to life than a career."

"I know that, Mom."

"Then why is a woman as beautiful as you not madly in love with the man of her dreams?"

There's no need to tell her about Vince. "It's not too late. I'm open to it."

"Are you?" She stares into my eyes as if she's

searching for truth. Perhaps she senses that I'm keeping something from her.

I think about Vince, but the thought of him is quickly wiped away by the memory of hearing him frolic through the lake with Cindy O'Lay and watching him watch me with that detached expression.

She pinches my cheeks and sighs. "You've always been too smart for your beauty."

I frown. "And what does that mean?"

"You figure it out."

"All right, enough of the talk about my eventual clash with spinsterhood. What's going on with you for real, Mom?"

"What do you mean?"

"You're all happy and glowing. You're giving me speeches on being in love instead of reaching the top. Are you in love?"

She takes her hands off my shoulders and walks to the door. "You'll find out soon."

I follow her. "Find out what?"

She pets my cheek. "It's good seeing you. I look forward to seeing more of you. I love you."

The way her eyes caress my face... it's been way too long since she's graced me with that look. It catches me off guard. "I love you too," I say, forgetting all about wanting answers.

She opens the door. "Don't take too long."

I watch as she closes the door behind her. What is she hiding? As I get dressed for the party, I wonder what man she's wrestled up now. Maybe he's twenty years older than her. That wouldn't be so bad. Maybe he's even younger than Cobey. Now that would be bad. Maybe he's one of my old boyfriends. Or maybe he's the fascist leader of a small country. Who knows! Whoever he is, I'm sure I won't approve.

12

THE NATURE OF OUR ASSOCIATION

VINCE

*V*ince's heart beat so fast he thought that seeing Maggie might have given him a heart attack. As soon as he made it back to his room, all he could do was stretch out on the bed and stare at the ceiling. He had left his wristwatch in the grass, so he'd gone out to retrieve it. He hadn't been prepared to see Maggie in her underwear.

Vince crossed his arms over his face. "Fuck."

"Fuck what?" Cindy asked as she walked into the room from the hallway. She stretched out beside him and fondled his dick. "Fuck me."

Vince removed his arms. "No, I mean, no."

Cindy massaged his dick, but he couldn't get it up. Even though Maggie was on his mind, he was quite aware that it was Cindy touching him. Fuck, he missed Maggie's smell and touch. If Cindy had stretched out beside him before he'd gone out, then she would've found what she was looking for. His dick still had no trouble getting up when he fantasized about Maggie Conroy. If only Maggie hadn't been intimate with Robert.

In the past, Robert had fucked just about all of Vince's girlfriends, but he never thought Maggie would submit to Robert's bullshit. Maggie was different. He'd known it from the first day he laid eyes on her back in high school, but even then she was a mystery to him. That hadn't changed when she'd walked into his office twelve years later. Maggie had the same sexy ass, luscious mouth, and intense eyes.

Vince believed that if he hadn't pursued Maggie the way he had, then she would've ended up with Robert Tango. At one point, he'd thought maybe he had altered the plans of fate. Maybe Maggie and Robert were meant to be. They were both pretty uncommitted to the idea of true love, although Robert's issues went deeper than love. As the founders of A&Rt Media Group, Robert and Vince were now multi-billionaires, and Robert still didn't know what the hell he wanted to do with his life. At least Maggie loved her profession. She would fuck her career day and night if she could. Nothing, not even her idol, Jack Lord, could get between Maggie and that fucking career of hers. That was another reason Vince had decided to call it quits. He just couldn't handle Maggie the way she was, not any longer. She used to call his ex-girlfriends debutantes. Well, maybe he wanted a debutante. They were less complicated.

Cindy rolled off the bed. "Oh well. We'll try again later." She winked as she sashayed to the bathroom.

Vince knew she could feel him looking at her backside. The way she shook her tight ass had always made him horny. Now all he could picture was Maggie's soft round ass against his erection. Vince looked down. That thought got him up. Instead of calling Cindy back to bed, he covered his cock with the blanket, wiped Maggie out of his mind, and waited until it deflated.

Cindy returned to the room twenty-minutes later wearing a tiny white dress. She always wore her clothes effortlessly. She had put her hair into a sexy bun so she could show off her graceful neck, and he could smell her sweet perfume from where he lay.

"Vince, what are you doing?" she asked.

He sat up. "Huh?"

"Get dressed, or we're going to be late."

That was one thing he liked about Cindy. Like Maggie, she was punctual. Cindy had risen to the status of supermodel for a reason. Also like Maggie, she put a lot of effort into her work, but unlike Maggie, Cindy knew how to balance her love life and career.

"Up and at 'em," Vince said and hopped out of bed and scurried off to dress himself for the evening.

Vince admitted to himself that he had Maggie in mind when he packed for the night's event. He put on a pair of heather-gray slacks and Maggie's favorite white shirt with his black leather sneakers.

"Wow," Cindy said when he returned to the bedroom. "You look like my man should." She wrapped her arms around him, and he rewarded her with a sweet kiss.

Vince took her hand. "Ready?"

Cindy squeezed his cock. "I guess so."

Vince chuckled. "Later. Give him some time."

Cindy winked, and they walked out of the bedroom holding hands. Vince couldn't shake the nervous feeling that at any moment, they would turn down a hallway and Maggie would be right there. But the house was empty. Everyone had already gone to the party.

They didn't run into a single person until they reached the bridge that led to Karina's house across a muddy field of wild grass and trees. Vince and Cindy quickly became part of the crowd. The music was set at the perfect volume. A variety of colors crisscrossed along the path, and Vince thought it was a nice light effect. Some of Angelina's friends danced in front of them. He could always distinguish Angelina's friends from Charlie's. Her friends were in tip-top shape and had a healthy glow. Charlie's buddies looked more like ragamuffins, frat boys, and beach bums. Cindy's eyes danced. It was her first party in Iberia. They followed the trail of lights through the backyard and down a narrow path along the side of the house, which led to the main party area.

Guests were already dancing in front of the cement stage. Canopies were set up along the outskirts of the dance floor and stage. Some of the canopies had tall tables and stools under them, and others had round tables and chairs under them. A full-service bar was also under a canopy. The caterers were set up next to the bar, but waiters and waitresses darted here and there, serving the guests. Angelina always enlisted a group of dancers to keep the dance floor lively.

Cindy tugged Vince toward the moving bodies. "Let's dance!"

Vince was on his way before he could object. He wanted to hang around the edges for a while, spot Maggie, then avoid her until he figured out how to ask her to represent his client, Kelly Simon. A&Rt Media had put a lot of money into shooting a full season of *Lightweight*, a new dramatic series on Prime D TV. Kelly played a sweet, lovable "all-American" girl who appealed to a certain demographic. The series had scored high in preliminary audience tests. A&Rt was on its way to being a real contender in the media world, which was a huge accomplishment for a company that wasn't owned by a major media conglomerate. He had to admit that Maggie had had a lot to do with *Lightweight's* preliminary success. She had been working on the package before she quit, and after she left, her former team constantly asked, "What would Maggie do," before making decisions.

Then Kelly's skeletons had started to fall out of

the closet. She used to be a stripper and went way further than lap dances, which was how she'd won her first role in TV. She was also engaged to a married man. Vince didn't know that was even possible! The man was her agent, Brad Bowers. The mere dots that connected her line of shit were enough to decrease her value. Vince knew that their competition was behind the leak. Major media conglomerates wanted to sink A&Rt. He needed Mo&Ma to keep them afloat.

"Have I told you how good of a dancer you are?" Cindy said.

"You have!" Vince said over the music.

She tossed her head back to laugh, and that's when he caught sight of Maggie.

MAGGIE

I search through the crowd for Charlie and Angelina. I'm supposed to say some words of endearment, and I want to know at what point of the night they want me to deliver them. I don't have anything written. I'm going to wing it. That means I probably shouldn't drink more than one glass of bourbon or Charlie's special brew before taking the stage.

I search through people flinging their arms, spinning, and kicking. There's no sight of Charlie or Angel. Then someone links an arm around mine, and I flinch.

"You made it!" Angelina says and kisses my cheek. She's beaming. Her dress is white and airy, and she's wearing a white rose in her hair.

I kiss her back. "So what time do I give the speech?"

One of Angelina's dancer friends does a jig in front of us, and Angelina kicks a leg above her head in response. "There's no set time." She laughs. She's already a little tipsy.

"Got it," I say. What I get is that they could ask me to give the speech in five minutes or five hours. So I shouldn't worry about being inebriated. No one cares. No one judges. "Have you seen my mom?"

"I have!" Angelina leads, shaking her hips and swirling her arms as we go.

We make it to a table beneath a canopy, and I can hardly believe what and who I see. "Dad?" I half choke on that word.

My mother and father have gotten cozy at a table. They're sitting with Jack and Daisy, who I'm happy to see but can't quite express it because of the shock of seeing my parents together.

"What the hell?" I say.

I can hardly believe what I'm seeing. I wonder if this is really happening. Leah and Isak, my dad, put me through hell when they divorced. Each and every day, they made me feel the fire of the deep, dark place. They insulted each other, hitting below the belt, and I was right in the middle. Mostly my mom tried to convince me how horrible my dad was, but I never saw my dad the way she painted him.

Even as a kid, I never thought they belonged together. I thought that perhaps they'd gotten married because my mom became pregnant with me. I soon came to accept that I was an accident child, but I never allowed that to fuck me up. My mom taught me from an early age that I was ultimately responsible for my own life, which was why I shouldn't put her on a pedestal. It was the best lesson she ever taught me, and the worst. There was nothing like being eleven years old and already burdened with taking care of my own psyche.

I look at my parents tonight. I have never seen

them sit that close to each other. My dad couldn't be the man responsible for the way my mom is beaming. I don't know why I feel betrayed. It's a stupid reaction but a strong one. My feet are stuck to the ground. I don't know if I should run away or join the family. Jack dips his head toward the empty seat beside him, suggesting that I sit.

My dad stands. "Maggie!" He's beaming like my mom.

I walk to him, feeling as if I'm carrying a heavy bag of bad memories on top of my head. He looks different. He shaved off his thinning blond hair, and now he looks much younger than fifty-eight. The way the candlelight on the table catches his eyes makes his face look stunning. His good looks were his downfall. Suddenly I understand what my mom meant by saying I had always been too beautiful for my brain. My dad was and is beautiful, which made it too easy for him to screw around on her. However, in my case, there's nothing I want that my looks can give me, not even Vincent Adams, who I haven't seen so far.

My dad and I hug. "Wow. You're here too?" I ask.

"Good to see you, lovely. It's been a while," he says.

I try to quickly calculate how long it's been since

we've last seen each other. I think of my life in eras—pre- and post-Cruella La Bitch, my ex-boss. I hadn't seen my dad since many years pre-Cruella La Bitch, which is too long ago to come up with a number.

I hug Jack and Daisy. I set my judgmental gaze on my mom. "So is Dad the big secret?" I sit in the empty seat beside Jack.

Leah throws up her hands excitedly. "Ta-da!"

I study how close they're sitting. I shift my finger from my mom to my dad. "What's going on here?"

My dad kisses my mom on the lips, a quick but soft and sensual kiss.

I'm flabbergasted. "So you're back together?"

Isak puts his arm around Leah and massages her bare shoulder. My mom is wearing a strappy black cocktail dress by some European designer. She looks exquisite.

"Perhaps," Leah says, making eyes at Isak.

They kiss. I watch as if two trains just collided before my eyes.

"Maggie, you're turning red," my mom says.

I'm speechless, although I'm trying to figure out why I'm so flabbergasted and uncomfortable. My parents are obviously together in a sexual way. I thought the sky would fall, hell would freeze over, and pigs would fly before that would ever happen.

"Things change, people grow, Mags. You know that more than anybody," Jack chimes in.

I shove my hands toward my parents. "I just don't understand how this could ever occur. You guys hated each other!"

"Well"—my mom leans in my direction—"you have to love someone to care enough to hate them."

"Perhaps," I sing in a cynical tone.

"Give them a chance. This is about them, not you," Jack whispers in my ear.

I know he's right. It's not as though I'm the teenager caught in the middle of an embittered divorce battle. "Sorry, Mom, Dad. Congratulations." To show that I'm sincere, I get up to give my parents another hug.

"Hello, Vince!" Jack says in the midst of me kissing my dad.

My stomach drops. I turn around. Vince and Cindy O'Lay are standing at the edge of our table. Vince and I lock eyes, and I feel like a deer trapped in headlights again. He's standing right beside the chair I abandoned. I look at my mom. She's watching me with a curious gaze. I don't want her to even suspect that I had once been involved with Cindy O'Lay's gorgeous boyfriend. If I choose another seat, then my mom will wonder why I'm avoiding him. So I put on the fakest smile I can muster and approach Vince.

"Hi, Vince!" I sing.

He shakes my outstretched hand with his eyebrows puckered.

Cindy is taken aback. "Oh, you know each other?"

I take my seat.

"Maggie is Charlie's cousin," Vince says.

I withhold a bitter snort. Did he not mention to Cindy that his ex-girlfriend would be at the party? Heck, I was more than his ex-girlfriend. He unofficially married me, albeit with his dick inside me. We made a commitment far greater than the average run-of-the-mill boyfriend and girlfriend.

After a moment of scrutinizing me, Cindy points at my father. "Isak Conroy?"

My father looks as if he's trying to figure out if he knows her. "That's me."

Cindy curls her arm around Vince's waist as if she's done it a million times. I'm gripped by sadness, but I can't show it because Leah is still reading the scene. So I hold this smile, refusing to let it drop, and turn to Daisy. She's smiling at me, but her eyebrows denote curiosity. I shrug slightly, and Daisy barely nods. I love that Daisy is wise enough to recognize the unspoken nuances during interaction.

"I've never shot with you, but I'm a fan of your work," Cindy says.

My father grins. I see he still loves to have his ego stroked. "Why, thank you."

My mom shakes a finger at Cindy. "You are…"

Cindy touches her chest. "I'm Cindy O'Lay." She sounds proud of it.

I look at the table to avoid Vince's stare.

"Yes!" my mom says. "You've shot a campaign for us."

"Oh?" Cindy's intrigued.

"*Damsel* magazine. I'm the executive."

Cindy gasps. "Holy shit, you're Leah Conroy!"

"The Conroys are a powerful trio," Vince says.

Now I look at him. I know Vince well enough to realize he's going somewhere with that comment.

"Maggie Conroy runs the top PR firm in L.A.—Mo&Ma?" he says.

My fake smile hurts my face. "Yes," I say so pleasantly that I'm inwardly rolling my eyes at myself for being such a great actress.

"I wanted to speak to you about a client of ours," he says.

I glance at Jack for support, but he and Daisy are whispering to each other. "Really?" I say.

Vince thumbs over his shoulder. "Do you have a moment?"

I lift a hand. "Sorry, but our client list is full."

He sets his gaze on my parents. "Is it?"

Fucking Vince. He knows me well enough to know that I'm hiding our association from my parents. I heed his warning.

"But sure," I say pointedly enough for him to get that I want him to stop looking at my parents that way. "I'll hear what you have to say."

Vince sets his mouth close to Cindy's ear. "I'll be back."

She kisses him then acknowledges me with a warning look before putting her focus back on my parents. I stand. Jack and Daisy watch me with amusement. Now I realize what they were whispering about—me. My head is dizzy. I can't believe I'm in this predicament.

"Lead the way," Vince says, his mouth so close to my ear that I can feel his warm breath. He's been sucking on a peppermint. He often freshens his breath with those little candies.

I smother the butterflies in my heart and avoid my mother's curious stare. *Vince and I are over,* I remind myself as I lead us through the crowd in search of a quiet place to talk. I'm curious to hear what he has to say regarding Mo&Ma. He sure doesn't want to talk about getting back together. He's moved on to a woman he seems to like very much while I'm still trying to figure out the rest of my life. However, that doesn't change the effect he has on me. I feel as though I'm walking through an alternate plane. Vince puts a hand on my waist. His hand is damp, which happens when he's nervous. Suddenly I have no idea which way to go.

"This way," he says.

I shake my head. He guides us in the opposite direction of where I was leading. We go down a narrow path between two brand-new brick walls. We pass a few couples who have stolen away for a moment of privacy. Vince hasn't taken his hand off my waist. I want to ask him to remove it, but I don't want to risk agitating him. He's holding all the cards. If my mom finds out he and I were involved, then she would press me until I admitted that I'd tried my hand at having a great love and failed. I would be a hypocrite for maligning her for running away with Cobey Miller when I fucked my boyfriend's best friend. I'm not ready to take my lickings for my hypocrisy.

We make it to the end of the path and turn toward the back of the house. This area is sparsely lit.

"Watch your step," Vince says, his mouth still too close to my ear.

I lean away from him. "Okay." My tone captures my irritation. He has to know he's being too intimate with me.

I rush up the steps to the porch, breaking away from him, and sit against the arm of the swinging bench. My goal is to leave space between us. "So what's this all about?" I use a stern voice to let him know this impromptu meeting we're having is all business.

Vince sits close enough that our thighs touch.

"Really?" I would scoot over, but there's no room on my end.

He fakes being oblivious to what he's doing. "Really what?"

"You're going to sit this close?"

"Does it bother you?"

"Do you think your girlfriend would approve?" I'm looking into his green eyes. He has such great lines on his face, so manly.

Vince takes a moment to contemplate. He moves over some. He's still too close for my comfort, but I welcome the tiny amount of breathing room.

"Like I said…" I swallow nervously. "Um, our client list is full."

"Maggie," he says.

I'm familiar with that tone. "What?"

"You don't want your parents to know about us. Why?"

"Because it's none of their business."

"Hiding isn't your style."

I have to look away from his gaze. "I just don't want them to know. That's all."

"Why?"

"I don't have to explain that to you."

He shrugs indifferently. "All right. I'll just tell your mother that you and I used to… you know."

"Fuck?"

Vince frowns as if I'd just slapped his face. "We were more than that, weren't we?"

I look at the wooden floor. This porch is old. "I thought we were." A long moment of awkward silence falls between us. "But you haven't told Cindy about me."

"She knows about you."

I'm shocked. "She didn't seem like it."

"She knows my ex... she knows you'll be here tonight. She just doesn't know who you are."

"That's confusing. You've never mentioned me by name to her?"

He shakes his head. "No."

"Charlie must've."

"No."

"What about your creepy friend who's always looking at my tits and ass?"

Vince grunts. "Which one?"

"The one who gave you the bad advice about using dominant and submissive tactics? He's here. I saw him."

He chuckles. "Thatcher."

I chuckle. "Have you tried any of your bondage moves on Cindy?"

"Don't have to. She's not you."

"Ouch." I wait for him to take the sting out of what he just said, but he doesn't. Vince clearly still wants his pound of flesh. "It's just not a good idea for us to work together."

"I know, but I need you."

I meet his smoldering gaze. Vince is playing mind games. "Lay it out," I say breathlessly.

"Lay what out?"

"The reason why you *need* me so much."

He tells me about the actress with a wild past. "We put a lot of money into shooting the first ten episodes."

"I can't believe you shot ten episodes back to back like that. Whose idea was that?"

"It was mine."

"You should've looked into her background before you invested all that time and money in her. Jeez. Hell, you could've called me!" I say.

"I could've?"

"Yes! I know that Kelly Simon is an effing train wreck. A quarter of the producers in Hollywood won't cast her, and that number is growing daily. I suspect by the end of the year, the agent she's screwing will only be able to find her a part in a porno."

Vince snickers. "Effing, Mags?"

I roll my eyes. "I just remembered that I made a deal with my mother. She wants me to find other words to use besides curse words."

Vince looks amused. "What did you wager?"

"She's going to stop smoking."

"Do you believe her?"

I narrow an eye curiously. "Why? Have you seen her smoke since about three hours ago?"

He's wearing the same naughty smirk that Robert Tango often uses. "No, I haven't."

I turn away from his gaze.

"Look," he says loudly enough to reclaim my attention, "if I had another option, I would take it. But I need this fixed."

The idea of cleaning up Kelly Simon's image doesn't appeal to me. "I don't know, Vince..."

"Come on, Mags. We need you. I need you. The big boys are coming after us, and they're willing to sink Kelly's career just to add another failure to our notch."

I frown. When I left A&Rt, they'd had some very good drama series lined up for the next season. The ratings on most of their existing shows were above average. We had been testing three new reality show series, and I'd left before we got the results. A&Rt had been on the verge of being a contender when I quit nine months ago.

"What makes you think they're coming after you?" I ask.

"I got an email from Tricia Dalton."

My eyes grow wide. "Of *OUR* magazine?"

"Yes."

I want to say fuck but decide to choose my words more wisely. "What did she say?"

Vince rubs the nape of his neck. I know that gesture far too well. He finds the topic stressful. "*OUR* is going live on Monday with photos of Kelly tonguing another woman while rubbing her ass against a top Hollywood agent's cock."

I sniff disdainfully. "You're referring to Brad Bowers. He's an idiot. But…" It's hard to believe that Monroe and I just started this business nine months ago. In the beginning, I jumped at the challenge of turning a public figure's personal shit into Shinola, but not anymore. All the lies I have to tell and sketchy deals I have to make are getting to me. "I don't know how much more of this I can take," I whisper past the tightness in my throat.

What's strange is that I feel as if I've finally confessed my truth to the right person. We fall silent. I clear my throat and smile just to pretend that I'm not as sad as I feel.

Vince winks. "You always have a job with us."

I'm a little taken aback by the offer. "Are you feeding me shit?"

He smiles. "Feeding you shit? Would your mother approve of such language?"

I chuckle and gaze out over the heavy tree line that marks the start of the forest. Vince sounds flir-tatious. I have to remind myself that he has a girlfriend. I wipe the tiny smile off my face and look at him. "So how well did the series test?" My tone is all business.

Vince pauses. I'm glad he remembers my personality well enough to know that I'm purposely changing the mood. "It's going to be a hit."

I nod, pondering his claim. "Are you positive?"

He's staring at me with that intense gaze of his. He does it so effortlessly, and I often thought he didn't know he was doing it. Then he smirks. "Even Maggie would agree."

I won't allow myself to be disarmed by Vincent Adams. I keep my expression stern. "Well then, I'll call Monroe. We're looking to fill an opening on our list."

He grins as if I've been caught in a lie. "Then your list isn't full?"

I rise to my feet, maintaining my composure. "Nope." I smooth the bottom of my dress. "All right then, I'll call you."

He stands. Our faces are so close that we've crossed into the intimate zone.

"You do that," he says.

I swallow the lump in my throat. "I will."

"By the way, you look stunning."

"Thanks."

"Light blue is your killer color."

"I'll remember that."

"I think you already have."

My heart is beating like a jackhammer. I snicker. "I guess so."

I step back and collide into the bench. Vince catches me before I can tumble over, and he squeezes me in an embrace. His package is rock hard against my lower abdomen. We're trapped in a moment of awkwardness. His breath still has a faint scent of peppermint. His chest is wide and solid. I used to love that about him. It reminded me that I'm a woman and he's a man.

The music winds to a stop.

"Charlie!" Jack calls on the microphone.

Vince lets go of me. "We should get back."

"I think so," I say breathlessly.

Jack says, "I want to congratulate my brother on finding *his* most perfect woman in the world. You see, my wife is the most perfect woman to me—always has been and always will be. It's a great feeling to wake up every morning and be in love with the person God made for you. Angelina was made for you, and you deserve her, brother."

Jack's speech wins applause. He continues to talk

about the sort of man Charlie was before he and Angelina met.

"You should go first," I say to Vince.

"We can just go together," he says.

I wrinkle my nose. "I'd rather not."

"Mags… come on."

"I'll go first, and you wait." I skip down the steps before he can respond.

I feel him staring at me as I retreat. I'm so confused about what just happened between us. I think I still love him, but it doesn't matter. I'll just have to get over him. We've bruised each other's egos way too many times to go back to the way we were. Being in Vince's presence still feels so effortless. It's as if we belong around each other.

I walk across a stone pathway that leads to the dance floor instead of returning to the table. The heel of my shoe gets caught in a crevice between the end of the pathway and the cement carport. I feel myself falling forward until two strong hands hold me steady.

"Are you okay?"

I'm looking into two bright brown eyes and one sexy smile. "I'm fine." I steady myself.

The guy flexes his eyebrows. "Wow, you're beautiful."

I frown. "Thank you."

He lets go of me. "Sorry if I offended you by saying that you're beautiful, but you are beautiful."

I look at his friend, who's smoking and grinning, admiring his friend's swagger.

"You didn't offend me," I say. "Thanks for the compliment."

He's about to say something else, then he looks past me. I turn to see what's caught his attention. Vince is glaring at the guy with a look that dares him to say another word to me. Jack offers his final congratulations to Charlie and Angelina and calls my name.

I smile faintly at the cute stranger. "That's me." I rush toward the stage.

Vince

VINCE POSITIONED HIMSELF IN THE MIDDLE OF THE crowd as Jack helped Maggie onto the stage. Vince looked around at the sea of bodies. Damn, a lot of people were present. He wondered how two people, Angelina and Charlie, could have so many goddamn friends.

"Be nice, Magnolia!" Charlie said, beaming at Maggie as she swept past him.

The man Maggie had flirted with under the carport gave Vince a challenging look as he stepped in front of Vince and positioned himself closer to the stage so that Maggie could see him. The asshole was on the hunt, and Maggie was his prey. Vince wanted to challenge the man, but he wasn't in the position to do that. He knew that once he broke up with Maggie, a whole slew of guys would try to take his place. However, he didn't expect Maggie to make it easy for them. But the way she'd smiled at the guy... Vince could hardly stand it. For a second, he wondered if he had been too hasty in ending their relationship. Maybe he should've struck a deal with her that they wouldn't see other people but remained apart until he figured out how to forgive her for fucking Robert. Truth be told, he was ready to take her back two months after they broke up.

Jack lifted Maggie onto the stage, and Maggie giggled as she took the ride. Vince was entranced by her. Her smile was as big as the moon. She was in good spirits all of a sudden, and Vince wondered if the other guy had anything to do with her mood.

"So..." Maggie said. "Charlie warned me to be

nice. But here's what I say to that." She flipped him the bird.

"Boo!" Charlie shouted.

Maggie laughed. "And that's why I love you, Chuck. No… I really do love Charlie. We've been through hell and back together. Fun times..." Maggie looked off nostalgically. "Not!"

Maggie paused while the guests laughed.

"I know why you laugh," she said once the laughing cooled. "You know exactly what I'm talking about. I won't go into the gory details—yet." Maggie smiled at Charlie while guests chuckled. "Charlie, I couldn't give you up to a better woman than Angelina Beauchamp. Chuck, you have always been my protector and my best friend. Let me tell you, if lightning were to strike me right now, I would die a happy woman because you have found true love. However…" Maggie raised a finger. "Let's take a moment of silence to officially say good-bye to *that* guy. Remember him?"

Her playful gaze rolled around the crowd. People snickered as they recalled their own Charlie Lord experiences.

"Yeah… him. But I loved that guy, and I still love that guy, and sometimes I even miss him, especially when I walk past that alley near 2nd Avenue."

"All right, Magnolia, get to the nice part!" Charlie shouted.

"I love you, Chuck! By the way, Angel, do you and Daisy have a brother or cousin for me?"

"I'll take you!" a guy shouted.

"Me too!" another one shouted.

The guy Maggie had flirted with raised his hand, and for a moment, Vince thought Maggie had acknowledged him. Vince seethed.

"I need a glass of champagne," Maggie said, ignoring all the want-to-be suitors.

Vince grinned. Now that was the Maggie he knew and loved. *Yes, loved.*

"Get her a glass!" Charlie shouted.

Charlie and Maggie grinned at each other. Vince knew Charlie was her favorite person. Jack was close to her heart, but Maggie and Charlie had a bond forged out of the fire.

"Here it comes," Maggie announced. She winked at the waiter as she took the glass from him.

Vince felt another pinch of jealousy.

Maggie raised her drink. "Okay, I would like to toast to my wacky cousin and his eccentric fiancée who are fun to watch and a hoot to hang out with! Congratulations!"

Two arms wrapped Vince up from behind. "Here you are," Cindy said.

Vince turned to acknowledge her. "Hey," he said in a lackluster tone.

Cindy looked at Maggie. "Is she your ex-girlfriend?"

Was he ready to call Maggie Conroy his ex-girlfriend? Did he really want that to be the case? Vince watched as Charlie lifted Maggie off the stage, cradling her as they hugged.

Vince looked at Cindy. She was still waiting for his reply. "Yes, Maggie's the ex that I told you about." However, he wasn't sure he wanted Maggie to remain his ex-girlfriend.

13

BEFORE THE PARTY'S OVER

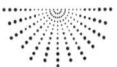

*a*s the night wears on, more of Charlie's friends take center stage to rag on him for "settling down". Angelina's friends recite poems, add expressive dance movements to their speeches, and some of them bawl about how beautiful love is. The guests are an eclectic mixture of nuts.

The guy from the carport's name is Ray. We've been dancing together from the moment the dancing commenced. Now the beat is slow and sultry, and I'm leaning against his chest. I've decided to pretend Vince isn't here, especially after I caught a glimpse of him and Cindy together. He loves her, I'm sure of it, and I have to move on. Ray's body is like a chiseled statue. He's good-looking enough, and I'm attracted to him. But when he spins me around and our lips nearly touch, my head doesn't turn woozy. His breath is tainted by slight halitosis.

"So…" he says.

"So," I say, shamelessly batting my eyelashes. The champagne and my determination to pretend that Vince doesn't exist are making me flirtatious.

"You want to go somewhere and talk?" he asks. There's a sexually suggestive look in his eyes.

If Monroe were here, she would rag on me for hesitating. She would say that I need to get laid and Ray looks as if he can get the job done. It would be nice to show Vince that I can move on too. However, I'm not sure I'm truly ready to move on.

I feel a tap on my shoulder. I spin around and end up facing my father's bright, shiny face.

"Hey, lovely, it's my turn," he says.

Ray looks at me inquisitively.

I shrug. "He's my father." Goodness, I feel relieved.

My dad gently but deliberately pulls me out of Ray's embrace, and before I know it, he's twirling me. I complete the spin and rest my chin on Isak's shoulder.

"So… you and Mom are two lovebirds sitting in a tree?"

He chuckles. "If that's how you want to put it."

"What happened to all the supermodels you used to bang? Have you given up the stick figures for good?"

Isak chuckles. "You always had a way with words."

"Don't evade. Have you?"

"Get ready for it."

Before I know it, my dad is dipping me. I can't help but chuckle as I fall backward.

"I love your mom. Always have—always will."

"Okay, but what about your dick?"

Isak flinches as if I just slapped him in the face. "You're asking me about my dick?"

I roll my eyes. "Come on, Dad. I've seen plenty of them and I know how wayward they can be."

He shakes his head. "Let's just say that your mom is the only woman who can satisfy me in that department. Count me older and wiser."

"It took you this long to learn that pussy doesn't come without a personality attached to it?"

Isak throws up his hands. "I give the fuck up."

I point at him. "You just cursed."

"I'm not the one who made the deal with Leah."

My smile hasn't been this intense in a very long time. "Okay, scratch out pussy and insert vagina."

Isak shakes his head, figuring there's no point in

trying to correct me. "Your mom sent me over to dance with you."

I gasp, pretending to be offended. "Dad, you didn't come on your own accord?"

"I figured you'd rather dance with your previous partner, but Leah sent me to you and her to him."

I follow my father's gaze to where Ray is dirty dancing with another woman. She's all over him, and he seems to have forgotten I exist.

My mouth falls open. "I can't believe her."

"She said he's not for you. Looks like she's right."

"But I didn't want to marry him. I just wanted to… forget it."

"All right, young lady." My dad dips me again, and I laugh my head off.

Screw Ray! I feel free. Tonight, I've made some kind of headway. At the moment, I don't know how much or what it is exactly, but I have a feeling I'm going to soon discover my growth.

I dance with Jack, then Charlie and Angelina take me for a spin. I head back to my guesthouse long before the party ends. I put on my pajamas and wash off my makeup. It's two thirty in the morning when I crawl into bed. I close my eyes and smile. I'm satisfied by how the night played out.

VINCE

Vince watched Maggie wave the pair of shoes she had taken off at her parents and skip cautiously up the pathway to Madame Beauchamp's property. One of Angelina's friends accompanied her. Vince had tried to keep his eyes on Maggie the whole night, and he'd done a good job of keeping track of her. He hadn't seen her make one phone call or check her cell phone once. She hadn't taken a break from the festivities to talk business with Jack.

The guy from the carport had shunned Maggie for another girl. The other girl had come on too strong for the guy to deny her, although Vince had a feeling that the guy wouldn't go away so easily. The guy had kept tabs on Maggie up until the point where the girl grabbed his cock and convinced him to follow her. Maggie didn't need to entertain assholes like that. Vince wanted to know his name. He wanted to make sure that guy never spoke another word to Maggie as long as he lived.

It was three in the morning, and Vince had just had sex with Cindy. He felt like a fraud. He'd had to fantasize about Maggie in that blue dress to even get it up. Was he ready to beg Maggie to take him back? He still couldn't forget that she had fucked Robert, but tonight, as he'd held her in his arms for those few seconds, Vince realized that he had forgiven her.

As Vince lay in bed, staring at the ceiling, he tried to stop wondering if the carport dude had been bold enough to track Maggie down and try to fuck her even after he'd fucked the other woman. Would Maggie invite the guy inside her cottage for a nightcap? The probability was driving Vince insane. He couldn't sleep a wink.

"Cindy?" he whispered.

She responded by breathing heavily. Cindy was out cold. She had drunk one glass of bourbon and two glasses of rum, and she wasn't a big drinker. She had been sort of out of it as they walked back to their bedroom. She kept mentioning how pretty Maggie was and wondering if he liked her better than Maggie.

"You two were gone so long," she slurred. "I thought you were fucking her. You want to, don't you?"

Vince hadn't answered. He'd just kept reminding Cindy that she was drunk and needed to sleep it off.

"But not without fucking me first," she said.

As soon as they were near the bed, she made her

move.

Vince sat up in bed. He took a moment to consider whether or not he should put himself out of his misery by going to Maggie's guesthouse. He jumped into a pair of trousers, slipped into his beach sandals, and tiptoed out of the bedroom. Before he knew it, he had gone out the back door, across the yard, and reached the sliding glass door to Maggie's bedroom.

"Damn it," he muttered, wondering if he had lost his mind.

He put his ear to the glass. There were no sounds of passion. Maggie didn't snore, so he listened for the sound of a man's snoring and heard nothing. There was no changing his mind and turning back now. Vince rapped lightly on the glass. He waited a few seconds then knocked a little louder.

He was just about to call it a bust when Maggie pushed aside the curtain. She was wearing a T-shirt and pair of baggy pajama bottoms. Vince struggled to keep his eyes off the way the material slid across her nipples and caressed the fleshy part of her breasts. Maggie had a way of being sexy even without trying. Her drowsy eyes were blinking him into focus.

"Vince?" she said. After she'd identified him, she

slid the glass door open. "What are you doing out here?"

"Just wanted to make sure you made it back safely." He curled his neck to see behind her. She was indeed alone.

Maggie rubbed her eyes. "Thanks, I'm okay."

"Okay," he said.

They stared at each other. Maggie was still blinking.

"Are you going back tomorrow?" he asked.

"Yeah," she breathed.

"So when can we meet? We never set a date."

She frowned, confused. "Oh. Kelly what's-her-face. I'll make some calls as soon as I wake up. We'll get the story delayed. Don't worry." Finally she seemed to focus better.

Vince wanted to kiss her. "Okay, but are you flying back to L.A. or New York?"

"L.A."

"Me too." That was an on-the-spot-decision he just made.

"Why don't we have lunch on Monday?"

Maggie nodded. "All right. Just have Langley call Mavis and set something up. Preferably after one in the afternoon and on Sunset in West Hollywood."

Vince couldn't stop grinning. That was one of

many things he liked about Maggie. Even while half asleep, she was on top of the details. "Mavis? I thought she was Robert's assistant."

"Not anymore. She couldn't work with him because Robert doesn't work. I told you that a million times."

Vince chuckled. He was still confused about how Maggie really felt about Robert. She'd never had much of anything good to say about Robert, yet she'd fucked him.

"How about I call you tomorrow?" he said. "We'll figure out a place together."

"I don't care where as long as it's in West Holly-wood after one. I don't want to get fuck—I mean, slammed by traffic."

Vince chuckled. "I see you're keeping to your word."

Maggie yawned. "I guess so."

Vince could see how exhausted she was, but he wasn't ready to leave her presence. "How did it feel seeing your parents again?"

"Good, I guess." She sniffed. "They're back together. Did I tell you that?"

"Get the fuck out of here!" he said, even though he'd already figured out they were together.

"After all the hell they put me through during

their divorce. Go figure."

"Things change."

"That's what Jack said."

They stared into each other's eyes.

"Is that it?" Maggie asked.

No, that wasn't it. Vince still didn't want to let her go. "Yeah, that's it."

"Okay, well, I'll get back to you."

"Tomorrow?"

She nodded.

Vince nodded. "Good night."

"You too." Maggie smiled weakly as she closed the door.

"Lock it," he said, pointing toward the lock.

Maggie locked the door and raised her eyebrows as if she were asking, "Happy?"

Vince gave her a thumbs-up. Maggie graced him with one more smile then disappeared behind the curtain. An unexpected feeling of loss hit Vince.

MAGGIE

I stop raking the toothbrush across my teeth and squint curiously toward the sound.

"Who is it?" I shout with toothpaste in my mouth.

The person bangs again. I rinse my mouth and trot to open the door. Charlie sweeps past me.

"Chuck? What?"

"Are you coming to breakfast?" he asks.

"Yes, just give me a minute to finish up in here."

Charlie looks around as though he's checking to see if I destroyed the place.

"What the hell are you looking for?" I ask.

"Nothing. Is everything to your liking?"

I narrow one eye suspiciously. "Yes. And why are you really here?"

He flops down on the sofa and crosses his legs, getting comfortable. "Good." He shakes his foot as though he's anxious.

Now I'm concerned. "What's going on?"

Charlie twists his mouth in that way he does when he's grappling with nervous energy. "I'm ready to just go through with it."

"You mean the wedding?"

"I don't need a ceremony. All I need is Angel. If I lose her, Mags, I'll fucking kill myself."

I sit beside him. "Now we're getting to the real reason you're here. What the hell have you done?"

Charlie looks me dead in the eyes. "Something stupid."

My mouth falls open. "Did you cheat on her?"

"No," he says as if he's offended. "Never. I just might need your services one day."

I frown confused. "For what? What did you do?"

Charlie growls and grabs his head. "Just give me some time, okay? Just know that there won't be some big fucking wedding. Last night was it. I'm marrying her as fast as she'll let me."

"You're trying to seal the deal."

"I have to. I can't lose her."

I take Charlie by the shoulders and make him look me square in the eyes. "Spill it, Chuck. You know your secrets are safe with me."

"I don't know. She could be lying."

"Who's the she you're referring to?"

"A girl. A woman."

"Did you get her pregnant?" I ask.

He looks at me with widened eyes.

"What the hell! Was it before you met Angelina?"

He shakes his head.

"Then you did cheat on her?"

"No, I didn't. I had a moment of weakness, and this girl took advantage of that. Angel and I were on a break."

I turn toward Charlie. "Okay. Tell me exactly what happened. Don't skip a damn thing. Got it?"

Charlie nods. He recounts how he met a cellist the first time he worked with Jacques in Los Angeles. The woman came on to him pretty strong, but he resisted her advances up until her stint was over. After finishing her portion of the soundtrack, she left the house but then returned to record revisions. They both lodged in the rooms on the same floor, and she would walk past his door with either her tits or ass exposed. One night she took advantage of his weakness.

I roll my eyes. "Took advantage of your weakness? Give me a break." It takes every ounce of my willpower to not say, "Give me a *fucking* break."

"That was after Angel had caught Monroe on my dick."

"I know, Charlie, but you're taking responsibility for your part, right? There would've been no cock sucking if it"—I point at his penis—"hadn't gotten with the program."

"You think my dick getting hard is an emotional response? Shit, the wind can blow the right way and up I fucking go. Believe it, Mags. My dick isn't attached to my brain. It's an independent agent. It acts on its own accord."

Silence lingers as I consider what Charlie said.

"You know what's sad? I believe you. You know Delta?"

"Delta Foster? The actor?"

I nod. "He'll fuck everything, including the kitchen sink, if you let him."

"The kitchen sink? The hole's too wide."

"And if he's lucky, someone will turn on the garbage disposal and turn it into mincemeat. I think he'd be happier if he were penis-less."

Charlie snorts. "The point, Mags, is that I made a mistake with this girl."

"You fucked her." I shake my head. "Shit, I'm not supposed to say fuck or shit. Listen, did you fuck her?"

Charlie looks at me askew. "You just said it again. And why are you not supposed to say fuck or shit?"

"I made a deal with Leah. I stop cursing, and she stops smoking."

"You'll be relinquishing eighty percent of your vocabulary if you stop cursing."

"Fuck you, Charlie."

"See what I mean?"

"Whatever. Back to you. Did you have sex with this girl or not?"

"Kind of," he says.

"Kind of? Did your penis 'kind of' find its way into her vagina?"

"For a short while. I hadn't fucked in a while, so I may have sprayed a little. I don't know. She says she got pregnant."

"By you?"

"That's what she says."

"And you haven't told Angelina about this?"

Charlie leaps to his feet. He stands at the window and looks out over the lake. "Angel knows Mita—that's her name. I would've told her back then, but she'd already caught Monroe and me together. I didn't want to look like some cheating moron who can't control his second head."

I join Charlie at the sliding glass door. I faintly remember standing at the sliding glass door in my bedroom last night. Vince and I had a whole conversation. I was so tired that I thought it could've been a dream, but the entire interaction was real. I'm supposed to have lunch with him tomorrow.

"Just tell her," I say. "Angelina's reasonable. She'll understand."

Charlie shakes his head. "She won't. I went over this a million times in my head. See, she hates Mita because Mita had been fucking Jacques."

I gasp. "Get out!"

Charlie and I turn to look at each other. He *is* in quite a predicament.

"What do you need from me?" I ask.

"I don't know. Can you figure out if she's telling the truth?"

"Probably. Maybe. I'm pretty sure I can. How did she get in contact with you?"

"She sent me a letter with pictures of a child inside."

"How old is the kid?"

"One or two. I can't remember."

"I'll need the letter and the pictures."

Charlie nods. "Thanks, Mags."

"You're welcome."

Charlie returns to the main house to join his guests for breakfast. I finish packing my bag then call Monroe and fill her in on Vince's ordeal. She's hesitant to take him on because she thinks it's a ploy to get me back. I assure her that Vince is happy and in love with Cindy O'Lay. If anything, he wants to be friends.

Monroe laughs. "You're too sharp to believe that."

I stuff my small makeup bag into my weekender bag. "Well, it's better than nothing."

Monroe scoffs. "Better than nothing? Mags, listen to yourself."

"What?" I look around the living room and kitchen to make sure I haven't left anything.

"Did Vince try to fuck you last night?"

"What? No." I'm utterly confused.

"I don't believe you."

I hang my bag on my shoulder and walk out of the guesthouse. "Then don't."

"Did you just slam the door?"

"Huh?"

"You're irritated. I just irritated you."

"You're irritating me now."

Monroe chuckles. "And the saga of Maggie and Vince goes on. Just marry him and get it over with already."

"Hanging up." My finger is on the end button.

"Wait!" Monroe calls.

"What is it?"

"Let me deal with *OUR* magazine. I'll call Rhonda Wexler. She owes me one."

Finally, a subject I'd rather talk about. "What are you going to ask her to do?"

"I'll try to use what I have to convince her to kill the story."

"What do you have on her?"

"I'll tell you when you get here."

"All right. See you in the morning."

We end our call. I already feel the pressure of seeing Vince again. My flight leaves in four hours. Last night I promised Charlie and Angel that I would join them and their guests for breakfast. I ignored the fact that Vince and Cindy O'Lay might be present, unless they decide to stay in and make love as Vince and I used to do. Regardless, my heart is beating a mile a minute as I approach the main house. I stop and take a deep breath. I close my eyes and let myself feel the cool, gentle breeze glide across my arms. This morning I put on a white T-shirt, faded jeans, and high boots. I want to pay homage to California when I fly back to the Golden State, so I put on classic Californian wear. Not many native New Yorkers will admit that they've fallen in love with the West Coast, but I have. If only I didn't have to deal with my clients' shit upon return.

I take a moment to try out telling Monroe I want out of Mo&Ma. I see myself taking her to lunch. She really likes Tantrum in Sherman Oaks. I would've called ahead and asked to have her favorite meal waiting for us. I'll order a bottle of their best wine when we get there. I'll let her babble on about her newest male conquest, and I won't cut in with a question about one of our clients like I usually do. Once the wine arrives and the waiter pours each of us a glass, I'll reach across the table, place my hand on hers, and say, "Monroe, I don't want to do this anymore."

She'll look surprised. "Do what?"

"Mo&Ma. It's ripping away at my decency."

She'll then accuse me of thinking I'm better than her because she doesn't feel the same way.

"Fine then," she'll say, not really meaning it.

I'll say, "That's okay. I take it back."

She'll say, "Good."

Dissolving our partnership without our friendship taking the ultimate hit would be nearly impossible. I shake the thought out of my head because it's giving me a low-grade headache. I open my eyes, walk up the steps of the back porch of the main house, and walk in. The sweet scent of breakfast sits in the air. I identify all the voices in the chatter. Jack is saying something about developing the marina in San Francisco. Charlie warns him that San Franciscans revel in the antiquity of their city and he's going to face resistance. The chatter stops as soon as I appear in the doorway.

"I didn't think you were coming," Angelina says.

I tap my bag. "I can't stay long. Are you still going to drive me to the airport?"

All eyes are on me as if they've been waiting for

my arrival. All my emotional baggage is seated around the table. My mom and dad are next to each other, their shoulders touching. Cindy O'Lay rests her head on Vince's shoulder. I can tell by the look on her face that she's letting me know Vince is hers. She doesn't look well. She's paler this morning than she was last night, and her eyes are red. I glance at Charlie's friend Thatcher, who's smiling at me.

Then I lock eyes with a familiar face. "Ray?"

He pats the empty seat beside him. "Saved you a seat."

"Right…" I search for another empty chair. There's one next to Cindy O'Lay. Sitting next to her isn't a good idea, so I take Ray up on his offer. "I can't stay long. My flight leaves in three hours."

"Actually, you can fly back in my jet," Jack says.

"Belmont and I are sticking around for a few days," Daisy says and spoons creamy grits into her mouth.

I set my bag on the floor. "I'll take it." No one ever has to convince me to fly private over commercial.

"Then you're going to sit there and relax and eat like a normal person?" my mother says.

I can always hear the criticism in her tone. "I'm sitting, aren't I?" I reach for a biscuit. The food is set up family style in the middle of the table.

"Here you go, Mags," Vince says, passing down the strawberry preserves and the basket of bacon.

The items go to Charlie, Angelina, then to Thatcher, and finally I take them from Ray. I want to say thank you to Vince, but I avoid looking at him because it's just so awkward that he sent the items without my asking.

"How did you sleep last night?" Ray asks.

"Fine. I bet you got no sleep at all." My tone is abrasive.

"I slept well," he says.

I roll my eyes. "I bet." Since I feel crabby about so many things at the moment, I focus on my parents. "So Isak, Leah, you never told me exactly how this picture of perfect felicity came to be?"

My mom glares at me. She hates when I'm sarcastic. "If you're asking how it came to be that your father and I resumed our relationship, then the answer would be you."

I nudge my chest. "*Me?*"

"Isak was in Las Vegas, and he called me. We made a dinner date." Leah rubs Isak's back, and he leans against her hand. Jeez, they truly have been having sex.

My brows are pinched. "What does *your* dinner date have to do with me?"

"We talked about you," Isak says.

"Really? What did you say?"

"Neither one of us knew what the hell was going on in your life, and we got a good laugh out of that."

"The conversation just flowed from there," Leah says.

My parents are caught in a moment. I hadn't realized I'd been leaning across the table. I sit back. "Well... I guess we're three people, one family, in love," I say without a hint of sarcasm. I've made my decision. From this point on, I'll be one hundred percent supportive of my parents' second go at a relationship. I take a bite of biscuit.

My dad grins. "Now that's a nice change of attitude. Don't you think so, Leah?"

My mom grins too. "I do think so."

I point at them and look at Charlie and Jack. "See where I get it from?"

We all laugh.

"Oh, Mags, I think you're the last to know that Daisy is opening a bakery," Angelina says.

"Oh!" That news hits me like a pillow in the face.

"Yes, and we found a space on State Street in Santa Barbara," Daisy says excitedly.

I throw up my hands. "Wait? Do you even cook?"

"Not only can I cook, but I can bake," Daisy says

in her normal affable manner. "However, the primary baker will be a little French woman named Ines. Her pastries are going to melt in your mouth."

I'm happy for Daisy and share in her enthusiasm; however, I'm still confused by her decision. "It's just that I thought you were a travel writer."

Daisy rubs her belly and winks at me. "No, I'm not a travel writer. I'm Daisy Lord."

I chew on those words as Daisy goes on about her plans for the bakery. My mom has a million questions for her, and Daisy is on top of all the answers. Every now and then, I feel Vince glance in my direction, but I don't look back at him.

"So you live in L.A.?" Ray asks.

I jump. I forgot he was here. "Sometimes." My tone is ice cold.

"I fly out to L.A. often. I'm an engineer. I work with Jacques Blanchard a lot." He smiles as if that's supposed to impress me.

"Right," I say before stuffing that last bite of biscuit into my mouth.

"Maybe we can have dinner sometime."

I swallow and take care to keep my voice low. "Listen, Ray, you're obviously a good-looking guy, but you have the attention span of a pocket puppy. Of course many men for many moons have proven that their private little friend is a hard thing to control, so I won't take personally the fact that you blew me off last night for a sure thing. But understand this—I don't want to have lunch or dinner or breakfast or even grab a bag of peanuts with you, and I find the fact that you're asking after what you did last night insulting."

Ray looks stunned. So does Thatcher, who was eavesdropping. My parents look stunned, and so do Daisy and Jack and Charlie and Angelina. Vince is smirking. Cindy looks worried.

I've officially lost it. Instead of sitting there and stewing in embarrassment, I stand and pick my bag up off the floor. "Angel, you don't have to take me to the airport. I'll call a cab."

"I'll take you," my dad says before Angelina can respond.

I feel so agitated as I hug and kiss my family good-bye. Jack lets me know that I'll see him and Daisy in a few days. I think they're worried that I've lost all my marbles. I don't even look in Vince's direction as I walk out the door. The verbal slap in the face I gave Ray worked. Even as I leave, he doesn't stop talking to Thatcher about their plans to visit the French Quarter tonight. His body language tells me "good riddance."

. . .

MY DAD IS DRIVING A FUEL-EFFICIENT RENTAL CAR, and he remains quiet as we head to the Baton Rouge airport. I close my eyes and rest my head as I ponder Daisy's answer about if she's still a travel writer. Her answer haunts me. Basically, she was saying that her job doesn't define her. Every single job I ever held, I've let it define who I am. I'm Maggie Conroy, and I make pricks, bitches, and egomaniacs easier for viewing audiences to swallow. Sometimes I just make shit up so that they'll appeal to the middle-American tastes. I've put three fake marriages together. Francesca and Delta even bred for their careers. That poor child will have the two craziest parents in the world. Add the fact that I slept with my boyfriend's best friend on top of that, and I come to the conclusion that somewhere along the road, I lost my soul.

The car stops, and my father cuts off the engine. I open my eyes. He's already watching me when I turn to look at him.

"Don't worry about it, lovely. You always figure it out."

"Don't worry about what?" I'm jumpy, afraid he may have just read my thoughts.

"Don't worry about being Maggie Conroy." He winks.

I smile faintly. "Is that your fatherly advice for my breakdown?"

"Breakdown? You aren't having a breakdown."

"Then what do you call it?"

"Growth."

"Growth?"

"You're demolishing the old so you can build the new," he says. "It'll look like a catastrophe at first. You'll clear away all the debris. Get some new wood and cement, all the material you need. You'll build a sturdier structure. Do you know why it's going to be sturdier?"

I shake my head.

"It'll be sturdier because it has to be. And that Vincent Adams…"

My eyes grow wide. I feel as if my dad may have uncovered my deepest, darkest secret. "What about him?"

"I like him."

"Okay. Why are you telling me that?"

My dad snickers before he leans over and kisses my cheek. "I'm going to get your bag. Make your mom happy and come visit us."

"What about you? Will my visit make you happy?"

"Always, baby."

My dad opens his door, but I grab his shoulder. "Wait."

He turns to look at me with a look that asks, "What is it?"

"Are you and Mom really back together, or are you fucking with me?"

He laughs. "I don't think I've ever had to tell you this, but not everything is about you."

I laugh. "No, you haven't."

"Then why would the fact that your mom and I enjoy being around each other be about you?"

"Is that all? You two are just 'enjoying each other'?" I draw quotes.

He nods. "Yeah, I enjoy Leah. I love her a hell of a lot too. I always have. She divorced me. I didn't want it."

"But you cheated on her."

"I was an idiot."

"And the house the idiot built has been demolished?"

My dad laughs loudly and studies me with glossy blue eyes. He used to give me that look whenever I brought home straight As on my report card or said something witty or savvy that proved to him I was the "genius" he believed I was. "I'm building a palace in the sky, baby."

I grin. "That's huge. Mom inspires this creation?"

"She's my one and only inspiration—and so are you."

"Then I think I want to build one of those too," I say.

"Build what?" my dad asks.

"A palace in the sky."

We smile at each other. My mom and dad are back together. *Wow.* Deep down, that makes me feel as if anything is possible.

I CALL MONROE AS SOON AS THE AIRPLANE TAKES OFF. She informs me that Rhonda Wexler has agreed to halt the article for forty-eight hours, and Monroe asks me to call Gray Lansing to have him go digging into *OUR* magazine's technical infrastructure. I feel a pinch of trepidation. I've never felt this way about a work task that's the right course of action. I shake off the anxiety and make the call. Gray's line rings twice and clicks on.

"Maggie Conroy. Jet three," I say and hang up.

Two minutes later, I get a call on the airplane line.

"How are you, Maggie?" Gray Lansing says.

I discovered Gray Lansing while working to prove that the woman who accused Jack of hiring prostitutes to win his land bid in Chicago was a fraud. Harold Doe put us in contact, and Jack has given me permission to contact Gray whenever I need to. Gray comes in handy. He has the ability to search through every single device a company has hooked up to a network. We've acquired pertinent information from him that has allowed us to make deals on our client's behalf. I've never met Gray in person, but I've wanted to kiss him a number of times for making my life a bowl of cherries.

"I'm very well, thank you," I say.

"What do you need?" He likes to get to the point.

"Have you heard of *OUR* magazine?"

"You mean filthy rag magazine? Yeah."

"I need to know what sort of information they have about an actress named Kelly Simon."

"Oh her. She's hot."

"Right."

"Computers, cell phones, land lines?"

"Everything they've got," I say.

"Give me some time."

"Six hours?"

"It won't take that long," he says.

"Right… my flight lands in four hours. I can pick up the packet from the same place?"

"It'll be ready and waiting."

"You're so damn good, Gray."

"That's what she said."

I laugh as he ends the call. I send Monroe an update via text, then I power down my phone, close my eyes, and force myself to think of nothing until I fall asleep. As soon as the jet lands, I disembark. Jack's car drives me to a P.O. box in an office building in Century City to pick up the packet that Gray promised. It's not too thick, which is a good thing.

The sun hangs all the way to the west by the time I make it home. I'm staying in Jack and Daisy's house in Malibu until I figure out what to do next—I had been living with Vince until our split. Jack and Daisy moved Montecito's grassy hills near the beach. As soon as I put on a comfortable pair of stretch pants and a T-shirt, I pour a glass of orange juice and warm up leftover moo-shu pork from Yang-O in Santa Monica. I sit at the dinner table to eat and go over the report Gray compiled. As the night goes by, I put together a plan of action for Kelly Simon. I think we can save Vince's television series, at least for season one. I'll suggest he figure out how to revise the storyline to hire a new leading actress for season two.

A snapshot of Cindy O'Lay with her head on Vince's shoulder bombards my thoughts. I think about my dad's house-demolishing analogy. Perhaps Vince is part of the old house I have to demolish in order to find true contentment. I don't know what sort of life changes the walls will be made of. Love? Before Vince came along, not one man, other than Jack, had convinced me that their species didn't suck. I think about Ray. He was cut, but he was a real jerk to think I would have anything to do with him after he ditched me for another woman.

"Damn it," I curse under my breath.

I fucked up, and now Cindy O'Lay is winning and I'm losing. I can't build a better house than Vince. Perhaps I should focus on building a better career. I turn off my computer, shower, and crawl into bed. The traveling and time changes have made me more tired than usual. Who knows what will happen tomorrow. I just might get the nerve to tell Monroe I want out of Mo&Ma.

Don't I want out of Mo&Ma?

I do.

14

I LIKE HER

*M*y alarm rings, and I shut it off. I look at the clock on the nightstand. It's seven in the morning. I have a meeting with Monroe in two hours. Our office is in West Hollywood. When I lived in the Canyons with Vince, it took me fifteen minutes to get to work. I could easily buy a place closer to the office. I haven't because although I've grown fond of Los Angeles, even with all of its irritating flaws like traffic and vastness that makes getting from point A to point B a one-day affair, every time I'm stuck in traffic, I feel as though I can never call the city home.

Thank goodness Jack and Daisy's house is a small paradise in smog-traffic city. All the rooms are filled with comfortable furniture. A maid comes to clean every day. She even makes my bed and picks my clothes off the floor. Their chef comes three times a day. If I'm not home, he leaves meals in containers in the refrigerator. I've been eating so well in the last six months that my body has grown stronger and my mind clearer. Chef Carlisle is a genius. Then there's the beach. I've walked from Malibu to Venice twelve times since moving in. The sweet, salty scent of the Pacific Ocean, the gentle breeze, and laid-back beachgoers are all so invigorating. The point is, ever since moving into the house Jack and Daisy abandoned, something inside me has changed. It's become more of a chore to prepare to go into the office, and this morning isn't any different.

I take a quick shower and put on a black button-front sweater dress because it's easy. On goes lipstick. I fluff my hair and take one last look in the mirror. For some reason, the Maggie looking back at me holds my attention longer than usual. She looks as though she's going to a funeral. I think back to Cindy. Would she ever let herself leave the house looking this way? *Get a grip.* I can't believe I'm comparing myself to another woman.

"Shit, I mean shoot," I mutter.

I rush to my closet to change into an aqua fitted

dress. I might see Vince today. Langley, Vince's assistant, hasn't called to set up a lunch meeting. She might call Mavis. Mavis is my assistant again. She worked briefly for Robert Tango, but he wasn't her cup of tea. She said he hardly ever worked and when something was asked of him, it was difficult to locate him. She left messages and of course Robert called back way too late, but in the meantime, people like Vince would put pressure on her to find him and make him respond. Every day she came into work, she felt anxious. One day she called me and asked if I still needed an assistant. I said, "I don't need an assistant, but I absolutely need you," and the rest is history.

It's been about five months since Mavis came onboard. Last Friday she said something very strange and life changing. I was sitting at my desk, staring out the door. I had just ended a phone call with a client, the actor Casey Blunt. He's thirty-five and releasing a new movie. He'd been doing press tours and was asked twice when he was getting married. The problem with Casey is that he's a commercial film actor. His viewing audience is looking for consensus in order to get off their asses and drive down to the movie theater and pay the box office to see his films, and they don't want to believe the rules of the world are different from what they think. A thirty-eight-year-old man who has never been married are specs that subconsciously turn off bankable demographics. So one Monday, I had Mavis get him a dog. She made sure he was a rescue dog. His audience base believes in that shit—being saviors to dogs and the downtrodden. By Tuesday, Casey had taken pictures with the brown-and-black German Shepherd-malamute mix, who had been homeless after his owner unexpectedly died. By Wednesday, Casey was telling the hosts of the morning shows that he had a new love in his life. They showed the pictures, and the audience swooned. The box office take was saved. By Wednesday, Casey called me to say thank you and ask who was coming to get the dog. He was going to Grenada for the weekend and he'd given his housekeeper the weekend off.

"Are we done with the goddamn dog?" he asked.

I was flabbergasted. During all his interviews, he'd talked about the dog with so much love and affection that he'd even had me fooled. "Let me make sure I'm hearing you correctly. You want to give the dog back now that she saved your ass?" I asked.

"What the fuck ever, Maggie. The fucking dog

whines and barks all night. I don't have time for this. Come get him, or her, whatever the fuck it is."

Mavis was so disgusted that she went to pick up the dog herself. She now owns the dog and has named her Fluff, but her nickname is Fuck Casey.

So I was staring out the doorway, trying to feel numb toward a request from Francesca Bell, the sexually fluid actress that Monroe and I coupled with Delta Kent, the sexually confusing actor. Francesca wanted out of the relationship with Delta Kent. She'd found a "real man," fallen in love, and didn't want to keep up the charade. The business side of me wanted to throw contracts and lawyers in her face. The human side of me wanted to wish her the best in love and tear up the contract. That thought led to "Fuck Casey," and suddenly I felt as if I were drowning.

"If you decide that you want to give up this line of work, I'll be fine," Mavis said.

"Huh?" I asked her.

"I know you, Maggie. You don't love what you do here. You've paid me very well, and so did Robert Tango, and I've invested my money wisely. Your next chapter in life will kick off my next chapter in life."

We stared at each other, speaking with no words.

My phone rings, interrupting my memory. I search every pocket of my satchel until my hand finds my cell phone. I look at the name on the screen. It's Vince.

I crack a tiny smile. "Hello."

"Good morning, Maggie. How was your night?"

He always asks me that when we're not together.

"Good. How was yours?" I ask.

"It was fine. Are you on your way to the office?"

I grab my keys off the hook near the door. "I am."

"How about we do lunch today at Spirits?"

I try to recall if I'm familiar with that place. "We've been there before, right?"

"You did some of your best work there."

I laugh a little. "Oh, you flatter me so early in the morning."

Vince chuckles. There's awkward silence between us.

"What time?" I ask.

"I know you said after one o'clock, but can we make it noon?"

I study the face of my watch to mentally fill in the hours between now and noon. My day will be jam-packed, but I'm pretty sure I can make it. "Okay, see you then."

"See you," he says.

We hang up.

Traffic never disappoints. It's exactly what I thought it would be—a nightmare. I sigh and grumble whenever the cars ahead of me come to a complete stop after moving at a decent pace. I roll down the windows because even though it's early January, the morning air is pretty comfortable. Today will be a warm one.

By the time I reach the office, it's two minutes after nine. Monroe and I bought a Victorian two-unit building, gutted it, and converted it into our offices. The first floor has three large meeting rooms, men and women's bathrooms, a kitchen, and a posh waiting area in the center. The top floor has my office on one side of the atrium and Monroe's on the other. Mavis's office is next to mine. Monroe's assistant, Bo, has an office next to Monroe's. We had two extra offices built because we knew we'd have to hire people, but we haven't had the time to discuss who we want to be part of our team. The builders paved a lane that leads to the backyard, where we have seven parking spaces circling a tiny round fountain.

I park my car and run inside. Monroe is in her office, laughing with Bo about something. He's not as good of an assistant as Mavis. I've asked Monroe to fire him a dozen times because when he drops the ball, Mavis has to pick it up and run with it. Every morning, Monroe and Bo spend the first hour or so gossiping about their nights. They're so busy doing that that they don't even see me walk in. I sweep past Mavis, who's typing on her computer.

"Morning, Mags," she says and jumps out of her seat to follow me into my office.

"Morning, Mavis." I sigh with relief when I see a cup of green tea, along with a bagel and lox, waiting on my desk. "Thank you."

She sits across from me with her notepad and pen. "You're welcome. So what's on tap for today?"

"Kelly Simon."

She scribbles the name on the pad. "The actress?"

"Yes. Vince wants us to represent her."

She narrows an eye skeptically.

"I know, but I told him I would look into it. She's definitely a box office and ratings wrecker." I take out the file that Gray Lansing sent to me and open it. "*OUR* magazine has enough dirt on her to keep them strapped with content for at least the next two years."

I show Mavis all the photos of Kelly having sex with different men, going down on women, and people going down on her. "Okay, this is the norm." I show her the final three photos. "He's married. This other boy she's screwing is fifteen. He's the married guy's son."

Mavis studies the photos. She points at the husband. "Wait. That's…"

"Brad Bowers," I say.

"He's married to—"

"Barbie Bowers."

"She produces that damn gossip show."

I nod. "You see the predicament."

Mavis nods. "I bet Barbie didn't give a damn that Kelly was fucking Brad, but fucking the fifteen-year-old son is an act of war."

I pick up a pencil and tap the eraser on the desk as I ponder. "You know, I don't even think Kelly Simon deserves our help."

"Do you think Barbie would press charges against Kelly for statutory rape if she knew Kelly had screwed her son?"

I sigh. "No. She wouldn't want the publicity. But I think she would leverage the information she has on Brad."

"But he's her husband."

"He's collateral damage."

Mavis's eyes beam in on a section of one of the

documents. "Wait, Kelly Simon is engaged to Brad Bowers?"

"Only in her own mind."

Mavis snorts cynically and shakes her head. "The stuff I've learned working here. I think I'd rather be oblivious to it all."

My cell phone rings. I read the name on the screen. "Humph." I answer the call.

VINCE

After Vince ended his call with Maggie, he felt more anxious than before. Yesterday, things had gotten tense between him and Cindy. As soon as they'd returned to their room, Cindy accused him of still being in love with Maggie.

"I'm going to always love her," he said.

Cindy snatched her suitcase out of the closet. "That's a fucking cop-out, Vince."

Vince sat on the edge of the bed, tying his sneakers. "It's not a cop-out. Maggie and I were together for two years."

Cindy slammed the suitcase on the bed. Vince

felt the vibration on his back. "Why didn't you tell me that *she* was your ex-girlfriend?"

"Because it wasn't a big deal."

Cindy snorted bitterly. "You're an asshole, Vince. Do you know who I thought your ex was? Angelina."

"Angelina?" He considered that for a moment. He definitely wouldn't have kicked Angelina out of his bed if he had met her before everyone they had in common came into their lives. "Why would you assume that?"

"Because she's always touching you."

"Angelina touches everybody. That's the way she is."

Cindy rolled her eyes and stopped putting her folded clothes into the suitcase. "So what happened?"

"Nothing's ever happened between Angelina and me."

"I mean between Maggie and you?"

Vince dropped his foot off of his knee. He let it slam hard against the floor as a memory invaded his thoughts. "She fucked Robert."

Cindy gasped, shocked. "Robert Tango?"

"Yeah."

"But he's your best friend."

Vince shrugged. The jury was still out on Robert

being his best friend. Things hadn't been the same between them since he'd caught him munching on Maggie's pussy. There comes a time when a man has to wake up and sniff the smelling salts. Robert had never been as good a friend to him as he had been to Robert. Five months ago, Robert had left A&Rt to pursue his own interests, and they hadn't spoken since their last handshake and good-bye. Vince hadn't missed him.

Cindy whipped over to the closet to collect the clothes she'd put on hangers. "Well, Maggie seems to be over you."

Vince felt the impact of her words. As far as he was concerned, Cindy couldn't know that She didn't see the way Maggie responded to him when they were alone, nor did she catch the instances where their eyes met and Maggie looked away in panic.

Vince's cell phone rang, and he saw that the call was from Pamela Dingy, their in-house PR person. He excused himself to take the call outside. Pamela had just gotten word that the article on Kelly Simon had been halted for forty-eight hours. She asked if he'd had anything to do with it, and Vince said no. He didn't want anyone to know Maggie and Monroe were on the case, so he left it at that. After the phone call ended, he stood on the porch and looked out over the grass. How many times had he studied those trees? For the first time in six months, he felt as if he was missing a very important part of himself.

"Hey you?" a woman said.

Vince turned toward the person who spoke. It was Leah, Maggie's mother. He nearly dropped his phone. "Ms. Conroy."

"Call me Leah," she said as she walked up the steps and leaned against the rail of the porch.

Vince took a moment to study Maggie's mother. She was nothing like he'd pictured. Leah Conroy had on a pair of leggings and a sweaty V-neck T-shirt. Her hair was damp. She must have just returned from a run. She was a thin woman but in good shape. It was evident that she exercised more than the average person. "Right, Leah."

"So how long were you and Maggie involved?" She winked.

Vince was still studying Leah's face, trying to discover the features she shared with her daughter. Maggie's mother was one of those people whose beauty had been sculpted from the American experience. Her cheekbones and straight forehead were reflections of her Native American ancestry. The slant of her eyes suggested a hint of Chinese blood. Her rounded face and button nose said that she was mostly Dutch. No wonder Maggie looked like no one else in the room.

"You two were once involved, am I right?" she asked.

Vince realized he had missed answering the question the first time she'd asked it. "Um..." He considered whether or not he had permission to confirm whether or not he and Maggie had been involved. Plus, he didn't like hearing their relationship referred to in the past tense. "Maggie and I are friends. She used to work for me, or work with me."

Leah snorted. "Is that so?"

Vince nodded. "It's so."

"I see. Well..." She stopped leaning against the rail and stood up straight. "That was a good answer. But I have a feeling that you're still in love with my daughter, so I'm going to give you a little advice. Don't put too much time and distance between you. Maggie loves you too, but she's the only person I know who can live with or without the ones she loves. Her dad and I are living proof of this."

Leah had taken two steps away when Vince called her name. She turned to face him.

"We broke up six months ago," he said.

Leah walked back over to lean on the rail, giving him her complete attention.

"I cheated on her, then she cheated on me with someone who was very close to me."

For a moment, Leah looked shocked, but she quickly dialed it back. "Humph. That doesn't sound like Magnolia at all."

Vince wanted to assure Leah that he wasn't exaggerating since he'd caught them in the act. Actually, he wanted to do more than assure her. He wanted to whine about it, rage about it. He felt as if Leah was the right person to tattle-tell on Maggie to. "Well, it happened."

Leah nodded. She was pondering something, and Vince desperately wanted to hear it.

"Vince, we're going to miss our flights!" Cindy called. She appeared in the doorway.

Leah stood straight and patted Vince's shoulder. "Good luck, Vincent Adams." She said good morning to Cindy as she walked into the house.

Cindy walked over to stand by Vince's side. "What was that about?"

Vince shook his head. "Nothing." He rubbed her back.

"One more thing... why don't you just come to New York with me?" Cindy asked.

"You know I can't. I have business in L.A."

"Why not? You've had no problems changing

your plans before."

Vince frowned. He knew what Cindy was insinuating. "I have to go to L.A."

"Is it because Maggie's in L.A.?"

Vince squared his shoulders. "Part of it. I'm in the middle of a crisis, remember?"

"Right. You need her to fix your problem, but you can do that over the phone." Cindy sighed and gathered his face in her hands. "I know that you still have feelings for her, but it looks to me like she doesn't share your affections."

Vince removed Cindy's hands. "You don't know what I feel for Maggie because I haven't told you."

"Well, I love you. And you haven't made any commitments to me."

Vince sighed with dread. He'd known the time would come when Cindy would hint that she wanted more. Up until then, she had been going with the flow.

"This isn't a good time to have this discussion," he said, knowing that wouldn't suffice.

"Then when is a good time?"

When Vince looked at Cindy, he took stock of his heart. Her nearness incited no deep emotions within him. He liked Cindy. She was nice and even-tempered. She was fun and pretty adventurous. She reminded him of Gabrielle, his ex-fiancée, in many ways, and even Emily. Those women were ideal in a way that made them artificial.

Maggie was flawed. She had never made him feel secure in their relationship. He never knew if she liked him as a person or not. Curiosity had attracted him to Maggie from the moment he first laid eyes on her. His interest built as he watched her from afar. Then, by the will of God, he found himself in a relationship with her. Sometimes their bodies were so close and their souls had merged, but other times, he felt as if he was still in high school, viewing her from the other side of the classroom.

Vince had a choice to make. He could take the less-complicated route and live an uncomplicated existence with Cindy O'Lay. Most men would kill to be by her side and to have her in their bed. He chose option two, electing to walk the more complicated path.

So Cindy flew to New York, and Vince gassed up the jet and headed to L.A. All night long, he lay awake, waiting for the right time to call Maggie. The sun rose. Light filled the bedroom. Vince put on his suit. He walked to the kitchen and made a cup of coffee. He swiped his finger across her name in his contacts list three times then placed the call. She answered. They spoke. Now he had to wait until lunchtime to see her.

Vince couldn't sit in his home office and work. If he stayed home, which happened to be the house he and Maggie used to share, he would climb the walls. So he drove to the office to conduct his first conference call of the day. However, he received a call from Maggie right before Langley dialed in. He was afraid she was going to cancel on him, so he asked Langley to take a message. Maggie insisted that he stop whatever the hell he was doing and get on the damn telephone. The way she imposed her will made his pants tight. He could picture her pretty red mouth barking out that order.

Vince braced himself for the worst. "What's going on, Mags?"

"Your fu... goddamn it!" She regrouped. "Your actress was arrested this morning. Excuse my language, I promised I wasn't going to say this word, but your fucking actress has been fucking arrested on a fucking DUI!"

The news was distressing, but Vince couldn't contain his smile. He was happy to get a taste of what he'd been missing.

"Meet me down at the precinct," she said curtly.

"Which one?" he asked.

"Santa Monica."

Vince leapt to his feet. He asked Langley to reschedule his meetings for early tomorrow morning and let the two department heads know that something had come up. Vince didn't let anyone impede his progress. He didn't have to wait another three hours to see Maggie. Luck was on his side.

VINCE TAKE ME AWAY

There's something absolutely demented about Kelly Simon. She speaks in a fake, high-pitched voice and flirts with anything that has a penis. I glance over my shoulder. She's standing too close to Vince's cock. I have a feeling she wants to jerk him off or something.

"I don't know, Maggie. You can't keep coming down here, asking us to give you special treatment and shit," Hector Ramos, the officer on duty, says.

"Oh come on, Hector, you're not a whiner, you're a winner." I show him my bullshit grin. "And in the end, I'm saving you from having to deal with douche bag lawyers and agents. The paparazzi hanging around. The antics. You don't want your department to turn into the big-top that other departments, which I won't name, in this city are."

He gives me a look. I raise my eyebrows, hoping I swayed him to see things my way.

"Just get her the fuck out of here. Next time, she's going to get booked, especially if she offers to blow my fucking officers again."

I shake my head. "If she does that shit again, then absolutely book her."

Hector grimaces at Kelly. "Fucking celebrities and their fucking issues."

I concur with a snort and turn in time to see Kelly squeeze Vince's bicep. She's gazing at him with a starry-eyed look.

"Vince, Kelly…" I point toward the exit.

"Are you coming?" Vince asks.

I look at Hector. "Is that it?"

"Until next time."

I smirk. "I have a feeling I'm running out of brownie points."

"You have one more left."

"I'll take it."

Hector and I share a chuckle. We say good-bye, and I walk toward the doorway. Vince is standing by the double glass doors, watching me with a scowl.

Since Kelly can't command his attention, she's watching me too.

"And you are?" Kelly asks when I reach them.

A snippy reply comes to mind, but I'm experiencing a peculiar shift in my mood. I take notice of the shiny, scuff-marked floor. Officer Ramos is on the phone. A couple who looks as if they haven't had a good night's sleep in a long time is pleading their case to the attendant. A number of stressed-out people are sitting in chairs, waiting their turn. It's as if I'm noticing the gravity of Kelly's situation and how easily I just waltzed in and flushed her shit down the toilet. If only those other people had me to wipe their blues away. I bet they would appreciate my services more than this ungrateful, spoiled actress. I blink at the light of day and walk toward it. I need to escape this whole ordeal, and never return to it.

Vince walks beside me. "She's Maggie Conroy."

"Am I supposed to know her?" Kelly's tone is snobbish.

"You're going to get to know her."

Kelly runs ahead of Vince and me, and now I'm privy to her provocative strut. Her bandage dress is so short that she's threatening to show the world her snatch. It's gross but mostly pathetic. She bats her eyelashes at two passing men. They accept the invitation to leer at her.

I shake my head. "Vince, we need to talk."

"We still have lunch, don't we?"

I sigh. "I don't know. This incident took up most of my morning."

"But, Mags…"

We're distracted by the sight of Brad Bowers, who's walking in our direction. Brad is a young agent. According to the specs Gray collected on him, he's thirty and has his coke dealer on speed dial. His looks are okay. He's not as tall, well built, or gorgeous as Vincent Adams, at least not at first sight. The longer my eyes dwell on Brad, the more attractive he becomes. He's a spiffy dresser. His cologne smells really good. His teeth are the perfect shade of white. People in this city tend to over-bleach their teeth.

Kelly runs to hug Brad. "Dolphin boy!" she sings in that irritating, high-pitched voice of hers.

"You called Brad?" Vince whispers.

"I had Mavis call and ask him to meet us at the station. She's his client. He should deal with her."

Vince nods in agreement as we watch Kelly rub her tits against Brad's chest; it's nauseating.

"Are you okay?" Brad asks her.

"I am now that you're here," she says in soprano.

I wonder how long she had to practice to master that irritating tone.

Brad lets go of Kelly and walks over to shake Vince's hand and mine.

"So you're Maggie Conroy," he says.

Brad holds my hand a fraction too long. I can tell by the way he's looking at me that he's the type of guy who loves a woman's pussy and tits and not the rest of her. Kelly rakes her hair across her shoulder. She seems bothered by the way he's searching my face.

"That's my name," I say.

"Maggie, it's a pleasure to finally meet you." His eyes drop to my tits. I have enough cleavage showing to feed his imagination.

I take my hand back. "Right." I choose to change the tone of our conversation. "Listen, you're going to have to control your client, or Vince will have to eat the cash he invested in her. She's not a cat. She doesn't have nine lives. Got it?"

"I'm right here, Megan," Kelly says.

"Her name is Maggie," Brad says.

I glance at Kelly dismissively. Brad's eyes dart to Vincent's face. I know he's worried that Vince may do something drastic, like kill the project.

"Nothing bad happened. Everything's still good," Brad says to Vince.

"Well…" Vince says.

I touch Vince's shoulder. "That's because I pulled some *magnificent* strings to get her ass out of trouble."

Kelly gasps as if what I said just offended her.

I take a deep breath and rub my temples to calm myself. I want to unload on her by telling her that a lot of money is riding on the fucking image she's determined to destroy. If she thinks she can fuck her way to the top for longer than a year or two, then she's going to meet a rude awakening, and sooner than she thinks. As a matter of fact, I can see her end in sight. It's staring her right in her fucking face. However, I too am facing a dilemma. I don't care about Kelly's situation—Kelly or any other pubescent-behavior/adult-aged box office/ratings sinker.

"Maggie," Vince says.

I blink until I'm back in the moment. "Vince, I don't think I can…" My cell phone rings. I lift a finger, asking for a moment. It's Mavis. Even though I feel burdened by the weight of the world, I step away to take the call.

"Lilly London has fallen deeper into the troll hole," she says.

It takes me a moment to focus what Mavis said. Lilly London used to be the queen of the A-list actresses. She was loved by conventional- and contemporary-minded women. Then one day, a troll decided it would be fun to ruin her popularity. For the last three years, questionable blogs have popped up, filled with articles that misquoted her to make her appear as if she was holier-than-thou. Her career took a steep downward spiral and hasn't recovered since.

I toss my head back and sigh. "What happened?"

"You know *Slipping on a Glass Slipper* hits theaters Friday."

I sigh tiredly. "I remember now."

Mavis pauses. "Well, a slew of suspicious blogs posted stories about Lilly advocating women dousing their twats with lukewarm green tea."

"And what's wrong with that?"

"Women are calling her a know-it-all who's out of touch with the average woman."

I grunt and shake my head. Lilly's a new client. I was actually excited to take her on because what's happened to her career is ridiculous and says a lot about how impressionable human beings are. But hearing that she requires my immediate attention makes my head spin.

"Maggie, are you still there?"

I had paused for too long. "I'm here," I barely say. "How bad is it?"

"Lilly-hate is trending right now," Mavis says.

I sigh. My feet are glued to the ground. Every nerve in my body is directing me to take one course of action, the decision that will mark the beginning of an era. Am I ready for it?

I set my gaze on Vince. He looks concerned. I have a flashback to the moment our eyes met for the first time in twelve years since high school. I had just finished my first day at A&Rt Media in Manhattan. I was waiting for the elevator to open, and when it did, we locked eyes, just like we're doing now. Back then, I would've never guessed we would end up in a relationship. After we found ourselves in love, or like, or maybe lust, I never imagined it would ever end, although I'd never thought it would last forever. His new girlfriend is Cindy O'Lay, but he's here with me. There's no special reason for it. Vince is a caring guy. He likes me. He really needs me to keep a lid on Kelly Simon, his stick of dynamite, which is on the verge of exploding. He broke up with me. I have to remind myself of that.

"Lilly's manager wants to meet in an hour. He's pissed," Mavis says.

I massage my temple. Vince is staring at me, and I can see the concern in his expression. Brad has just said good-bye to Vince, and now Brad and Kelly are walking down the grassy hill toward the parking area along Ocean Avenue.

"Maggie, are you there?" Mavis asks.

My anxiety dissolves into an eerie calm. "Mavis."

She pauses. "What's going on, Maggie?"

"I'm ready to give up this line of work."

"You sound like you mean that."

"I do."

Mavis takes a deep sigh. "Okay… when?"

"Right now."

"Maggie?" She sounds worried.

"I know. I'm not coming back to the office, at least not today. Hand Lilly's file to Monroe. Or you can handle her case."

"No," Mavis says emphatically. "I meant what I said. If you're out, then I'm out."

My eyes meet Vince's. "Then we'll talk soon," I say.

She goes silent until she says, "Maggie?"

"Yes?"

"About time."

My breaths flutter as I try to keep myself from falling apart even more. I end the call.

Vince's frown intensifies. "Is everything okay?"

I shake my head. "No."

My feet are carrying me away from him. I see my car parked along Ocean Avenue. I'm running and speed-walking. Vince is right on my heels. I leap over the grassy patch in the sidewalk.

As soon as I make it to my car door, Vince takes my shoulders and turns me around to face him. "Maggie, who were you speaking to? What's going on?"

I shake my head. "Nothing... I'm... I have to go."

"Go where?"

He's staring into my watery eyes. "I don't know. Home, I guess."

"It's just, this is so sudden."

"Not for me it isn't."

"Talk to me, Mags."

"I can't right now. I just want to go."

He scratches the back of his neck as he always does when he's frustrated. "I'm not going to leave you alone like this."

I take a deep, cleansing breath. "I'm just going home."

"Then let me take you."

I point my hand at my car. "I can't leave my car here."

"I'll take care of it."

"How?"

"Maggie, come on…"

We look deep into each other's eyes. I consider climbing into the driver's seat and telling Vince that he doesn't have to worry about me. He dumped me, and rightfully so, so I'm no longer his responsibility. Cindy O'Lay is his responsibility. But I don't want to be alone right now. I could drive up to Montecito and stay at Jack and Daisy's new place for a little while, but I'd have to explain myself to them. Plus, Monroe would be knocking on their door by nightfall to chew me out for abruptly quitting. She won't take whatever the hell's going on with me very well. I can't explain to her why I can't do the work that Mo&Ma requires anymore. I love Charlie and Angel, but you don't run to their house when you need space. Vince… I'd rather be with him than anyone else in this great big world.

"Okay… I'll go with you," I say.

Vince seems taken aback. "Yeah?"

I nod.

"Good," he says with a sigh of relief. "Good…"

We walk to his SUV. He opens the door for me, and I get in. Soon we're on the road, but we still have nothing to say to each other. However, the air is thick with the energy we're emitting. We're breathing in confusion, nervousness, and desire. I feel the pressure to start some small talk, but before I can, my cell phone rings.

We both jump, startled. I look at my screen. It's Monroe. Vince studies me as if he's curious to how I'll respond. I send the call to voicemail then power off my phone.

"Wow," he whispers. Vince has never seen me turn down a business call.

"I can't go on like this," I strain to say.

"Go on like what?"

I stare dejectedly out the window. We're trapped in a parade of high-end cars slogging west up Sunset Boulevard. "This job. This business. It's devoid of decency."

"But…"

His car phone rings. We both look at the number on the panel. Vince frowns as he tries to figure out who the caller may be.

"Mom?" I mutter.

He nods at the console. "That's your mom?"

"Yes. How did she get your number?"

The phone rings for a third time. "I gave it to her." Vince answers the call. "Hello."

"Hello, Vincent. It's Leah."

It's strange hearing my mother's voice through speakers.

"Hello, Leah."

"You said you were having lunch with Maggie."

Vince looks at me. "Yes."

"Is she with you?"

"I'm here, Mom," I say as tears rush to my eyes. I force myself to keep my composure.

"Maggie, are you crying?" she asks.

"No!" My tone is as joyful as I can make it.

My mom pauses. "Okay well, I just tried to call your phone, but the call went straight to voicemail. I need to speak to you right away."

I lean toward the console. "About what?"

"I'll just cut to the chase. Your dad and I are getting married."

I sit back to process that. "Married? But you're divorced."

"Oh, stop it, Magnolia. You're not a child, for goodness' sake. Like it or not, your dad and I are getting married, or remarried, tomorrow in Las Vegas, and we'd like for you, our only child, to be there. Capisce?"

My fucking head hurts. I rub my temples. She's right—I'm not a child, and they are adults. If they want to get remarried, who am I to stop them?

"Capisco, but I can't fly out to Las Vegas tonight. I'll check flights for early tomorrow when I get home."

"I can drive us up to Vegas this afternoon—right now actually," Vince says.

I quickly face him. "Really?"

"Yes." There's not an ounce of doubt in his tone.

"That'll be perfect," my mom says. "You'll stay at my house."

"We'll be on the road soon," Vince says just as I'm about to respond.

"Ha! Vincent Adams, I knew I liked you the first time I laid eyes on you. I'll text you the address. I expect you for dinner tonight." She's talking so fast that I can't keep up, which isn't like me at all.

"We'll be there," Vince says.

The call ends, and seconds later, my mother's address shows up on the dashboard panel. I settle into my seat. We can now add awkwardness to the blend of moods trapped in the car with us.

"You don't have to do this," I say.

"Don't worry about it," he says.

"What about Cindy?"

"No need to worry about her either."

We've reached the hillside, nearing the 405 Free-way, where the roads are narrow and winding. I hold on tight because Vince is driving faster than most people do through these parts. Perhaps I hit a nerve when I mentioned Cindy.

"She's your girlfriend, isn't she?" I steal a glance at Vince. He's tightened his jaw and squared his shoulders.

"Like I said, I'll deal with Cindy," he says.

His answer is infuriating, but I don't have the energy to argue with Vince at the moment. I have too much going on inside me. I'm skipping out on my responsibility to a client under contract with Mo&Ma. I could help Lilly quite quickly actually. I would have Gray hit the comments sections of those pop-up and insignificant blogs with comments in favor of Lilly. But first I would count the negative comments and hope to find significantly less than before. I would book Lilly on a few "Good Morning" shows. Lilly's delightful and likable. I would ask her to take pictures of her and her six-year-old son baking cookies or a cake with lots of sugary frosting and festive colors. The kid would have to be covered in flour and the kitchen cluttered. Her hair would have to be messy. She's already sent us pictures of her and her dog. We could use some of those too.

It would take two days to help Lilly recover from the damage, but that's only until the next time. I don't know if I'm weary of the work or the people my clients are forced to appeal to. With the help of the Internet, the average person is getting meaner and meaner, brain-farting comments about celebrities, who are people too. Being a professional actor offers a glamorous lifestyle, but it's not an easy job. The people. The guy stopped at the light in the car to our right. *That guy.* The woman in her car across the intersection, waiting for the light to change. *Her.* I'm fucking tired of the fucking consumers for being too simpleminded.

The light turns green, and Vince takes the ramp to the 405 Freeway. I rest my head on the seat. Did I get good sleep last night? I can't remember. Traffic is thick, but Vince will be turning onto the 10 Freeway and traveling west in less than a mile. I close my eyes. "Thanks, Vince."

His "you're welcome" is music to my ears.

16

OFF THE BEATEN PATH

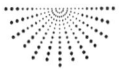

*V*ince waits in the car while I'm inside the house, packing a bag. The house phone is ringing over and over. It's Monroe, I'm sure of it. I change into a royal-blue sundress made of T-shirt material and pack as fast as I can. I know Monroe is on the way over. Traffic will slow her down some, but the last thing I want to do is end up in a confrontation with her.

"What in the hell am I doing?" I mutter as I shove my nightdress, three pairs of panties, a pair of jeans, a T-shirt, and a dress to wear to the ceremony in my bag. Since I'm staying at my mom's house, I needn't take anything else with me. Whatever I don't have, I'll just borrow from her.

I rush out the front door and lock it. I can feel

Monroe nearby. We have to get out of here and fast. I trot down the steps, hop into the front seat of Vince's SUV, and strap the seatbelt around me.

"Let's get out of here," I say.

Vince is staring at me as if I'm a ghost.

"Drive," I say urgently.

"Are you running away from someone?" he asks.

"Monroe is on her way. I don't want to run into her right now, so can you just get us the hell out of here?"

He nods as if he gets it. "Aye, aye, Captain."

His lopsided smile is infectious. I feel like holding his hand like old times, but I have to remind myself these are new times. Vince drives down the hill, and I lose sight of the ocean. Now that there's nothing for me to look at but the dashboard, it dawns on me that my ex-boyfriend and I are driving to Las Vegas in order to attend my divorced parents' wedding. On top of that, I, Maggie Conroy, am avoiding my business partner and my clients. In all my years, I have never neglected work duties.

"By the way, I handled your car," he says. "Tyler is going to drive it to my place."

I frown. I don't get what Vince is trying to do. "Why couldn't he drive it to Jack's house?"

"I don't have the key to Jack's garage. I didn't

want to leave a car like yours just sitting in front of the house for who knows how long."

He's right. Deep inside, I know I don't plan to return to L.A. for some time. I've never visited my mom's house in Las Vegas, but growing up, she was the best roommate I ever had. Leah knows how to settle on her side of the house and give me space to move freely on my side.

"You've got a point," I say.

"And you don't have to worry about Monroe. We talked," Vince says.

I whip my gaze onto his face. "You did? When?"

"She called me while you were in the house."

I snort. "I guess you're still at the top of my emergency contacts list. Anyway, what did you say to her? What did she say to *you*?"

He grins. "First, I'm okay with being at the top of your emergency contacts list. Second, she was mad as hell, but I explained that you need a break."

"You explained?"

He nods. "I did, Maggie, and lo and behold, she understood."

I narrow an eye. "Really? What did you say?"

Vince takes a right turn onto the main highway. I can relax more now that I know Monroe isn't hunting me down. She can be relentless, especially when she thinks I'm in the wrong and I owe her an explanation.

"I told her you need a break, and I'm going to see that you get one."

I laugh facetiously. "You told her that I lost my marbles, didn't you?"

Vince comes to a stop at a red light and turns to look at me. "You haven't lost your marbles."

He said that with such authority that I want to believe him. "How do you know?"

"You were bound to burn out."

A car honks from behind us. Vince peels his eyes off my face and puts them on the road. The light has turned green. Now that the ocean is visible again, I watch the beach until Vince turns onto the 10 Freeway.

Suddenly I'm back in my old office at A&Rt in Manhattan. The lights are dim. There's no one here but me. I glare at Vincent's office, which is past the aisle cut between two rows of cubicles. I wait with bated breath. My heart is heavy. Tears well up in my eyes. I feel as if when I finally see Vince, he'll hurt me. Regardless, I can't look away. I incline my body forward as the door to his office creeps open. My heartache intensifies. I don't want to see. I try to shut my eyes, but they won't close. A woman with a high-pitched voice laughs. I think I hear Vince laugh too, but I'm not certain.

I cover my ears. "No." I feel Vince's hand on my thigh, and I open my eyes and look down.

"Maggie," he says as he tries to keep his eyes on the road and me too.

I fell asleep. I sit up. The leather crunches beneath me. "Bad dream, I guess." I squint out the window. "How long have I been asleep?"

"About an hour and a half."

A blur of dry fields, bushes, rocks, and sand pass before my eyes. I feel loopy but hungry. "I could eat a horse."

"There's a diner not too far away. We'll stop there and get a bite to eat."

I rub my eyes until I'm able to focus. "Thanks."

I turn to look at Vince. I want to ask if he stopped by his place to get anything for an overnight stay, but maybe he isn't planning on staying the night. It would be very much like Vince to drop me off. He's truly playing papa hen with me. It's sort of refreshing, but I think that once we make it to Mom's and we part ways, it'll be best if we sever all ties. However, for the moment, I try to think of him as a good guy who did a favor for a woman in her moment of weakness—and a silly weakness it is.

"So, Maggie," he says as if he's about announce something very important.

"Yes?" I'm jumpy.

He glances at me. "I want to tell you that I have no hard feelings, and I hope you don't either."

I shrug. "I don't." I think.

We fall silent. I'm kind of stunned that he would say that.

Vince touches the stereo. "Do you want to listen to some music?"

I don't want to hear any noise except the low hum of the engine. I have to figure out my damn life —what will it be from this point on? I lower the back of my seat, curl up into a ball, and face away from him. "Not really."

He moves his hand from the stereo to my hip. "I hate seeing you this way, Mags."

I should tell him to move his hand, but I don't want to. "I hate being this way," I mutter.

"So you don't like the work you do, is that right?"

I nod.

"You're good at it."

"A prostitute's good at... sex, but it doesn't mean she enjoys it." I wanted to say fucking, but I remembered the deal I made with Leah. "I just..."

"You just don't want to do it anymore. And you

know more than anyone that it's your choice to make. That's what I like about you. You're brave enough to make hard decisions. Even if they're crazy as hell."

We chuckle. I flip over to face him. Vince removes his hand, and I curl back up into the fetal position.

"I can't believe I left A&Rt the way I did."

Vince keeps looking straight ahead. "You had your reasons."

"I guess I did."

We go silent.

"We had a good thing, didn't we?" he asks.

"I thought so." I feel as if my answer isn't adequate. I sigh. "I've had time to give *us* some thought." Vince keeps stealing glances at me, and I pull my seat up. "When all I had left was work, my life felt like a lot of work. I don't know. That felt insufficient somehow."

I'm waiting for his response, but he keeps his eyes on the road. I have a slight panic attack. What was I hoping to accomplish by revealing that? Do I really want to rekindle my relationship with Vince? He has a girlfriend. I can see by the way he's tightened his jaw that he wants me to remember that.

I face forward. "Anyway, I've been thinking about

Daisy opening that bakery. That's such a drastic shift from being a travel writer."

"Remember what I said the other night?"

I'm relieved when he finally glances at me, but I'm confused.

"I said you can come back to A&Rt whenever you felt like it. I meant it."

A face comes to my mind. "I don't want to rain all over Linda's program."

"I know you wouldn't. That's not your style."

I smile at him. "It isn't."

"Now that Robert's gone, I could use a solid VP of Acquisitions."

"I never thought Robert's leaving would result in such a hefty promotion. I still don't know what the hell he did all day long, besides pretend to be an executive."

Vince's expression turns intense. I certainly get it. I don't get to slam Robert anymore, not after I fucked him.

"There's the diner," he says.

I retreat into myself. I feel as if Robert is in the SUV, sitting right between us. Vince steers the vehicle off the highway toward the diner set in the middle of nowhere. It looks like the kind of restaurant depicted in slasher films. Its only saving grace is the number of cars in the parking lot. There aren't too many, but I see enough to make me believe that they aren't going to go all chainsaw murder on us and grind Vince and me up for tomorrow's double-cheeseburger special. Vince finds a parking spot near the entrance. I'm relieved when he smiles at me after he turns off the engine.

"By the way, you look pretty," he says, staring into my eyes.

I can only hold his gaze for a few seconds before looking away bashfully. "Thanks." I open the door and hop out.

My feet hit the ground, and I hear Vincent's door slam. I close my door. He's already waiting for me to walk alongside him. I'm too starved to worry about what sort of conversation I can drum up to keep the awkwardness at bay. The closer we get to the entrance, the more I can smell the fried foods sizzling on a flat grill. Every now and then, it's good to put the arteries to the test. Vince opens the door for me and touches my waist to halt me before I walk past the hostess station. I'm quite aware that this is the third time he's touched me since I climbed in his passenger seat and agreed to let him drive me to Las Vegas.

A pretty young lady with jet-black hair and an

over-made face shuffles from the kitchen to the hostess station. "A table for two?"

"Yes," Vince says.

She flexes her eyebrows at his gorgeous face then looks at his hand, which is still on my hip. "This way, please."

We follow. Vince's hand is warm and heavy. He only takes it off of me when I sit on one side of the booth. He takes the other side.

The young lady focuses her attention totally on Vince. "Your waiter will be over shortly."

I'm used to being ignored by women when I'm with him, but I've never conceded to it. I lift my finger to get her attention. "Excuse me, I'm not invisible. I'm a customer too."

She flinches, taken aback. "Oh."

Vince's smile grows.

"Just making you aware that at the moment, you're not being as polite to me as you are to him," I say to her.

"Oh," she says again.

I shrug. "Hey, I say this from woman to woman— I wouldn't devalue your presence and legitimize his."

The woman grimaces as though she has to really think about what I just said. "Right," she says, still looking confused. She walks away wearing a frown.

Vince chuckles. "Just couldn't let her get away with it, could you?"

I throw up my hands. "What?"

"Nothing. It's just one of many things I like about you."

I pause to think about what he just said. "Well, you're the one man besides my dad, and Jack, and a bit of Charlie, who likes my crazy."

"Ha!" Vince says, grinning bigger than I've seen in ages. "I think Charlie likes your crazy more than you like your crazy."

I smirk. "You think I like my crazy?"

"You love your crazy."

I grunt thoughtfully. I don't really want to talk about what's wrong with me or not. I rub my belly. "Damn—dang—jeez, not shit, I'm hungry."

Vince laughs again. "Why did the deal Leah made with you entail you not cursing?"

I furrow my eyebrows. "Leah? You say her name as though she's your old friend."

"Hi!" a tall lanky guy says.

Vince and I rip our stares away from each other and look at our waiter.

The waiter nods at our closed menus that are still sitting on the table. "Do you still need time to decide?"

Vince shakes his head. "You have the standard diner food?"

The waiter snorts. "Pretty much."

"Then we'll order. She'll have the cheeseburger with grilled onions, mustard, and ketchup..." Vince narrows one eye at me, waiting for consensus.

I shrug. "That's it. With french fries and a cup of coffee."

"And I'll have the double cheeseburger with fries. Get us two bottled waters and two coffees."

"Bottled?" the waiter asks as if that threw him off.

Vince winks at him. "Unless you've got cocktails."

The waiter laughs and swipes our menus off the table. "Two bottled waters and two coffees coming up."

Once he's gone, Vince and I smile at each other. It's just like old times. I've racked my brain trying to figure out what made Vince and I tick, besides work. Well, it was moments like this.

"So are you driving back tonight?" I ask.

Vince looks at me as if I'm insane. "What do you mean?"

"You didn't stop by your place to pack a bag, so I thought you were just going to drop me off and drive back. I mean, you do have Cindy at home, I guess."

"Cindy isn't at my place in L.A., and I'm not driving back tonight or tomorrow morning. It sounded like your mom extended the invitation to the both of us."

"Okay." I'm certainly happy to hear that I'll be spending more time with Vince. "Are you going to wear what you have on to the wedding tomorrow?"

"Mags, I have a penthouse in Vegas, remember?"

"You keep toiletries and the like in the penthouse?"

Vince smirks. "What do you think?"

I go back into my book of Vincent Adams. His chateau in Aspen is furnished and stocked from end to end. So is his chateau in the Alps and his apartment in Manhattan. I nod as I get it. "So you're going to stay at your place on Las Vegas Boulevard?"

He shakes his head. "I'm going to stay at your mom's house." He nudges his chest. "I'm her guest too, Mags."

"I know. You said that already."

"Well, it sounds as if you're trying to get rid of me."

I roll my eyes. "Give me a break, Vince. You're being dramatic."

Vince smirks as he studies me.

"What?" I ask.

He shakes his head.

"It's something," I say.

"It's just I miss this?"

I gaze out the window. The sunlight reflects off the mountain range on the horizon. It's beautiful. I've never taken the time to notice something like that. "So where's Robert Tango these days anyway?"

Vince is silent for too long. I turn to look at him. He's tightened his mouth.

"He's in San Francisco," he says.

"Doing what?"

"Do you care?"

I shrug. "Just making small talk."

His furrowed eyebrows go from showing anger to curiosity. "When was the last you spoke to Rob?"

"Oh man, a long time ago." I scrunch up my face. "Not since when I was in London with Delta Lunatic and Francesca Frightening."

That gets Vince chuckling again. "You're naming your clients?"

"Yes. There's Ed Dickhead, Fiona Effing Airhead, Silly Sam Edging-fuck." I slap my hand over my mouth. "Oh shit, I said fuck."

Vince tosses his head back and laughs. My eyes dance as I watch him. I think making him laugh is my favorite thing in the world. He simmers down, and now we're caught in a moment.

"I never thought you would sound bitter when it comes to work," he says.

I roll my eyes. "Me neither. But I am. I'm just... I'm burnt out, Vince. And I don't know what to do about it other than selling my interest in our company."

He lifts a finger. "Sorry, but really, you haven't seen or spoken to Robert since London?"

"No, not since London." I snicker. "What? You thought we've been getting it on or something?"

"I didn't know what to think."

It's time to nip this in the bud. If we're going to exist as friends, associates, or two people who live on the same Earth, then we really have to put the whole Robert Tango incident to bed.

I sit back and square my shoulders. "Vince, I'm sorry I had sexual relations with Robert Tango."

He lifts his hand. "Mags..."

I lift a hand. "No, let me finish. I guess I could've banged someone else to get back at you for how you were making me feel. I know that screwing Robert was the lowest of the low blows." My mind travels back to that night. "When you caught us, I felt bad but justified."

We're staring at each other.

"How long had you been wanting to fuck Robert?"

"The truth?"

He shrugs.

"Sometimes I wondered, but I never would have ever gone through with it if it weren't for all the shit that led up to me doing it with him."

Vince sniffs cynically. "You're saying it was my fault."

I shrug. "Kind of."

This time we're engaged in a stare off, locking horns for the very first time since our breakup.

Vince sighs as if he's giving in. "All right, I fucked Emily first…"

The waiter approaches with our coffee, cream, sugar, and water. "Sorry for the delay. We're having a problem in the kitchen, but your order will be up real soon."

"That's fine," Vince says.

We watch the waiter until he's out of earshot.

"You did fuck Emily first," I say. I don't want to lose momentum. "Not only did you fuck her, but you made her your new girlfriend while I was still your girlfriend. I mean, who does that?"

Vince rubs the back of his neck. Good. I've

gotten to him. "Okay, what I did was stupid. But you know, Mags, I just didn't think you were going to change."

"Change into what? A debutante like Emily? Like Cindy O'Lay?"

"What the hell do you mean by debutante?"

"A woman whose goal in life is to be presented to the world on the arm of some fine stag like yourself."

"You say that like being in love is the seventh deadly sin."

I rip open a packet of raw sugar. "Did I mention being in love? Lassoing a stag rarely has anything to do with love."

"I felt like I was fucking begging you to marry me."

I sigh forcefully. "Can you not curse? Because if you curse, then I'm going to want to curse."

Vince tilts his head as if he can't believe I said that. "Deal. I won't curse."

"All right. You know about the marriage thing. Maybe I was afraid. Life gets into your cells and affects your brain and emotions. My mom and dad didn't have an amicable divorce. She did the most unwise shit. I mean stuff. She talked about how bad of a dad and husband Isak was. Told me all about his affairs. I had to hear all their court action blow-by blow. And my mom just wanted to take and take from him, bleed him dry. And to me, my dad wasn't a bad guy. So if he was the worst husband, then hell, other women's husbands must be horrible as hell."

"You're not your mom, and I'm not your dad."

I empty the sugar into my coffee and pour in cream. "You can say that again. And they're getting remarried. Here's what I'm afraid of… my dad is the one making a mistake by remarrying her. I mean, he got out while the getting was good."

Vince narrows one eye. "Are we talking about them or us?"

"I don't know, maybe us. Maybe you too got out while the getting was good."

Vince snorts and shakes his head. "You can always find a way."

I'm confused, but Vince doesn't have to explain himself because our burgers arrive. We're both so hungry that we do more eating than talking. He feels comfortable enough to feed more details about Robert Tango.

"I think he partnered with Jack in commercial real estate," Vince says.

Thank goodness I hadn't swallowed just before he said that; I would've choked. I had hoped Robert Tango would get so far away from my life that I would never have to think about him again. I can't blame him for ruining my happiness by seducing me. "Really?"

"I'm surprised Jack didn't say anything to you."

"Well, he's got himself all wrapped up in business with Daisy and her cousin."

"Anton?"

"The good-looking French guy."

Vince shifts and scratches the back of his neck. "Have you met Anton?"

"Fourth of July on Martha's Vineyard."

Vince stares at me. I can see that he's wondering if I slept with Anton or not.

"He brought his girlfriend," I say to put him at ease.

"Oh."

"And I'm not his type."

"You're every guy's type, Maggie."

"Says you."

We share another lingering look. Why does Vince affect me so? He makes my heart gravitate out of my chest and merge with his. It's easier to be over Vince when he's on the other side of the country and poking a supermodel named Cindy O'Lay. Our breakup seems more definite that way.

To change the subject, I make a comment about

how picturesque the mountains are. "I never noticed stuff like that before."

"I can show you some picturesque places," Vince says.

I feel my eyebrows pull together. Once again, Cindy O'Lay comes to mind. "Why didn't you wait at least a year to acquire a new girlfriend?"

Vince seems caught off guard by my question. "I don't know. Is Cindy my girlfriend?"

"What does Cindy think?"

Vince tosses one of his last few fries back on the plate. "I don't know, Mags. I can't be by myself like you can. I need love."

"Then you love her?"

"That would be impossible." The waiter passes, and Vince waves. "Excuse me, can I have the check?"

I let go of the last thing he said and dig into my purse. "I'll get half."

Vince snickers. "Are you fucking kidding me? I appreciate the reach, but I got it."

"What do you mean? I was going to throw in a twenty."

"Keep your twenty-dollar bill." He digs his wallet out of his pocket and takes out a hundred-dollar bill.

"Do you want change or something?"

He winks. "I'm feeling generous."

"He wasn't that good. He was late with the coffee and the water had no ice."

Vince looks at me with one eye narrowed. "Are you messing with me, Maggie?"

I wink. "I am." Vince is normally a generous tipper.

The waiter returns with the check, and Vince gives him the hundred and tells him to keep the change. I feel more comfortable being alone with him now than I did before we came into the diner. We both go relieve ourselves before hitting the road again. Once we're in his SUV, I turn on the stereo. He has satellite radio, and he's very patient as I switch through channels and settle on the standards channel. Frank Sinatra is singing that he did it his way. I sing along to as many words as I can remember.

"You know that song?" Vince asks once it's over.

I bop my head merrily. "Monroe's mother used to have this old Hollywood fantasy. That was the universe she really wanted to live in, so she played standards all the time. Monroe and I didn't mind."

"Monroe is really like your sister, isn't she?"

"She is my sister."

"Then whatever decision you make regarding the business, she should understand."

I twist my lips thoughtfully. "Monroe would never abandon me. She's always been the unstable one of the two of us, and I feel as if my ego won't allow me to fall off the pedestal she puts me on." I fall back in my seat with a sigh. "Hell, do I need that from her? Worship?" I look to Vince for the answer.

He glances at me then puts his eyes back on the road. "Hell, I hope not."

I take a moment to really get in touch with my emotions. Am I really running away without telling Monroe what's going on inside me because I'm afraid that she'll think we're more alike than different? Is my shit really not as together as I thought? I rub my temples and close my eyes. "Route 66" by Nat King Cole plays. It's one of my favorites, and I sing a few lines, letting the song take precedence over my emotional dilemma.

"Hey…" Vince turns down the volume. "You should call Monroe when we get to your mom's. You should tell her exactly what you told me. I think it's time she hears it."

I study Vince's profile. He can't say things like that to me while being the one man I can never love.

"I will. But you should call Cindy O'Lày later tonight and let her know that you're with me," I say.

He side-eyes me. "Don't worry about Cindy. I'll do the right thing as far as she's concerned."

Suddenly my heart flutters. "I'm going to do the right thing too."

"What's that?"

I grin. "Take the good advice you gave me."

Vince steals a glance at me. He's smiling. I love his smile. I turn the volume back up, make myself comfortable, and really let those old standards that formed Monroe's and my childhood take me away.

17

TRUTH NO LIES

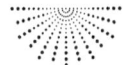

I tell Vince about living at Jack and Daisy's. I mention the walks on the beach, the blackout curtains, and the personal chef, who has made me way healthier than I was before I moved in. For a very short while, Vince tells me about the new projects they're considering for Prime D TV. I try to think of something constructive to lend to the subject, but I have nothing. Instead I smile and listen.

"Prime D TV is costing us more money than we're bringing in, but I don't want it to fail." For the first time, Vince pauses and waits for my response.

I sigh. "Just acquire less costly programming."

"That's easier said than done."

"It just takes more patience and less cronyism."

"You didn't have any reaction to my vague offer."

"You mean the Vice President of Acquisitions suggestion you made?"

"It was an offer, Mags. I'd like to have you back on our team."

I gaze out at the Vegas landscape, which now lingers in the distance. It's early evening, and the lights compete with the diminishing daylight. I've never been a fan of Vegas. I wonder if there's anything significant about Las Vegas other than the booze, gambling, and prostitution, legal and illegal. I've never been willing to discover the answer until now. Actually, I'm ready to discover anything and everything. The sky is the limit, and I'm not sure if returning to A&Rt Media is regressive or progressive.

"I don't know," I say. "I'll think about it."

"I'll be waiting for your answer," he says.

Vince transfers my mother's address from his messenger to his GPS and starts the navigator. Since it's late Monday, the second wave of weekenders are leaving, making traffic very thin. We take the 215 Freeway, driving away from all the excitement. I'm surprised my mom doesn't live closer to the Strip or out in the middle of nowhere in an oasis in the desert. She used to hate Aunt Carlotta's affluent neighborhood. The houses were luxurious and there was enough space between neighbors to offer a morsel of privacy, but my mom used to say that she could smell the consensus. I never cared to know what she meant by that, but after listening to her continuously recite her list of issues about why she couldn't bear to remain in Colorado for more than three months, I sort of figured out what she meant. She called Aunt Carlotta's neighbors a bunch of people who were as small-minded as they were wealthy.

My mom's neighborhood in Las Vegas looks an awfully lot like that neighborhood. However, I don't have the will to needle my mom about it. People live and learn. Vince lived in Aunt Carlotta's neighborhood. Yeah, he loves dating supermodels, but he sure doesn't concur with some stagnant way of seeing the world. Of course, his mom and sisters do, but not Vince.

We pass three-story adobe-styled homes and modern Spanish mini-mansions. The yards are nicely landscaped with rocks and clay. The GPS announces that our destination is on the right, and Vince pulls into the driveway of one of the three-story adobe-styled houses. He drives slowly up the roundabout, which gives my mom time enough to run out the front door and wave from the veranda. She's really happy to see us, and I'm happy to see her too. Vince comes to a stop. We grin at each other.

"Thank you for bringing me," I say.

He winks, gazes into my eyes for a long moment, and hops out of the driver's seat. I wonder what he meant by not responding to my gratitude. Regardless, I hop out of the vehicle. Vince retrieves my bag out of the backseat.

"Hi, Mom!" I call.

Leah walks toward me with her arms outstretched for a hug. She looks so happy—genuinely happy. When she ran to Vegas with Cobey years ago, her happiness seemed more like that of someone running off to practice some strange new religion. I give her a hug, and she holds me tight. I close my eyes and let myself receive the warmth she's emitting.

"How are you doing, lovely?" she asks.

"I'm fine," I lie, sort of. The drive with Vince was pleasant, but I'm still confused about how to proceed with my future.

"I spoke with Roe," she says, meaning Monroe.

I glance at Vince.

"Oh, Vincent," she says as if she's just seeing him.

Leah hugs him. "Thank you for driving Maggie here on such short notice."

"It wasn't a problem," he says.

"I bet it wasn't," she says slyly then pulls me along. "Come on in, you two. Let me show you your new family home." My mom has always led me to believe that her home is my home.

The inside of the house is decorated in the Southwestern style. She has Navajo blankets across her brown leather sofas and Navajo rug art on the walls and floors. I remember that she used to be more into overloaded bookshelves, purple velvet furniture, and black-and-white stills of New York City. She used to decorate with trinkets, including modern art pieces she picked up from here or there but cost an arm and a leg, nude statues, and chandeliers. In here, there's more but less. She has two light stick trees in two corners of the living room, cute wooden end tables at each end of the U-shaped sectional, one furry white arm chair, and a few trinkets like glass ravens, metal baskets, and crystals.

"This is different," I say, admiring the warm lighting throughout the house.

"I'm different, lovely. That's what happens when you grow up."

I hold on to those words.

"You have a nice house," Vince says.

"Thank you," my mom replies.

"So where should I take Maggie's bag?"

"You're not staying?"

Vince thumbs over his shoulder. "I have to make a run to my place on the Strip."

My mom studies him as if she's assessing him. "I see..."

I take the handle of my bag. "I can take my bag from here."

Vince puts his hand on mine. "I got it."

I quickly remove my hand as I try to downplay the sparks shooting up my arm. "Okay."

My mom shows us to our rooms on the third floor. Vince and I are semi-neighbors; a huge bathroom separates our rooms. When Vince sets my bag on the bed, the moment is awkward. We've never slept in such close proximity without sharing the same bed. On top of that, as we make our way back downstairs, my mother tells us that her bedroom is on the first floor, facing a mosaic-tiled swimming pool, which is the next stop on her tour. Basically, Vince and I will be alone upstairs. Just thinking about it makes me anxious.

Vince and I admire the swimming pool, which resembles a healing pool. My mom was never spastic, but she was never close to being the tranquil individual standing beside me now.

Leah claps. "So... dinner! Will you be back in time to join us, Vince?"

"Of course," he says, looking me in the eyes.

I force myself to break eye contact and focus on the shimmering water. "Where's Dad?"

"He was working as of"—she checks her watch —"five minutes ago. He'll be home for dinner."

"You cooked?"

"Don't sound so surprised, Magnolia. It's not hard to season a steak, blend some soup, and toss a salad."

She's bragging, and I like it. "Look at you, Mom."

We smile at each other.

"Well, I'm going to head to my place and gather some things," Vince says.

The practical side of me wants to suggest that he stay on the Strip. It doesn't make sense for him to stay with my mom if he has a luxury penthouse at a five-star hotel—unless we're together. However, my mom's house does offer a more tranquil environment. I should stop deluding myself. Vince seems to be here for me. Does he want me back? I'm not sure. Do I want him back? Yes.

"All right," I say, playing it cool, and turn to

address my mom. "Do you need any help in the kitchen?"

"I don't need help cooking, but I do need tons of your attention."

VINCE

Maggie's scent lingered in the car. Vince took in a deep breath of her smell as he drove. He hadn't felt this good since they were together. He had walked behind her as Leah led them upstairs. Her ass was monumental. All he'd wanted to do was grab two handfuls of it and slam his dick so deep inside her that he would come on first thrust. There was no way he would last long if they fucked again. Vince wanted her. He wanted her bad.

He flipped his thoughts so that his dick would get softer. Leah Conroy was an interesting woman. She was nothing like Maggie had described her. According to Maggie, Leah had suffered a mental break and run to Las Vegas to immerse herself in the depths of debauchery in Sin City. He had suggested twice that they take a weekend to visit her mother, but Maggie was always too busy. In a way, one of the reasons he had chosen to end their relationship was that Maggie didn't value family more than business. It made him believe she was genuinely cold-blooded. He most definitely loved Maggie, and hot damn did he lust her, but Vince always wondered whether or not he liked her.

Then he'd seen her at Chuck and Angel's party. Vince wasn't convinced that not liking Maggie, or the fact that she fucked Robert, was enough to keep him from needing her. He had been driving all day with an engorged dick. At one point, he'd wanted to stop the damn vehicle and ask Maggie if she was interested in stopping at the first hotel they found and getting a room for an hour or two so they could flat-out fuck and get it over with.

Vince grinned from ear to ear as he exited the highway. Maggie hadn't spoken to Robert since London. That was a long time ago. He'd often driven himself crazy wondering if they were still fucking. Imagining Maggie getting it on with Robert had made him prolong his relationship with Cindy. Vince wiped the grin off his face. Shit. He had to end it with Cindy.

Vince thought of a number of ways to tell Cindy it was over without hurting her. He wasn't opposed to the popular "it's me, not you" spicl. That was guaranteed to work. He could tell her that he needed to be a single man and figure out what he really wanted. What he wanted was Maggie. He considered telling Cindy the truth. Apart from being in love with Maggie, he just wasn't that into Cindy.

Vince stopped in front of the main doors of the hotel. The valet ran over to assist him, and Vince informed him that he would be in and out within fifteen minutes. He strolled quickly into the hotel, keeping his head down to make sure he didn't run into anyone he might know. He often ran into business associates in the lobby, but he didn't want anyone or anything to impede his progress. Vince reached the elevators that would take him to the residents' floor. He presented his pass to the operator, a college student in a black suit and funny hat.

"Mr. Adams?" he said.

Vince nodded.

"You have a visitor waiting for you. Cindy O'Lay."

For one second, Vince thought he may have gotten trapped in the *Twilight Zone*. He rubbed the back of his neck. Hell, Cindy could ruin his whole night. "Who let her in?"

"I let her in. She said you were expecting her," the elevator operator said.

"Is that all it takes to get the hell inside of my apartment?"

The guy's eyes grew wide. "Oh... I'm sorry, Mr. Adams. I didn't know."

Vince sighed forcefully. He wanted to choke the guy for being stupid. "Just forget about it. What's done is done."

The elevator was getting closer to the top floor. Vince considered telling the operator to take him back to the lobby, but it was better to deal with Cindy now, while he had a chance.

"I'm really sorry, sir," the operator said.

"I said forget about it."

"I mean, she's Cindy O'Lay."

Vince ruffled his eyebrows.

"If you don't mind me saying, she's not just some random chick. You know?" He looked at Vince as if Cindy's mere physicality should get him off the hook.

The elevator stopped, and the doors slid open.

"Right," Vince said. He dug into his pocket and gave him a twenty-dollar bill anyway. He took two steps before he was struck by illumination. The elevator operator had given him a valuable piece of enlightenment. "Hold up!"

The operator quickly opened the doors.

Vince took three twenty-dollar bills out of his pocket and gave them to the operator "Thank you."

"For what?" The operator held the cash, looking bewildered.

"For your wisdom." Vince spun around and strolled to the door of his penthouse.

The guy had hit the nail on the head. Cindy wasn't just some random chick. She was a sought-after supermodel who could get just about any man she wanted. Unlike Maggie, who could do the same, Cindy threw her appeal around like a wet rag at a car wash.

Vince braced himself then smashed his thumb on the lock-plate. The door unlocked, and he entered. The house lights were off, but the lights of the Las Vegas skyline reflected off the walls. For one second, Vince hoped that Cindy had come to her senses and left, but the elevator operator would've told him that. He heard a sniff and looked at the back of the head of the person sitting on the sofa.

"You didn't take my calls." Cindy's voice quaked. She had been crying.

"Oh," Vince said.

"What are you doing in Vegas?"

Vince felt trapped where he was standing. "I'm here visiting some friends."

Cindy stood. "You're lying! You're here with Maggie!"

Vince looked at the light switch and rushed over to flip it on. The makeup around Cindy's eyes was smudged, and her face was patchy. He checked her hands. She sounded as if she'd brought a gun and was planning on shooting him for cheating on her.

Vince didn't want to make a bad situation worse, so he lifted his hands in surrender. "I'm here with you now."

She slapped her chest. "I love you, Vince, and you love me."

"Let's just talk about it. How about I fix us a drink?" He slowly moved toward the bar.

"I don't want a drink. I want you to tell me that you're not going to leave me for her."

Oh hell, did he need that drink. "Let's just have a drink."

"I'll kill myself, Vince. I promise I'll kill myself."

"Don't say that, Cindy," Vince said.

He realized that he was trapped in the hellish depths of Cindy's breakdown. He needed help, but he had no one to call other than Maggie, and the situation wasn't safe for her. Desperation was written all over Cindy's face. He poured himself a vodka and tonic with more tonic than vodka. It was important to maintain a sober mind. The trick was to convince Cindy she was better off without him.

Vince took a hefty gulp of his drink.

Cindy walked toward him. "It's true. You're the one for me." She wrapped her arms around his neck and held on tightly.

All Vince could think about was the taste of Maggie's tongue in his mouth and her body against his. He needed to hold her. Nothing was going to get in the way of him making love to Maggie tonight, especially Cindy.

"You can't even hug me," Cindy spat.

She pushed his chest, but he didn't budge, so she did it again and again. After the fifth time, Vince grabbed her by the wrists.

"What are you going to do?" she snarled. "Hit me! Hit me!"

Vince let go of her and took two big steps away. He grabbed his phone.

"Who are you calling?" she asked.

"Security." He dialed.

"No! Please hang up."

Vince clung to the receiver. He needed to think fast. Cindy was shaking, and her eyes were glazed over as if she'd lost her ability to reason. Would she abuse herself and scream rape?

"What the fuck, Cindy? You're beautiful, and I'm just some guy," he said in a desperate act to get her to appear normal.

"Is that what you think?"

Not really, but he'd already said it, and it was clear from her reaction that talking her up and putting himself down wouldn't work. "I think we met at a bad time in my life."

Cindy's gaze fell to his hand, which was still wrapped around the receiver. She was still freaking him out. Vince hit the zero.

"Hang up," Cindy pleaded.

The operator asked if she could help him.

"Could you please get security to Penthouse 6502? I need them now," Vince said.

"Yes, sir," the operator said.

"Could you stay on the line with me until security gets here?" The last thing he needed was to be falsely accused of physically abusing Cindy O'Lay.

"Um, yes, sir. Do you need emergency assistance?"

"I'll figure that out after security arrives."

Cindy calmly sat on the sofa and stared out the window. "You didn't have to do this."

Vince looked around the living room. The place had marble floors, luxurious furnishings, and vivid wall art of the Las Vegas city and desert landscapes. He'd hired someone to decorate it and couldn't remember who. It occurred to him that he'd treated Cindy like the objects in the penthouse, as if she was an expensive arm-piece. But she wasn't an arm-piece. She was a fucking woman with feelings and a heart and her own insecurities, and he'd fucked up all of those things.

"Call off security," he said to the operator. The operator was speaking, but he hung up on her.

Cindy turned her head. "You don't have to treat me like this."

"I don't know, Cindy. You said you were going to kill yourself."

She wiped her eyes. "I was being fucking foolish. Are you really going to break my heart, Vince?"

He studied her profile. Two months they had been dating, and it was as if he was finally seeing her for the first time.

Someone pounded on the door. "Security!" said a deep, burly voice.

Cindy faced forward as Vince went to answer the door. He told the two oversized ex-athletes that all was good and thanked them for answering his call. Then he sat beside Cindy, who was very still. Tears flowed from her eyes like a leaking faucet.

"I'm sorry, Cindy," he said.

"You didn't love me?" she asked in a quiet voice.

Vince remained silent. He didn't want to hurt her with truth.

"I need you to say it. Own it." She took a deep breath and wiped her eyes.

"I didn't love you. I couldn't, because I already loved somebody else."

Cindy whimpered then caught herself. She gulped. "Can you just sit with me for a while?"

Maggie was waiting. Dinner was waiting. Vince had looked forward to a pleasant evening of getting to know Leah and Isak a lot better. But he owed Cindy at least this. He put his arm around her shoulder, and she shrugged away.

"Don't hold me. Just sit."

Vince was surprised she had rejected his affection. He put his arms at his sides. "Okay. I'll just sit."

They both gazed out across the Vegas skyline.

"Do you think she's prettier than me?" Cindy's voice disturbed the settling silence.

Vince didn't want to answer that, because he had learned a lesson that Cindy hadn't yet learned. "It's not about that."

"A lot of men were looking at her at the party.

She's too smart to notice. Is that what you love about her?"

Vince could see the self-degrading road Cindy wanted to travel down. She was looking for an easy reason why Vince loved Maggie and not her.

"Love is rarely about how the other person looks. We all have beauty. We all work hard. You work hard, don't you?"

Cindy frowned. "I guess I do."

"You do. You see what you want out of life, and you go for it. That's why you're Cindy O'Lay."

"She's Maggie Conroy. I've heard of her, you know."

"That's not it. What Maggie and I have is different."

"How?"

"Maggie and I connect on different level."

"But how?"

"I'm the me that I want to be when I'm around her. And if I lose that better version of me that being around her makes me, then I'll feel lost."

Cindy watched him as if everything he said had confused her. She was still in her early twenties. She had no idea how to wait for the real thing. She wanted the evidence of love but not the truth of love. Vince had often smiled while she spoke of her ticking biological clock. She wanted to be married before she turned thirty and have her first child before she turned thirty-three. Cindy was looking for a man with means so she could end her lucrative modeling career. Vince had no doubt she would find the man who would marry her for her beauty, give her the kids she wanted, and learn that there's rarely a true happily ever after when one makes the life choices that she was hell-bent on making.

"Is she good in bed or something?" Cindy asked.

"For me she is. The best way to explain that is that my soul makes love to Maggie's soul."

Cindy snorted as if some sort of subtle illumination had just struck her.

"What?" Vince asked.

"I don't want to believe it," she whispered.

"Believe what?"

"That she could be your soul mate. I want that for myself."

Vince heaved an internal sigh of relief. "Then you just might have to wait for it."

Cindy ruffled her eyebrows as if the thought of waiting for true love was a notion she couldn't quite wrap her head around.

WAKE ME UP

*M*y mom is cooking a peach tart for dessert. Not too long ago, I excused myself to call Monroe. I was in a good place after I got Leah up to speed about how Vince and I met, and now I'm lying on one of the wooden lounge chairs that surround the pool. Steam rises from the tranquil water. I fight the urge to pull off my dress and go for a swim, which sounds a lot more appealing than having this unavoidable conversation with Monroe.

I slide my finger down my contact list until I reach "Roe." It's time. No more delaying. I tap her name. The call rings twice, and she picks up. I wait for her to speak, but her silence says it all.

"Hey, Roe," I say squeamishly.

"Maggie." She's seething.

"I'm so sorry." I hope I say it like I mean it.

"No, you're not."

Silence falls between us. I think Monroe is hoping I'll rebut her claim. I love her too much to do that.

"You're in Vegas?" she asks, or more like states.

"Yes." My throat is tight.

"Leah and Isak are getting remarried?" There's a little joy in her voice, but only a little.

"Yes, they are."

"How did you get to Vegas?"

She already knows the answer. Monroe is going somewhere with this line of questioning. I would normally stop her by finding some way to get the upper hand, but I screwed up. She deserves the pleasure of making me sweat.

"Vince drove me," I say. "Listen, I don't know what's going on with me, but—"

"I do," she declares.

I balk. "You do?"

"Fix the shit between Vince and yourself, then get back to me," she says.

I shake my head at how utterly ridiculous that sounds. "I don't think Vince has anything to do with me not wanting to do this anymore."

"You're being vague. Do what?" She's back to all-the-way cold.

I sigh hard. "Care about the people we work for. I don't care about them."

"Do you care about them, or do you not care about them? I can't understand exactly what you were saying."

I think about our clients' skinny faces. They're all underweight and have large heads. "I don't care about them. Not one of them. They have fucking wealthy people's problems."

"Last time I checked, you were wealthy. Your cousins are wealthy. And your boyfriend is wealthy."

"Ex-boyfriend and—"

"And our clients are only wealthy, Maggie, because we keep them wealthy."

Her aggravating attitude makes me bold enough to just say it. "Well, I don't want to keep them wealthy anymore."

Monroe heaves a long, drawn-out sigh. "I'm going to hang up," she says, enunciating clearly. "Let's resume this conversation after you resolve your shit with Vince and the two of you have fucked until you both are all fucking full of fucking."

I roll my eyes, even if that last part sounds fun—as well as inevitable. "Vince and I are just friends."

Monroe chuckles facetiously. "Right. Good-bye." She hangs up.

"Hello?" I blow a hard breath. "I can't believe she just hung up on me."

"Who hung up on you?"

That voice sends bolts of joy through me. I spring to my feet. "Isak!"

My dad has on trendy jeans that fit him perfectly, a white button-front tailored shirt, and leather sneakers. Most men his age can't get away with dressing that way, but he can. Other than having an abundance of sex with loads of women, he's always believed in taking care of his body. Isak and I hug. He smells like expensive cologne and a long day of maneuvering his body to wield a camera.

He kisses my cheek. "Happy you came."

"Do I have a choice?"

"Yes, you do."

I study his face, looking for any sign of cold feet. "Are you absolutely sure you want to do this? I mean, Leah has certainly changed from the old days. But I think an alien has invaded her body, and once you're married, the alien will leave and the old Leah will return."

My dad snickers coolly. That's about as far as he

goes in the laughing department. "The old bait-and-switch."

"Precisely."

My dad ruffles his eyebrows. "The old Leah wasn't so bad. I liked the old Leah. Hell, I married her."

"But you divorced her too."

Isak looks at me cockeyed. "Sit."

I sit back down on the wooden lounge chair, and my dad sits on the one next to me.

"Until we got back together, I hadn't been involved with your mom since six years ago."

I grimace. Six years ago? They've been divorced for fifteen years! "What do you mean by 'involved'?" I ask.

"We run in the same circles."

"Are you saying you two were fucking up until six years ago?"

He sniffs. "You said fuck."

I roll my eyes. "Sorry."

"Keep your side of the bargain. Leah's been keeping hers."

"You're telling me she hasn't had a cigarette since Saturday?"

"Not one."

"How do you know?"

"She told me, and I trust her. You should try it sometimes."

I grunt as if what he just suggested is ridiculous. "I trust Mom."

"Then trust that she loves me and I love her. We've already wasted too much time being apart."

It dawns on me that I know exactly what he means. I bend over and start playing with my toes.

"Hey." Isak guides me to sit up straight. "What was that about?"

"What was what about?"

He sniffs. "You just checked out on me."

I frown, confused. Hell, I guess I did check out. I didn't even know I'd done that. "Oh…" I sigh. "It's just that you said something I can relate to and it…" I shrug.

"You're referring to Vincent Adams?"

I twist my mouth and nod.

"He told your mom you cheated on him."

I nod. "Did he tell her all of it?"

"He told her all of it."

I fight the urge to bend over and play with my toes again. "What do you think?" I shift in my seat.

"I think you are two intelligent individuals."

"Why do you say that?"

"Because you didn't get married first then end up

doing shit to each other. Marriage isn't a big Band-Aid. Loving each other as far as you need to in order to be ready to make that commitment is the Band-Aid. Sometimes it takes one year, sometimes two, and in your mom's and my case, it has taken fifteen years."

My dad studies me as I ponder his words. I think about all those good guys whose calls or visits I refused because they farted in bed, drove too selfishly, left goop in my sink, talked too much, didn't talk enough, were too close to their moms or their nosey sisters, and the list goes on. Vince has done everything on my "dump them for it" list more than twice—heck, more than ten times! Perhaps I didn't dismiss those pretty good guys for those actions. Most of them were successful, stable, and good-looking, but deep down, I knew they weren't *the one,* which was why I couldn't tolerate the things they did that irritated me. I smile at my dad, relishing my father's words of wisdom. I'm lucky. He's the reason why I didn't take the first decent guy who had all the things a girl looks for in a life partner. My dad and my mom taught me to go with my gut in every aspect of my life, including finding and being in love.

I kiss my dad's cheek. "I'm really happy for Mom and you. And me! I'm lucky to be your daughter."

Isak plants a tender kiss on my forehead. "Let's go see if your mom needs our help."

We stand, wrap an arm around each other's waist, and walk into the kitchen.

VINCE HAS BEEN GONE FOR OVER THREE HOURS. I TRY to phone him, but the call goes straight to voicemail. I suspect he never powered on his phone after powering down earlier. I'm worried, but a tiny voice inside me convinces me to let it go. I thought he and I had made a little progress, but maybe it was all in my head.

I carry the weight of disillusionment on my shoulders as I walk downstairs, gripping my cell phone. I make it to the dining room. Isak and Leah stop in the middle of laughing and look at me from the table.

"Well, is he on his way?" Leah asks.

I force a smile to hide my disappointment. "I couldn't reach him."

Leah's jolly expression settles into a frown. "What do you mean you couldn't reach him?"

I sit in front of the full glass of chardonnay I left at the table. "His phone was still off."

"And you're not concerned?" my mom asks.

"Well, yes, I guess."

She tilts her head, giving me the "disappointed mother" look.

"What?" I sigh. I already know why she's studying me that way. "I guess I can call his house phone."

"Well, that's an option." She's being facetious.

I get up.

"You don't have to leave to make the call. We're all friends."

I roll my eyes and sit back down. I search down the list of twenty-three numbers where I can reach Vince until I find *Las Vegas Flat – House*.

"Is it ringing?" my dad asks.

I glare at him, and he chuckles. He's screwing with me. The phone rings for the sixth time.

"He's not home," I say. I look at my parents, waiting for their permission to hang up.

"Then he must be on the way," my mom says.

"Or he isn't coming," I say.

"He's coming."

I'm on the tenth ring. "Well, can I hang up?"

"Hello," Vince says. His tone is lifeless.

Now I'm concerned. "Did I wake you?"

"Maggie?" he whispers.

"Yes. Listen, if you can't make it to dinner…"

He pauses. "It doesn't look like it."

I'm caught off guard by how short he's being. "Okay."

In the background, a woman asks who he's talking to. I'm sure it's Cindy O'Lay.

"Maggie, I'll call you back," Vince says.

I end the call, power off my phone, and slam it on the table. "He's with Cindy. Let's eat. I'm starving."

The disappointment I've been carrying on my shoulders has doubled in weight. I work hard as hell to not show my heartbreak on my face. I'm not even sure if I have the right to be heartbroken. She's his girlfriend, not me!

My mom's frown intensifies. "Do you mean Cindy O'Lay?"

"Yes. His girlfriend Cindy O'Lay."

"But she's in New York."

"Apparently she's not."

Mom gives my dad a look. "Isn't she shooting the Chiaroscuro Campaign for *WOF* magazine?"

She's referring to *Whispers of Fashion* magazine, the most popular fashion publication on the market. For a second, I think I might have misread the situation, but I'm sure I heard Cindy.

"Yeah, she is," my dad says.

I throw up my hands. "Mom, Dad, please can we eat dinner? Vince is with his girlfriend. I'm fine with it. Tonight is about the two of you. Please, can we let it drop?"

Thankfully my mom respects my request. She insists on making our plates because she's never done it before, and my dad and I tease her about it. We have a good laugh, and from that point on, I'm able to bury Vincent Adams way in the back of my mind.

"SO WHAT NEXT FOR YOU, LOVELY?" MY DAD ASKS.

When we're halfway through dinner, my parents tell me about their plan to sell their homes and buy a new one off the Kona Coast in Hawaii. They've already looked at six properties and are torn between two of them.

"We're flying to Hawaii the day after tomorrow," Isak says.

"We'll make our decision then," Leah says.

I notice the way they're looking at each other. They're speaking without words. Although I can't see under the table, I can tell that my dad just crossed his legs. He does that when my mom is in the room, they've had a discussion about me ahead of time, and he's ready to initiate the interrogation.

"Hey, lovely, what are your plans?" my dad asks.

I straighten up and keep on my toes. Things can get tricky during these interrogations since my mom and dad are excellent at prying and manipulating me, especially when they're working together.

"I don't know." I would love to leave it at that, but I'm positive my parents won't allow it.

"When do you plan on going back L.A.?" my mom asks.

I shrug. "Soon."

"Sweetheart, it's not like you to skip out on your work the way you did this morning," Isak says.

I slouch in my chair and stare at the lines in the table. They've done it. Score one for my parents for getting me to regress to my teenage years. "Don't I know it."

"Well, I do worry," Leah says cautiously.

"I'm worried too, Mom. I mean, I invested money and time into building Mo&Ma. Monroe and I made our company successful in a matter of months." I feel more like an adult, so I sit up. "I think we all have gifts. I thought mine was my ability to understand and affect public perception. I'm good at it."

"You're damn good at it," Leah says. "I've been following you career."

I smile. Of course she has. My mom has always had a way of keeping tabs on me without being physically or emotionally imposing. "Thanks, Mom. However, I think I'm over."

"Over?" Isak says, encouraging me to be less vague.

"Over affecting and persuading the public. I'm starting to become cynical about it."

"In what way?" he says.

"The fact that there's a need for what I do depresses me."

"Then do something else," Isak says.

I narrow an eye curiously. "Can I just leave my success behind like that?"

Isak pounds his fists on the table. "Yes, you can. Success is happiness, and if your work isn't making you happy, then it isn't success."

"Yeah," I say with a weary sigh. "I get your point, but I still don't know where else my talent lies."

"Then take some time to find out. Life isn't going anywhere. It's not a rat race."

"Maggie, you've been on full throttle ever since graduating from high school. You've never taken the time to figure out what you love about this world," Leah says.

I look from my mom to my dad. "I guess you're right."

"You have money saved up?" my dad asks.

I nod. "I do."

"Enough?"

"More than enough."

"Then take the year off to gain some perspective. Could you do that?"

I'm so full of happiness that I just might burst. For the first time in my life, I feel as if the sky's the limit. "I can!"

"And don't just gain perspective on your profession. Gain perspective on every aspect of your life— especially love," my mom says.

I smirk. "Wow, Mom, when did you become a romantic?"

She takes the bottle of wine and tops off my glass. "While you weren't visiting me." She points the top of the wine bottle at me. "Do not be a stranger ever again. Understand?"

I lift my full glass of wine. "I won't be a stranger, and I'm going to drink to that." I guzzle the entire glass.

I'm buzzed. I agree to fly to Hawaii with them the day after tomorrow and stay until Sunday. Then I'll return to L.A. and begin the process of giving Monroe complete control of Mo&Ma. I don't want to take Vince up on his offer to become VP of Acquisitions at A&Rt Media. His offer is tempting, but I just want to take the year to explore other parts of myself.

We spend the rest of the night talking about all my parents' old friends and who's divorced, who's remarried, and the terrible shit the divorced couples did to each other in the process of getting a divorce. They relish the opportunity to tell me how bad the kids of their divorced friends are doing and take every opportunity to pat themselves on the back for me not ending up that way. I let them take the credit.

And so, despite being brushed off by Vince, tonight is a good night.

ROCKS IN THE WINDOW

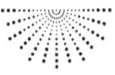

VINCE

*M*aggie's call to his house phone sent Cindy back over the edge. She paced in front of the floor-to-ceiling windows, begging him not to leave her. Vince felt trapped in a nightmare. He didn't know what to say, so he kept asking her to get control of herself.

"I will, but you have to say you love me first," Cindy said.

Vince studied Cindy's face. It finally dawned on him that the main issue was that she'd never had to deal with being rejected by a man. The dramatics weren't sparked by the fact that Cindy loved him. She just didn't want to lose to Maggie.

"I will always love you," Vince said. It wasn't the truth, but he was speaking to an unstable person.

"Just... how about we go get some dinner?" He wanted to get her out of his place and thought the fresh air might do her good.

Cindy agreed. She slipped on her sandals, Vince grabbed his keys and stuffed his cell phone into his pocket, and they headed out. He felt as if they were making real progress when they walked down the hallway to the elevator. The same elevator attendant was on duty, and he studied Cindy O'Lay with ruffled brows. Her face was patchy from crying, and her mascara and eyeliner were smudged. Vince didn't look his best either. His hair was messy from running his hand through it in anguish. He was exhausted and eager to get back to Maggie.

The operator peeled his stare off Cindy and pasted it on the control panel. "Lobby?"

"Yes," Vince said.

The residents had express elevator service, so they didn't have to worry about making any stops along the way. Vince and Cindy got to the lobby and walked past a small casino and closed high-end shops. The jewelry shop caught Vince's attention. Two guards stood alert outside the door. Nicely displayed diamond necklaces, bracelets, and rings sparkled in the window.

Vince remembered the ridiculous business of

forcing the engagement ring he'd bought Maggie on her finger. She didn't like to wear it, and that had bothered the hell out of him. He had once come to conclusion that he'd rather have her without the ring than not have her at all, but as time went on, he stopped deluding himself. The truth was that he wanted Maggie to be his legal wife. He wanted the wedding day complete with a best man, bridesmaids, and a minister. The fact that Maggie didn't want all the "hoopla," as she called it, made her look untrustworthy.

He was still so very thankful that she had been out of touch with Robert. He'd thought Robert would pursue her and that Maggie would let herself be caught. At least that was what he had hoped. If Maggie had gotten into a serious relationship with Robert, then that would've put a stake through the heart of Vince's love for her. He would've been able to move on and fall in love with someone like Cindy O'Lay—at least for the moment. He often wondered if falling in love with another woman was even possible post-Maggie.

"What do you want to eat?" Cindy asked.

Vince blinked himself back into the moment. "We'll go to the deli."

Just about every guy they passed took a moment

or longer to notice Cindy. She wore the tightest skinny jeans and a tight deep-cut V-neck T-shirt. Cindy had a way of walking that made men pay attention and women regard her with envy.

Vince remembered when they'd met at the Met Gala in Manhattan. They'd attended with separate dates, but he noticed Cindy staring at him past the sea of publicity-starved celebrities in skimpy attire. Cindy didn't have to try hard to get attention. She wore a black lace cocktail dress that dipped low enough in the back and front to make a man wonder. Vince smiled and winked at her. Cindy tossed her head back and chuckled before she made her approach. They introduced themselves, and he led with his profession, as always.

"A&Rt Media! I've been vegging out on reruns of *Not Like My Mother* on Prime D TV," she said.

"And you're a model?" Vince asked.

"You already know that I'm Cindy O'Lay, don't you?" she asked.

"I do now," he said.

At first she couldn't believe he didn't know that she was a famous model, but it wasn't Vince's style to convince her. Since he didn't try to convince her that he didn't know who she was, she believed him. He listened as she talked about how she'd just returned from living in Paris for a year. But she spent most of her time on the road, chasing one fashion week at a time. That was why, when she returned to the United States only a week before they met, she had locked herself inside her apartment to veg out on all the television shows she had missed.

Vince had kept her talking about herself because that was the subject that made her the happiest. She wasn't narcissistic, but talking about herself was easier. All he wanted to do was fuck her. It had been three weeks since he'd had sex with a woman whose name he couldn't remember—she was a model too. He usually found himself rubbing off to memories of Maggie's ass and face. He needed real pussy from a woman who could take his mind off his sexy ex-girlfriend, and he figured Cindy could make that happen.

They'd exchanged phone numbers. As soon as Vince left the ball and slid into the backseat of his limousine, he'd called Cindy, and she answered on the first ring. He asked if she'd like to come over for a drink. She said yes. They fucked that night, and it was good enough to make him forget about Maggie. The second time was just as good. Soon they were dating and in a full-blown relationship where no serious questions were asked as long as they were having fun.

Vince and Cindy stood quietly in line at the deli. When he looked at Cindy, he noticed that she was staring at him. She opened her mouth to speak but decided to not say anything since everyone around them was watching them. She ordered the avocado on whole grain with kale juice and Vince ordered the pastrami on rye. They found a seat in a quiet corner, and he was free to speak freely.

"Listen, Cindy, I'm sorry if I hurt you."

"You have hurt me."

Vince could tell she was definitely not going to let him go so easily. "But I love Maggie."

"You're forgetting that she fucked your best friend."

Vince closed his eyes to absorb the impact of Cindy's words. "I haven't forgotten, and neither has Maggie. We talked about it."

Cindy grunted with disdain. "And since you talked about it, now you think what she did to you was okay?"

Vince flinched. Cindy was making Maggie out to be some sort of monster. He had never explained to Cindy that he had cheated on Maggie first because

Cindy never cared to know the gory details. "Maggie and I are adults."

"And I'm not an adult?"

"I didn't say that."

"But you're insinuating it."

Vince paused. Cindy wanted to fight. Perhaps she realized that she couldn't change his mind about Maggie, so she just wanted to fight. "I'm not insinuating that you're not an adult. You're obviously not a child."

"Then stop treating me like a child," she snapped.

"Okay. I won't."

"Good."

Vince wanted to walk out of the deli and leave her sitting there, but he couldn't. He took a bite into his pastrami sandwich. It was good.

Cindy nibbled on her sandwich. "I thought you were the one, that's all." She kept her eyes on the table.

Vince rubbed the back of his neck. He didn't know what to say. He didn't want to break her heart more than he already had. "You're beautiful. You'll find someone else." He hoped that would make her feel better.

"Don't fucking patronize me."

He sighed. It hadn't made her feel better. "I'm not patronizing you. I'm just stating a fact."

"I'm beautiful. Is that the reason you've been with me?"

"No," he said emphatically.

"Then why?" Her tone was pleading.

"Well, you are beautiful and that's nice, but you're fun too. I guess I could've loved you if my heart—shit, my soul—didn't belong to Maggie. Shit, Cindy, I love her. How many more times do I have to say it?"

Cindy kept her eyes on the table. He could see her thinking.

"You did nothing wrong," he said to help her process his thoughts. "You did everything right. I was just the wrong man for you."

Cindy raised her face, and tears rolled down her cheeks. "You said that I was fun."

Vince shook his head. "Not in a sexual way. You know how to enjoy yourself." He smirked. "I'm stuffy, and you're not."

She chuckled softly. "You *are* stuffy."

She seemed caught off guard by the moment they were having, and the tension between them dissolved. By the time they'd finished their sandwiches and drinks, it was after two in the morning. Vince knew Maggie well enough to know that she had written him off. She would feel that he had blown her off and wouldn't cry about it. He had a lot of making up to do for missing dinner, and he couldn't wait get started.

"So where's Maggie?" Cindy asked with a hint of scorn.

"She's at her parents' house."

Cindy got rid of the sneer. "Oh, they're in town?"

"They're getting remarried tomorrow." He looked at his watch. "Well, later today actually."

Cindy gasped. "Good for them! I really like her parents. Isak Conroy, wow…" She gestured as if his name elicited a deep, joyful feeling. "No wonder Maggie is who she is. Look at her parents."

Vince chuckled. He knew that if Maggie had heard Cindy say that, she would ask, "Who do you think I am?"

"Right," he said. Vince picked up a napkin and wiped his mouth. He didn't want to seem too eager to leave because he could sense how delicate the situation still was. He threw the napkin onto the tray. "So."

Cindy's shoulders curled, taking the wounded bird posture. "Is this good-bye?"

Vince was exhausted, emotionally and physically. "Yes, Cindy, it's time we say good-bye."

She nodded and looked off. The crowd in the diner had thinned out some. The line to enter the nightclub across the walkway had dwindled down to nothing. The only people still out were hardcore gamblers.

"I left my luggage in your apartment," Cindy said.

Vince had to think fast. He didn't want Cindy back in his penthouse. He took out his cell phone and placed a call to the concierge. "Don't worry. I'll have a car waiting for you and your luggage already brought down."

"You're trying to get rid of me?" Cindy sounded so dejected.

"There's no use in dragging this out any longer." The concierge answered the call. "Hello," Vince said.

"You're a jerk!" Cindy shot to her feet and stormed out of the diner.

Vince was stunned for a moment, but he quickly recovered. He gave the concierge strict instructions to not let her into his penthouse no matter what. He let them know that he was not happy they'd let her in earlier, and he ordered a car to take her to the airport. The concierge said they would take care of everything. He felt bad about how he'd ended things with Cindy, but at least now he could breathe easier.

Vince had no intentions of running after Cindy.

That was what she wanted—more drama. Instead, he called Maggie, but the call went straight to voicemail. He pondered whether or not to make the second call. It was awfully late, or early in the morning, and he'd already been a no-show for what would've been a delightful evening, but Vince had no choice. He called Leah. He nervously tapped his fingers on the tabletop, waiting for her to answer. Leah answered on the fourth ring.

Vince scooted to the edge of his seat. "Hello, Leah."

She yawned. "You're a little late with the call, aren't you?"

"I'm sorry I missed dinner. Cindy showed up, and I had to stick around until she evened out enough to not do anything drastic."

"Oh, dear." Leah sounded concerned. "Is everything okay?"

"I'm making sure she gets to the airport safely. How's Maggie?"

Leah sighed. "You don't have to worry about Maggie. Just make it right with her, and everything will be just fine."

"I will."

"Good."

"See you at the wedding?"

"Is it too late for me to come over now?"

Leah chuckled lightly. "It's never too late for you."

Vince felt extremely relieved. He hung up, jumped out of his seat, and trotted down the walkway, not caring who saw him. He passed that jewelry shop again. The two guards studied him with the curiosity of a disturbed grizzly bear. Vince slowed his pace. He thought about the last ring he'd bought Maggie. No, he wouldn't dare give her that ring again. She needed a new one.

"Excuse me?" he called to the guard. "What time does the store open?"

One of the guards told him nine o'clock. Vince couldn't possibly wait that long, so he let his money open the very expensive doors to the most beautiful and expensive ring he could find to put on Maggie's finger before sunrise.

MAGGIE

Shit, I woke up again. I just had a dream about Vince, and I'm thankful I can't remember it, but the emotions from the dream are still with me. I've already woken up numerous times. The three glasses of wine weren't strong enough to battle the angst I feel about Vince ditching us for Cindy.

"He's with his girlfriend," I say until I get tired of repeating it.

Regardless of the oath, the taste of his tongue from six months ago lingers in my mouth. I caught a whiff of his breath a few times yesterday. His smell always draws me to him. We're bonded by our pheromones. We belong together.

I turn on my side and close my eyes, hoping that changing positions will make me sleepier. Minutes pass. I do a number of rounds of deep breathing, but thoughts of Vince won't let me sleep. I kick the sheet and blanket off of me.

"Forget it," I mumble.

I strip out of my tank top and panties, put on a robe, and head to the swimming pool. The hallways and staircase are nearly lightless, and it's pitch black outside. I walk carefully, feeling the walls until I make it to the brighter side of house. I open the glass door to the patio, softly walk to the edge of the pool, take off the robe, and sink my feet onto the porcelain-covered bottom. This is the shallow side. The pool gets deeper as I walk forward.

I sigh as I continue to submerge myself in the lukewarm water. Once I'm shoulder deep, I push off my feet and swim underwater to the other end. I flutter on my back all the way back to the shallow side and rest on the surface with every part of me submerged except my face. I'm relaxed enough to yawn. One lap is all it took to make me sleepy, but just in case, I swim two more, then I use one of the towels on the wooden rack to dry off.

That short swim felt so good that once I make it back to my bed, I decide to go for another swim as soon as I wake up. I curl up into a ball, and minutes later, exhaustion overpowers my inactive mind, and I fall asleep.

VINCE

When Vince arrived at Leah's house, he called her from inside his vehicle. She had been on the verge of chewing him out for arriving three hours after his last phone call, but he explained his tardiness and she let him in pronto. And now he stood in the doorway of Maggie's bedroom, watching Maggie breathe deeply. The curtains were open, and the light of dawn filled the room. A white towel was loosely wrapped around her head, and she had kicked off the blanket. His gaze fell on her perfect ass, which wasn't too big or small. Vince got hard quickly. He didn't want to grow a boner, but the excitement of what was to come had overpowered him.

"Hey, Maggie," he called.

She didn't stir, so he walked to her bed and sat on the edge. Vince ran his hand up and down her shoulder. She felt warm and soft. He hoped Maggie wouldn't deny him her body.

"Maggie?" he said louder.

She opened one eye then slowly flipped onto her back. "Vince?" she asked throatily.

His hand slid up from her shoulder to pet the side of her face. Oh, how he wanted to kiss her sexy mouth. "Hey."

"What time is it?" she asked.

"It's early."

She blinked rapidly until she could focus on his face.

"Sorry I missed dinner last night. I really wanted to be there," Vince said.

Maggie was about to respond, but then she looked down at her nakedness. She pulled the blanket up, covering her beautiful body. Her eyes were wide open now. "What are you doing here?"

Vince's breaths came quicker. Only a thin blanket separated him from what he needed.

Maggie ruffled her eyebrows then turned to look out the window. She seemed very confused. "Are you really here?"

"I'm right here, baby," he replied.

She parted her soft lips, and Vince couldn't help himself. He went in for the kiss. Their lips touched, and their eyes locked. Their tongues met and circled each other. Vince thought his bulge would pop right out of the crotch of his pants. He wanted to devour Maggie, and with the greedy way they were kissing, he was close to doing just that.

20

SAY IT AND MEAN IT

*V*ince drops his face, and our mouths pull apart.

"Wait," he says, breathing heavily.

Even though we're no longer kissing, I still feel as if I'm a feather floating gently through the atmosphere.

"Maggie, do you forgive me for all the shit I've done to you?" he asks.

I feel as if I'm nodding in slow motion. "Will you forgive me?"

"I already have. Maggie, can I make love to you?" he whispers.

I skip a breath. I can still taste him, and the flavor sweetens my tone. "Yes, absolutely."

Vince sucks in a deep breath. With the reflexes of

a tomcat, he takes my knees and spreads them. He breathes deeply as his gaze devours my body. His desire makes my sugar walls pulsate. He slips two fingers inside me to indulge in my wetness.

Vince's breaths tremble, and he pulls off his shirt and the white T-shirt under it. His wide chest and tapered waist make me hornier. He tugs his belt loose, undoes his pants, and eagerly pulls them off. Our fiery gazes meet. Are our lusts too high to truly relish the moment?

I'm so wet. Vince slips between my legs and presses my thighs to the mattress. I tilt my head back, knowing what's coming next. His wet, warm tongue licks up my slipperiness. His grunting and moaning tells me that he loves the way I taste. Eager fingers press deeper into my thighs. Vince's tongue flicks the side of my engorged clit, and I whimper and twist. The pleasure is nearly unbearable. I cover my face with my forearms, snatch up the sheets, and grab Vince by the scalp. I want to scream, but we're in my parents' house, so I grit my teeth.

"Hurry up, baby, because I'm going to…" Vince mutters then goes back to sliding his tongue against my clit.

The sensation peaks. I lift my pelvis. With one more lick, the pleasure gusts through my sex. I scream even though I'm not supposed to. Vince comes up and smashes his lips on mine. I taste myself on his tongue. The fact that he drank me, ate me, and licked me without reluctance is erotic and makes me want more and *more* of him.

Then he impales me, sinking his hard-on deep inside me. I gasp when he hits the wall deep in my belly. He's so engorged, and I'm so turned on. Vince grabs two handfuls of my ass and flips me on top of him. Although I'm on top, Vince is squarely in charge, crashing my wetness against his rod. Every thrust feels so damn good. Our lovemaking is a symphony of moans, grunts, sloshing, and skin slapping skin. His fingers sink so deep into my butt cheeks that it aches so good.

"I'm going to come," he cries.

He shouts, shakes, buries his face into the side of my neck, and nails me with his erection. I hold his strong frame as he lets loose.

"Oh baby," he whispers once it's all out.

Vince sucks the side of my neck, up to my chin, and sinks his tongue into my mouth. We roll around the bed, kissing, groping, and tangling our limbs. Overcome by emotion, we embrace tightly. Vince only loosens his grip on me when I cough for air.

"So are we back together?" I ask breathlessly.

Vince's eyes shine just as big as his smile. "I have something for you." He kisses me on the mouth once then twice, and he extends an arm over the side of the bed, reaching for his pants. He scoots closer to the edge, bringing me with him.

I chuckle. "Do you really have to take me on this ride?"

He seizes his pants. "I'm not ready to let you go."

I gently press my lips against his bare chest. Vince responds by guiding me onto my back. His lips are parted, and he's staring into my eyes.

"I can't get enough of you," he says.

"Me neither. But…"

He ruffles his eyebrows. "But what?"

"Forget it."

"No, we're not going to forget anything. This time around, we're going to communicate and shit like that because we're not breaking up again, Maggie. Never again."

I nod. "Never, I agree."

He's still lying on top of me as he digs through his pants pocket and takes out a ring box. I gasp from surprise.

"What?" He looks worried.

I grin from ear to ear. "Nothing! If you're going

to do what I think you're going to do, then I'm happy."

Vince comes in for a kiss, and then forces his lips away from mine. "Um…"

I suck my bottom lip so that I can continue tasting his delicious flavor.

"Maggie…" He opens the ring box, and I'm hypnotized by the most beautiful diamond I've ever seen. "Will you marry me? For real, this time. I want a real wedding, Maggie."

I wait for the fear to overcome me. It doesn't. So I extend my ring finger. "Yes, I'll marry you for real."

When he slips the ring on, it doesn't feel like a weight on my finger. It feels right. Being without Vince for six long months, which felt more like six long years, made me realize that I don't want to ever live without him. We study the diamond on my finger. It fits perfectly. Vince kisses the ring then my lips.

"How long have you had it?" I ask, admiring the fine piece of jewelry.

"I bought it this morning." He reads the surprise on my face. "I had to grease the palms of two security guards and a store manager."

I chuckle. "I'm not going to ask how much it set you back."

"Baby, you're worth every dime and more."

I roll my eyes a little. "You're such a charmer."

Vince gets ready to insert himself inside me.

"Wait." I squeeze my knees together as close as they can get with him lying between my legs. "Why don't we wait?"

He frowns. "Wait for what?"

"Wait until we're married."

"Wait until we're married to do what?"

"Have sex."

His frown deepens "Ha! You're kidding, right?"

I shake my head. "No."

"That's not what you were going to say before I asked you to marry me again."

Vince's rod feels harder, not softer.

"Well no… I was going to ask if we could go away somewhere, just the two of us, and spend some quality time together. Remember how we said we'd never done that?"

He rubs his engorged cock against my pubic bone, and it feels so good. "I don't remember."

I take a quick sip of air between my teeth. "Vince, come on."

"You come on. I've been dreaming about having you ever since I saw you at the party. No…" He shakes his head. "No deal."

I pat his chest and wriggle out from under him. I don't get very far before he pulls me back beneath him.

"I'll never make it, Mags."

"Then we'll get married soon," I say.

"When? Today? Right now? We're in Vegas. I'll marry you right now if you want." He's spastic.

"Vince, you're thinking with your penis at the moment."

He sighs hard. "Because my penis misses your vagina."

I laugh, but he doesn't. "Come on, Vince, it'll be fun. All we've done since we've been together is work and fuck. I want to make different memories."

"We can have sex and make different memories."

"No…" I shake my head. "We can't, because sex is too good between us. We do it, then we can't stop. It's like when we were on the Vineyard. We hardly went out with the others. We were always holed up in the bedroom, fucking."

Vince sighs hard. I recognize the tone of his sigh. I'm getting through to him.

"We have to strike a deal then," he says.

I grin victoriously. "What are your terms?"

"I need to make love to you one more time, and

then after two weeks, that's it—we're getting married."

I grimace. "Two weeks? Where, in Manhattan?"

"If that's what you want."

"Deal. Deal. And deal. Hey, I can plan a wedding in two weeks."

Vince rolls off of me. "I bet you can. Now get on your knees."

I chuckle, remembering the last time he asked me to do that. He wanted me to go along with that dominant/subordinate crazy business. Although the situation was weird, it was sexy then, and it's sexy now. I get on all fours, and Vince positions himself behind me. He grabs two handfuls of my ass. The anticipation makes me cream, and he knows it because he's sliding his fingers down my dripping pussy.

"Oh," he breathes. "I can't believe you're going to make me wait two weeks to do this again."

Before I can respond, his tongue forces its way into my asshole. I sigh because it feels so damn good. Vince's mouth goes everywhere. It's wet, soft, and hot. His fingers find my clit and jerk it off. Fuck, we've already forgotten where we are. I'm whimpering like a porn star, and I'm about to come so hard that I'll see white. Vince doesn't let up until I scream. That's when he smashes his dick inside me.

"Ah!" I scream.

"Did I hurt you, baby?" he whispers.

"No." I sigh.

Regardless, Vince takes it nice and slow. He stops, holds it there, and shifts positions whenever he feels as if he's going to come. He's drawing out this last session before we make love again as a married couple for as long as he can. I think an hour passes before my mom calls from downstairs.

"Maggie! Vince! Breakfast!"

"Shit," I mutter. "Do you think she heard us?"

"Hell, yes." Vince humps me faster. "Our two weeks…" He goes faster. "Starts…" His dick jabs me. He grunts and quakes. "Now," he says breathlessly after settling down.

The journey continues. Read the next book In the LOVE in the USA series now!

He's So Bad: A San Francisco Love Story, **Book 6**